Daughter of a Queen Pin

Daughter of a Queen Pin

Treasure Hernandez

www.urbanbooks.net

Urban Books, LLC
300 Farmingdale Road, N.Y.-Route 109
Farmingdale, NY 11735

Daughter of a Queen Pin

ISBN 13: 978-1-64556-342-6
ISBN 10: 1-64556-342-1

First Trade Paperback Printing June 2022
Printed in the United States of America

10 9 8 7 6 5 4 3 2 1

*This is a work of fiction. Any references or similarities
to actual events, real people, living or dead, or to real
locales are intended to give the novel a sense of reality.
Any similarity in other names, characters, places, and
incidents is entirely coincidental.*

Distributed by Kensington Publishing Corp.
Submit Orders to:
Customer Service
400 Hahn Road
Westminster, MD 21157-4627
Phone: 1-800-733-3000
Fax: 1-800-659-2436

Daughter of a Queen Pin

Treasure Hernandez

CHAPTER ONE

It was hot. Not just regular hot weather, but miserable heat that had even skinny women uncomfortable in their clothes. The mid July temperature made the funeral procession seem longer than it truly was. Countless vehicles passed through the often-turbulent neighborhood. The rays from the sun blinded the residents crowding the streets. It was as if they'd come to see a superstar perform, instead of a zip code legend being laid to rest. Cars both new and old were lined up for miles. People from all walks of life—gangsters, pimps, priests, politicians, policemen, whores, drug dealers, and even dope fiends were posted. One would think a president, a mayor or a United States senator was deceased. For sure, this was a special kinda day in the hood that could not be missed. Each person was there in the scorching sun for their own individual reasons, yet the bottom line was to bear witness that this person was indeed dead.

As goes life in the streets, the game had snatched another soldier. Although feared throughout the community, ironically, the person was also well liked. Cold, hard cash was easily loaned to many, or at least to those who, without a doubt, could repay it. Far from being a rumor or tall tale, countless clients had come up missing after defaulting on agreed-upon payments. They never settled their debt, and subsequently, they paid with their lives. Each knew the risk they had taken on when asking for the money, so their mournful families had to turn a blind eye to the deadly consequences or risk the same fate on point and principle.

The blocks of cars seem to take forever to go past the neighborhood greasy spoon where the infamous crew had made their headquarters for the past ten years. Strangely, the hearse followed the cars.

I never understood why the casket was always last in the funerals in our neighborhood. My uncle once explained to me, "This is the Bottom Barrel, and in our neighborhood, there are only three ways to get out. Dead, jail, or leave and be successful." The other residents still living in the neighborhood were like walking zombies moving from day to day just existing until their number was called. Therefore, the casket was always last around here, signifying the end, the final ride through their stomping ground. For the people who lived in this poverty-stricken community, it was the end.

The last few cars before the hearse were designated family cars. I was in the last car by myself. I felt like I was having an out-of-body experience. I couldn't believe I was in this car. *Am I dead too?* I thought. *No, the hearse is behind me. But I'm in here all alone.*

I'd always felt I was in this world all alone. My parents died when I was young, and I was always a loner. I had one brother, Kurt, who got killed three years ago slanging drugs. My brother and I were raised by our uncle, who provided a roof over our heads and food on the table. He never stayed home to counsel us on the pitfalls of life. He, too, was a major drug supplier.

The car I was riding in passed some familiar people that snapped me out of my thoughts. I could see faces of people I didn't get along with, yet they were here to give their respects to me, or to the person in the hearse. I tried to relax and go with the flow. It seemed like I was looking outside from a box. It took all my strength not to just bolt out of the car and run.

The hearse was painted gold with black trim, and the interior was lined with black satin. That made it look soft and comfortable. The sides of the hearse had wide windows, so you could view the casket. Of course, the casket was gold.

When the hearse passed a crowd of people, they would raise their right hands that were covered with white gloves. It was a tradition in this Bottom Barrel neighborhood, supposed to signify cleansing in hope that all the sins of the person in the casket would be forgiven with unity from the community.

The family car and the hearse pulled up to the church. My body was there, but my mind seemed to be watching from afar. The pall bearers one-stepped with the casket to the front of the church as if they were on Bourbon Street in New Orleans. Once again, I was reminded how alone I was. No family, no close friends were with me. I sat alone on the front row as people streamed by to give me their condolences. My mind wanted to get up and see who was in the casket, but I was too scared it might be me. The line finally ceased. The hugs and kissing stopped, and the envelopes of money being dropped on me stopped as well.

The reverend got up to speak. The casket was slowly closed by the grim-faced funeral director. Tears and sobs continued for two grueling minutes as all waited patiently. The organist played softly in the background.

The so-called man of God began with, "Another young life shortened by utter violence. We live in a community that raises our youth not to care about another human soul as long as they achieve that street dream. That thirst for power and money. This allows them to buy all the materialistic things in life—jewelry, big cars, clothes, and even a person's soul." Everybody's attention was on what was being said. It was hitting home for everybody.

Out of nowhere, the thunderous sound of gunshots rang out. Screams overshadowed the tears. Mourners hid, seeking refuge. People ducked for cover while others panicked, trying to sprint for the door. I saw bodies fall and people being trampled attempting to get out of the sanctuary. Some young men returned gunfire. I kept hearing screams for God's supreme mercy through the barrage of flying bullets.

CHAPTER TWO

Abruptly I was awakened out of my deep sleep. I was annoyed. I despised being snatched out of my dreams. I looked out the window to see Chuckie banging on the door.

"Damn! What?" I yelled.

"Hey, get up, girl. A guy got a few dollars. We can go get some blow." He continued to knock as if he were already high. "Get up, girl. I got cash money." Chuckie was anxious and full of excitement.

I yawned and stretched. "Damn, what time is it?" I looked out the window at a frail man I had come to know as my friend. He was smiling but had no teeth in his mouth. The years of drug use had rotted them out and pulled the sense of real life from him. Now he was only a surviving corpse that moved along in life until the man upstairs said it's time to check out.

"Its seven thirty," Chuckie replied. "So, you going to go get this blow or what? You know Malcolm don't open this time of day, but he'll let you in. Come on, Charday. Get up."

I gazed at Chuckie for a few seconds as if I weren't going to move. "Slow down, fool, and give me a damn minute," I barked. I knew I had to start my day off right so I could hustle up money to feed me and my unborn child.

I sat motionless for a good minute, trying to figure out why I had this same dream repeatedly. What was the dream telling me? Who was in the casket? It seemed so real.

The thought of the strong blow brought me back to reality. I opened the door to my temporary home, an old two-door Tempo, which was sitting on bricks, taking in the early morning hood air. Since it had broken down, it had been my home sweet home for two solid months. Sometimes, I allowed Chuckie stay with me when he got locked out of the homeless shelter, or when he was too high to move, which was a frequent occurrence. This was home for my unborn child and me. At least I wasn't out in these wicked streets like some.

I got out of the car with a good long stretch because I had to sleep in the fetal position in the rear seat. It was not big enough to lay extended. "Okay, let's go." I finally gave in as I led the way to Malcolm's.

Chuckie gave me the money and urged, "Don't take too long."

Everybody in the neighborhood knew I used to be Malcolm's woman, so nobody bothered me. He was also the father of my unborn child; however, he didn't believe me. He was in denial. Either way, we were still cool.

My using drugs destroyed our relationship. He always told me if and when I wanted to stop, he would help me. At the age of eighteen, I thought I knew it all, yet these drugs were getting the best of me. Malcolm claimed if the child was his, he would raise it.

I rang the bell for what seemed like forever. When Malcolm finally looked through the peep hole, he opened the door. "What you want this time in the damn morning?" he asked in a dry, husky voice, trying to wipe the sleep out of his eyes while holding himself as though I still excited him.

"Come on, now. You know what I need, and you know what I want." I gave him my sensual smile.

"You need to leave that shit alone, girl. You knocked up and still using that bullshit," he lectured.

"Well, I'm only sniffing a little bit," I exclaimed, not one bit ashamed.

"Charday, you are still the finest girl in the hood, but you're eighteen and using hardcore drugs. It can't get any better. Trust, only worse. I promised your brother I would look out for your crazy ass." Malcolm frowned as he lowered his head like he was ashamed of the poor job he'd done.

"Yeah, you looked out for me all right. Got me pregnant and hooked on drugs, then put my ass out on the damn streets. I'm sure my brother would be proud of you." My words cut him to the core.

"I didn't make you do no drugs or put a gun to your fucking head. That was your damn decision," he yelled.

I could see the hurt on his face. He went to the back room and came out with a plastic bag of what I needed and threw it at me.

A bright smile came across my face. "All of this for me?" I held the money out, even though I knew it wasn't enough for what he had just blessed me with.

"Go ahead and get out of here so I can get some sleep." He spoke with a calm and cool voice. He opened the door wide with annoyance.

"Thanks, Malcolm. I'm sorry if I said anything to hurt you. And yeah, I need to use the restroom."

On my way to the toilet, I thought I saw a tear fall from his face. He was one of the most feared dealers in the hood. He killed one of his workers for coming back from the store late with his beer. But I think I was his weakness. I knew he truly loved me, yet I was too busy chasing parties and highs to realize something good for me.

Once in the bathroom, I opened the dope and snorted some. Then I put some in an empty cigarette pack.

Whenever I saw Malcolm, he always gave me more drugs than I paid for.

When I left the bathroom, I passed by Malcolm's bedroom and noticed a picture of my brother Kurt with Malcolm. I guess this was really hard for him. Malcolm was waiting at the door. I gave him a hug and left.

Chuckie was waiting for me around the corner. "You get it?" he asked in between loud sniffs. I think his jones was coming down. He needed to get high.

"Yeah, be cool. You wanna go back to the car or what?" I knew Chuckie was a mainline user. He shot drugs straight into his veins, so he needed a spot to fix up.

When we reached the car, I gave him what was left in the plastic baggie, and he smiled.

"Malcolm be hooking your ass up," Chuckie said with a smirk as we climbed into the car.

"Yeah, he cool. But he's always talking shit about me using." I couldn't let my homie know how much my soon-to-be-baby daddy was hooking me up.

Chuckie pulled out a small can used to sell mints. It was wrapped in rubber bands. Opening it up, he pulled out a needle with an eye dropper on it, then a bent-up spoon. He took the contents from the bag, tapping it onto the spoon. He opened a small pill bottle he had with water in it. Using the eye dropper, he sucked a few drops of water and put it on the spoon. Chuckie then took a lighter and put flames under the spoon, melting its contents. Chuckie got excited pulling a piece of cotton from his filtered cigarette. He put it onto the spoon as well. In seconds, the powered drugs had become liquid form. Easily, he sucked the drugs through the cotton with the needle and the eye dropper. Removing his belt, he tied it around his upper arm. He tapped his arm while balling up his fist.

"You want a hit?" Chuckie asked, surely hoping the answer would be no.

"Come on, now. You know that's not my thing. I'ma do a couple of lines." That's what my mouth said, but I always paid attention to the difference in the high I got and the high Chuckie got.

"You sure?" He smiled as he stuck the needle in his arm, watching the blood come up from his vein into the eye dropper. With expertise, he pushed the top of the eye dropper so the contents would go back in his vein.

I glared Chuckie with admiration and nervousness. *Is this where I'm headed?*

His eyes closed slowly. He loosened the belt as the drugs started to take control of his inner soul. My get-high buddy sat there in a trance with the needle in his arm.

"Chuckie!" I yelled as he drifted off. "Nigga, wake up!" I was terrified as I shook him.

"Damn, girl, you blowing my damn high," he complained as he woke up from his deep nod to take out the needle. He started scratching his nose, then his nuts. Every time I saw those actions, fear came across me, halting my thoughts of shooting up.

I snorted a couple of lines Chuckie left in the bag for me. Like him, I was out the gate and nodded out as well.

CHAPTER THREE

It was well after one o'clock when I woke up. Chuckie was long gone. The neighborhood was alive. On a warm summer day, the temperature was 80 degrees. The sun was hot, and there was no breeze to speak of. I opened the trunk of the Tempo to get something halfway decent to put on. Even though I had a drug habit, I still kept myself clean. My home, I mean my car, was in the far rear of a police precinct with a lot of old discarded police vehicles. So, no one messed with me or my things.

I picked out a nice green outfit. Like normal, I had to make sure my top fit loose so no one could tell I was pregnant. I went to take a "ho bath" at the gas station across from the station and changed my clothes. I returned home and put my dirty clothes in my closet. Okay, my trunk. I must admit I was looking good for a homeless semi-addict. My caramel skin put an accent on my short haircut that I usually kept wrapped up to make me look older. My mature body could catch any man's attention.

I was ready to go get my hustle on. I didn't have an everyday hustle. I just went with the flow of the day and whatever came my way. However, the last thing I wanted to do was have sex with some random dude. So, I'd explore all my options. I wasn't greedy. I just wanted my kid and I to eat and me to get high.

With no shame, I walked up on the avenue. A candy apple red Cherokee pulled up to me and the driver rolled down the window. It was Duane. He was a young drug runner who worked for Malcolm. He liked me, but he knew Malcolm would give him a short stay on earth if he got caught up with me. I think Malcolm had scared the whole neighborhood. That's why I didn't have any real friends or a man.

Duane pulled his truck close to the curb. I kept walking to allow him gaze at my voluptuous body that I knew he lusted for. Duane followed my walk with his eyes and his vivid imagination. He inched the vehicle forward to keep up with me.

"What's up, Charday? Where you going?" Duane inquired, trying to be cool.

"I'm just gonna get me something to eat." I put that out there just in case he had enough nerve to try his game knowing there would be consequences.

"Oh, word? I was just going to have lunch too. You wanna go with me?" Duane spoke in a strong, I-don't-give-a-fuck voice.

"Naw, that's okay. I don't want you to get in trouble with your boss." I stopped, putting my hands on my hips. I gave him my stern look, waiting on him to give some excuse and back down.

"Look, baby, I'm my own boss. I don't answer to nobody. Malcolm got me started, but I got my own game and my own money. Now, do you wanna go eat, or are you scared?" Duane put the truck in gear.

"No one owns me," I shot back at him as I opened the passenger side and got in the car.

This was the beginning of a long friendship and relationship with Duane. We started off by having lunch twice a week. He seemed to always come down the street when I was walking. We talked a lot and got to know each other. One day, he asked me to go out with him, dinner and a movie. I always thought he only wanted to see me during the day so we wouldn't look like we were dating.

"Why you never asked me before?" I challenged him.

"All my work is done at night, and I didn't trust my crew to do it without me," he replied.

"Oh, but now you do?"

He looked me up and down. "Yeah, now I do. So, you wanna go or what?"

There was no mention of Malcolm or my big belly that was now showing. I was well into my seventh month.

"Uh, you do know I'm pregnant with Malcolm's baby, right?" I finally asked.

"I've always known. But hey, that's Malcolm's problem, not mine. I think he treated you wrong. I see you as a beautiful sister that I want in my corner. I will be in yours no matter what. That is, if you let me."

Duane had me stunned with that. I just thought he wanted to have sex with me. However, he never asked.

"What do you think is going to happen if we get together and the baby is born? Do you think Malcolm will accept that," I asked flatly, waiting for a response.

"Let me tell you something, Charday. I'm a man that lives for now. I can't predict the future, and I don't try. I see what I want in life, and I do what I have to do to get it," he proclaimed. "See, I really don't care about what Malcolm accepts or don't accept. I want you and whatever comes with you in my life. Now, do you want to be down with me or what? I'll help you get off drugs and the whole nine." Looking deep in my eyes, Duane demanded a truthful answer.

I really liked Duane and enjoyed being with him. I would be looking forward to seeing him twice a week. "Yes, I wanna be down with you," I answered in my most sincere voice.

That day, my life changed.

Duane picked me up around seven o'clock. The sun was just setting, and the cool breeze made the coming night mystical. The moon was full, and I had a tingle in my heart that I couldn't explain. I hadn't spent any time with a man in two months since I'd moved from Malcolm's.

We drove and talked as he got on the expressway. Duane was much smarter than I thought. Come to find out, he had his own business on the other side of town. He just needed someone he could trust who would watch his back. I knew he must have had a lot of trust in me. He knew I used drugs, but I vowed if he believed in me, I'd be down with him all the way.

We came up on a tree-lined street. Duane had a weird smile on his face. He hadn't said much in a few miles. I just assumed he had a lot on his mind. We soon pulled up to a beautiful house, and we both got out. When we made our way to the door, Duane pulled out a key and looked at me.

"Are you down with me, Charday?" he quizzed.

I looked deep in eyes and answered, "For life, if you want me to. I'll be whatever you need me to be."

With that, he opened the door. We stepped inside a nice three-bedroom ranch-style home with a huge backyard.

Duane looked at me and kissed me. "I want to put this house in your name, just in case something ever happens to me. This is yours forever."

I can't believe this. I must be dreaming again.

"Duane, I can't afford this house." I broke down and started crying, then I confessed about my current housing.

Duane took me in his arms and held me tight and whispered in my ear. "I always knew where you stayed at. I knew you wouldn't take any help from anybody, so I had to make my own plan to get you in my life."

I pulled back out of his arms. "You planned all this?" I was shocked.

"Girl, I've loved you since elementary school. Whatever I've done in my life, I did for you. This house is paid for. If something should happen to me, it's yours."

"Why do you keep saying that? Are you expecting something to happen to you?"

Duane took my hand and looked in my eyes. "Charday, I'm in the game, the life. One day I may be here, and one day I might be gone. Can you understand where I'm coming from?"

For the first time in my young life, I could actually imagine a possible future. "Yes, baby, you don't ever have to look back, because I will always be there. You concentrate on moving forward. I got your back," I promised before my dress magically dropped to the floor, my naked body exposed with my belly sticking out. It was a daring move for me. I gave him my most inviting look and most sensuous, sexy smile.

Duane took a step backward, looking me up and down. "You are a beautiful, strong black woman. I will always be there for you."

We made love for the first time in our empty house, neither caring about Malcolm's possible reaction.

CHAPTER FOUR

My life was forever changed. At least for the time being. I stopped sniffing dope cold turkey, which amazed us both. I guess I was so busy getting the house together for the baby, decorating and doing whatever Duane needed, that I didn't have time for drugs. I was truly happy. The next month, I had my child, a beautiful baby girl. I named her Krystal. Duane was the man that I loved who'd help raise her. He meant the world to me and my baby.

Duane had become one of the biggest dealers in the Bottom Barrel. He showed me how to make money and how to watch your money. Because he didn't trust too many people, he had only one true friend, Renard Thomas. They called him Nardo for short. He and his girl, Rose, would visit a lot. Over time, Rose and I became good friends.

The years seemed to fly by. I think it was because I was really happy. I didn't want for anything in life. I had everything I wanted—or thought I wanted.

It was Krystal's ninth birthday. We were having a party at the house for her and her little friends. Nardo and Rose had three daughters. With them and some kids from school, the house was full of children.

Nardo and Duane were not there yet. They were supposed to have been at the house by three o'clock. It was now five, and I began to worry. I kept checking for them out the window while Krystal kept asking, "Where's my daddy?"

Those two had a tight bond. Duane's love for Krystal was so pure, and he was the only dad she knew since Malcolm, her biological father, only saw her on her birthdays. His hurt over Duane and me being together was a deep wound.

"Daddy is coming, baby. Go play with your friends," I assured her.

Rose who was helping with the party, asked me, "Are you okay?"

"I don't know, Rose. My chest is hurting, and my heart is beating fast. Duane is never late. He wouldn't miss Krystal's birthday party."

"Just relax, girl. Everything will be all right." Rose tried to ease my mind.

"Something is wrong. I love this man with all my heart, and it just doesn't feel right. Please call your man to see if he has talked to Duane."

Rose called Nardo. When she got him on the phone, her eyes grew wide while she was talking. She tried to play it off as she left the room. When she returned, Rose had tears in her eyes.

Just then, the phone rang. I jumped to answer it with a nervous feeling in my stomach—a woman's intuition. I keep my eye on Rose, and my tears started to flow before any words were spoken on the phone.

"This is Detective Willis. Do you know a Duane White?" the voice on the phone said.

"What's wrong? No, no, it can't be. He is supposed to be at home!" I stumbled over each word as my heart shattered.

Screams and tears from Rose and I brought the kids running in.

Krystal started crying. She must have had the same gut feeling I did. "What's wrong, Ms. Lady? Where's Daddy?" My soul was forever ruined as I listened to my daughter call me the pet nickname Duane had created.

"Your daddy's not coming home, baby."

Tears flowed like a faucet. Rose was crying, her three kids were crying, and Krystal and I were sobbing. That is all I remember. I must have passed out after that.

I had a mental breakdown, and I was in a hospital for eight months. Rose and Nardo would visit every week, and after a while, I started to remember their faces. Rose took care of my daughter while I was there. She talked to me and revealed the truth of what happened only after I was released.

Duane had gone to the store to get Krystal a cake for her birthday. Malcolm decided he was going to finally be a father to his child, and he had gone to get a cake as well. They started arguing in the store, and the tension carried out to the street. Malcolm pulled a gun and shot Duane, and then as Duane lay there in the street, Malcolm came near to finish him off with two to the head. Before Malcolm could shoot, Duane squeezed the trigger on the gun in his coat pocket. He got off five shots and he hit Malcolm in the heart. Malcolm fell on top of Duane. They were both pronounced dead at the scene.

They said Duane had a smile on his face.

How could I lose two of my child's daddies at the same time on the same day? I would never be the same.

Luckily, Duane was a very smart man, so he left me in a good position. Everything was in my name—the house, the cars, and our bank accounts. He even had an insurance policy. Krystal had a trust fund for fifty thousand dollars that would mature when she turned eighteen.

I was not hurting for anything, except Duane. All the money I had and all the materialistic things couldn't make me happy. I loved him so deeply. He was my whole world. I felt I couldn't survive without him.

I started on a downward slope. Soon after I was released, I started using drugs again.

CHAPTER FIVE

My life was in shambles. I slumbered through the years, using heroin, cocaine, and smoking weed. I used up most of my money and started to turn to men friends to help me pay my bills.

Krystal was fourteen now, and we talked about everything in life. The only thing I had in this world was my daughter. I vowed to teach her everything about the streets so she wouldn't get caught up. I told her about my addiction. I told her about what men wanted and what men would do to get it. I even showed her how to handle and shoot a gun. Since we were the only two people living in the house, we had to always protect each other.

My drug habit was getting worse. I would go in the streets late at night and bring guys home with my daughter in the next room. I gambled with her life as well as mine.

On Krystal's fifteenth birthday, I wanted to get her something special. I couldn't believe that I had gone through one hundred thousand dollars so fast. I was broke and desperate, so I picked up a large man at the neighborhood bar. He had a pocket full of money. I think he worked in the factory close by.

I took him to my house, where we had sex. Afterward, he fell asleep. I reached in his pocket and took some of his money. He woke up just when I was putting his pants back.

"Yo, what the fuck are you doing?" He started yelling and cussing, then he raised his huge arm and gave me a fierce backhand to my head, knocking me over the table.

I got up to run, but he caught me by my hair, slamming me through the kitchen door. Blood ran down my nose as I thought about Krystal. I was glad I had made her go to school, although she wanted to stay home.

Another blow from his fist brought me back to reality. He lifted me in the air, upside down and naked. Then, he threw me on the floor, jumped on top of me, and started swinging. He hit me in the face and in the head repeatedly. Then the sick fucker attempted to kiss me. His breath smelled like stale liquor.

I tried to bite his lips off, so he hit me again. When he tasted the blood from his lip, it sent him over the edge. He was a big man, six foot three and weighing over two hundred fifty pounds. I felt like a rag doll in his arms as he flipped me over and then went to grab a broom that was nearby. I screamed, knowing his intentions, and tried to brace my body.

Suddenly, I heard an explosion, and I blacked out. The next thing I knew, I felt someone gently touching my face.

"Ms. Lady, Ms. Lady, it's me! Please don't leave me!"

It was Krystal, holding my head in her lap. She must have thought I was dead. Her salty tears were dropping on my face.

I got control of myself and lifted up to look around. The house was a mess. The large man was slumped on the kitchen floor with a pool of blood around him. I could see bullet holes in his head and chest.

"What happened, Krystal?" I asked.

"Ms. Lady, I'm sorry. I didn't want him to hurt you."

"I'm not hurt. Krystal, you saved me. I am proud of you."

"He was beating you, Ms. Lady. He was gonna hit you with that broom. So, I shot him until he fell."

Krystal sounded panic-stricken. We hugged and cried and got our stories straight, then called the police. My daughter grew up on this day, her fifteenth birthday.

The next couple of years, I got worse, and Krystal grew stronger. She began to hang out in the streets, but she always came home and talked to me about what she was doing.

One day, she came home and told me, "I wanna hustle. I wanna sell drugs." Her mind was made up.

We talked for hours about her biological sperm doner, Malcolm, who sold heroin, and her real daddy, Duane, who sold crack cocaine. I knew as a mother I was supposed to discourage her, but it was in her system. Krystal got it from her fathers. She was going to do it anyway, so I wanted her to have the knowledge and the heart for the game.

CHAPTER SIX

Ms. Lady gave me a lot of knowledge about the life I was about to enter. What she didn't know was my daddy had already schooled me a lot. I remember on my eighth birthday while on our way to get my present, daddy picked up Uncle Nardo. He was not my real uncle, but he and Aunt Rose were the only family I had. Uncle Nardo was bleeding, and his eye was swollen.

"I got jacked by some young dealer," Uncle Nardo said.

Daddy Duane was furious. "Was it one of Malcolm's people?" he asked. I knew they were talking about my biological father. He didn't mean anything to me but a gift on my birthday.

I heard Daddy say, "We gonna take care of it." I knew that meant trouble. My dad didn't get mad or angry on the regular. However, when he did, you knew something was going to happen.

They looked at each other, and nothing else was said. We rode in silence until we came to a stoplight, where some guys were on the corner.

Uncle Nardo nudged my father. "There they are. They really got some balls still out hustling with my stuff. They must think I'm weak."

"Calm down. I got Krystal in the car, and I don't want her to get hurt. I'll let you out a block away. I'll take the car around the block and park at the other end. That way, we can catch them in the middle."

He let Uncle Nardo out and went around the block. "Krystal, you stay in the car. I'll be right outside. I promise I won't go too far."

"Daddy, I'm not scared. Can I help you?" I proudly asked. I was always with my dad, so I watched him handle business. He also let me hold his little gun sometimes. We nicknamed it Tick Tock. He taught me that if anybody messes with you, shoot first and ask questions later. Strangely, I always thought I was protecting him when I was holding Tick Tock.

"No, Krystal. I'm good. I'll talk to you when I get back. I always explain what I'm doing and why when I'm with you, don't I?" he asked.

"Yes, Daddy, just be careful. Where's my Tick Tock?" I asked.

"It's in the glove compartment," he responded.

Daddy Duane got out of the car. He bent down, gun in hand, closing the door behind him. I reached in the glove compartment and got my Tick Tock. I slid down in the back seat so no one could see me. I held Tick Tock with both hands close to the side of my face. My two little fingers were on the trigger. I know this was unusual for an eight-year-old, but my dad was a man of sheer reality. He didn't try to hide his life or any part of it from his family. He said he wanted us to be aware of what was going on. He always said it was better to know what to expect than to not expect it and get caught. Then it was too late.

Uncle Nardo walked right up to the three men and started shooting. One man fell, and the other two took off running in the direction of where Daddy had parked. Uncle Nardo chased one man, and the other man came toward the car. Daddy stood up, and the man stopped, fear on his face with his hands in the air.

"Did Malcolm send you?" I heard Daddy ask the guy. "Tell me the truth and I'll let you live."

The man sounded really nervous when he answered. "N–naw, man. I owe him some money, and I'm tryin' to get some to pay him back, but he ain't sent me."

At that moment, Uncle Nardo came running up the street. I could hear sirens blazing in the background, and they were getting closer. "Come on, man. We got to go," he yelled at Daddy, his adrenalin pumping.

"Is this the guy that robbed you?" Daddy spoke up as he held the gun on the young man in front of him. "Nigga say Malcolm had nothing to do with it. So, you believe him, or what?"

Uncle Nardo looked Daddy Duane straight in his eyes. I guess friends always know what their friends are going to do. "Yeah, dude, I believe him," he laughed.

Daddy shot the man four times, bringing him down to his knees. They both got back in the car and drove right past the approaching police.

On the way home, after he dropped off Uncle Nardo, he explained to me why he had to do that and what had caused the situation. He also told me to never pull a gun on somebody unless I was going to use it. "If you decide to shoot someone, shoot to kill them," he said.

When we got, home Daddy Duane was back to his normal self.

I was now seventeen. I didn't claim to be the finest girl in school, but I held my own. I was not interested in boys; they were interested in me. I only had one thing on my mind. I wanted to finish school and start my business. I wanted to be like Daddy Duane, a mover and shaker.

Most kids want to be like their parents, and I was no exception. My parents always taught me you must have a plan in life for where you want to go and where you want to be in ten years. I know I was kinda young to be thinking about this, but ever since I first put my hand on that gun, Tick Tock, I knew what I wanted. After I killed that awful man that was hurting my mother, I felt the power the gun gave me, and I wanted to feel more of it. Something in me knew that night where my life was going. So, I spent all my time planning how to make it happen.

There was this senior in school named Cedric. I could tell he liked me a lot. He was the school hustler. He always had girls and guys around him. Every time he saw me, he'd always speak. no matter whom he was with. One particular day, he was with four girls. One girl, Mae Mae, didn't like the idea that he came over and started talking to me.

"Yo, you wanna go out wit' me?" Cedric asked.

I looked him up and down and then said, "Nah. No thanks." Like I said, I had no time for guys and their bullshit games.

Mae Mae looked at me and then at Cedric. She looked back at me and rolled her eyes, giving me a look that said she wanted to fuck me up. I knew there would be trouble.

That afternoon, I told my mother what had happened. "What should I do?" I asked.

As I said before, my mother and father were close to me, and I always took their advice.

My mother gave me a bag my daddy had told her to give me when she felt the time was right. "Do what you gotta do to protect yourself," she said.

The next day, I went to school with my bag. We got out of school earlier than usual. On my way home, I saw Cedric and some other guys that were buying something from him and a couple of his friends that I recognized.

"Yo, ma," Cedric said to me.

While my attention was on him, I didn't notice four girls come from across the street. Before I could speak to him, I got shoved in the back. The guys started laughing, and Cedric, not wanting to act like he liked me, remained silent.

Mae Mae pushed me to the ground. "Bitch, don't you speak to my man again!"

The whore tried to kick me, but with catlike moves, I jumped up and was in her face with my old friend Tick Tock pointed to the side of her head. "What did you say?" I shouted as everybody froze.

"Come on, Krystal. Don't do this." Cedric pleaded for his girl's life.

The three other females were so scared they didn't move or even blink.

"So, yeah, I asked you what you said," I growled, getting in Mae Mae's face. It was like I was in a movie. My heart was beating fast, but I wasn't scared. "I should blow ya head off right now. But let me guess—you sorry now, right?"

The girl looked at me as pee started to flow down her pants leg onto her gym shoes.

"That's my sister," one of the guys yelled as he picked up a bat and started moving toward me.

I had to make a decision. Daddy Duane always said be ready to kill. So, I told myself, *Her first, then him.*

He was swinging the bat, and he was getting within striking distance. I cocked Tick Tock and was getting ready to pull the trigger.

"Anybody moves, and I'll kill you all." This was a new voice.

Everybody's eyes turned, searching for the person that spoke. I saw two familiar guns pointed, one at the guys and the other at the girls.

"Let it slide this time, Krystal. This is their only warning. Next time, we play for keeps." It was Ms. Lady. She saw the surprised expression on my face and smirked in response. "Uncock Tick Tock and let's go."

I was the only one who knew what she was talking about. I lowered the gun and kicked Mae Mae dead in the stomach. The other girls backed up so I couldn't reach them. I passed the guys and rolled my eyes at Cedric.

Ms. Lady put her guns to her side until I was safely in the car. Just like Daddy Duane, Ms. Lady explained what she was doing and why she did it.

"Find someone you trust to always have your back, like I had your father's. You don't pull a gun to show off. When you pull a gun, expect to use it, or keep it in your pocket. Only time you need it is when somebody disrespects you or you are trying to build a reputation.

"You said you want to be a player in the game. You cannot go off on somebody just 'cause you mad. You must think and then react. I want you to be calm and cool. That way, nobody can pull your strings. They can't catch you slipping if they don't know what makes you fall. Now, you understand me, Krystal?"

"Yes, Ms. Lady. Do you think what I did was wrong?" I asked.

"No, you were disrespected, and now you will have a rep at school. No one's going to bother you again."

I loved it when we had those heart-to-heart talks. Ms. Lady didn't pull any punches with me. Like Daddy Duane, she was always straightforward with me, teaching me about real life.

That was my junior year in school. By my senior year, I was running the school. I was supplying the weed and the pills. I had a crew, and Cedric was kinda my competition. He had graduated or dropped out, but he was at school every day, selling drugs. Our paths didn't cross much because he sold heroin.

I was making enough money to keep my supply going and take care of the bills. Ms. Lady had gotten worse with her addiction. She needed heroin in her body in the morning, then she used cocaine to bring her up from her jump-off high. I loved my mother deeply, but I vowed I would never use any kind of drug. I wanted my mind to be free to see what was coming at me. Ms. Lady had become blind to the world.

CHAPTER SEVEN

I was about to turn eighteen in three months, and I was graduating in six. My plan for my life was working. I would receive the money Daddy Duane left me and finish setting up my empire. I searched for a house to buy to no avail. So, I went back to the Bottom Barrel and talked to Uncle Nardo. He also had a plan for me that his best friend had put in place before he got killed. That was, if I decided I wanted to hustle. Daddy Duane must have known it was in my system early on.

"I have enough money to retire," Uncle Nardo had said, "so if you want it, the greasy spoon is yours." Uncle Nardo and Daddy Duane had owned the restaurant together.

"Cool," I answered. "I'm ready to hustle."

Uncle Nardo nodded his head. "Duane always said he thought you had it in you. I can turn you on to my supplier if you want."

"I do."

Uncle Nardo stared at me for a second with a concerned look on his face, and then he laid out the reality to me. "You know that as a female, dudes is gonna test you repeatedly. So be ready, build your crew, keep them loyal, and pay them good. Don't try to make all the money yourself. Yours is going to come. As always, I will always have your back if needed."

Just then, there was a knock on the door. Uncle Nardo opened it, and a chick walked in with an attitude. I didn't know her name, but she looked sorta familiar. She looked like a high-class model.

"You forgot our appointment. You were supposed to meet me," she said to Uncle Nardo. The young lady looked over at me and frowned. I guess she thought I was his girl.

"I'm sorry. I did not know you were expecting company," I said.

"Damn, y'all. Aren't you gonna speak?" Uncle Nardo said.

We both looked each other over and just shrugged our shoulders.

"This is your cousin Krystal," he said to the other chick, then he looked at me. "And this is Sable, my oldest daughter. You act like y'all didn't play together as kids or when Krystal stayed with us," he announced matter-of-factly.

I jumped up. "Sable!"

She ran over and hugged me. "Krystal, I haven't seen you in nine or ten years."

We were truly happy to see each other. Although we weren't real cousins, we always said we were. Sable was two years older than I was. She always protected me from the girls and the boys in elementary school. She was rough.

"You are beautiful, girl. What you been doing? Modeling?" I inquired.

"I was until my sister was killed last year," she stated.

"Okay, Sable, not now, please." Uncle Nardo stopped her, looking at the ground, not wanting to talk about it.

"Girl, what you been doing?" Sable asked, changing the subject like her father wanted her to. "Why you down here?"

"Getting ready to graduate. I just wanted to talk to Uncle Nardo." I didn't know how much Sable knew about Uncle Nardo's lifestyle, so I decided not to tell her my real reason for coming to the Bottom Barrel.

"I'm trying to get my pops out of the Bottom Barrel. He don't need to be here. He sometimes can't remember things, and people take advantage of him. So, I've been running his business with him." Sable stood proudly.

Uncle Nardo got out of his chair and approached us. "I'm glad you're both here. I want to talk to you ladies." He sounded serious. "Sable, I am retiring next month. I'm leaving the shop to Krystal. That was her old man's wish." Sable didn't look too bothered by what he said.

Then he told me, "I'm leaving Sable with my business."

I didn't say anything. That was his daughter, so of course he would give the business to her before me. But he wasn't done.

He continued, "I can't tell you ladies what to do, but Duane and I always dreamed that we'd stay in business long enough for our kids to take over. But we never thought about you being women. You girls already have a bond, and if you stay close like your father and I did, nothing could or should come between you."

"Daddy, are you really leaving?" Sable sounded like she was praying his answer was yes.

"Yes, baby girl. I couldn't leave you here alone, but with everything I taught you and everything Duane and Charday taught Krystal, I feel you girls will be all right. You must remember that we are family and always, I mean always, have each other's backs."

This was the start of building the foundation of our empire, which we called Family First Enterprise. For the next three months, we planned, recruited, and laid the groundwork. Every step we made, we talked about it.

We hustled out of the greasy spoon, and we always kept guys around us. That wasn't hard for Sable because she was so beautiful. Ms. Lady was still using drugs, so we set her up in the greasy spoon. She could use all the drugs she wanted, and we could keep an eye on her.

Sable and I became like sisters. All I had to do was think about it and she knew my thoughts.

On my eighteenth birthday, we had a party at the greasy spoon. This was my birthday and also our coming out party. We invited everybody in the neighborhood who we knew used drugs. We gave out free samples of Family First, the new heroin in the Bottom Barrel. The bags were labeled and distinctive in color. Everybody at the party, passing out the new drug, would have a dope house in a certain area. We told them where we would be and the hours.

Our business took off better than expected. The twenty thousand dollars I had spent as an initial investment was given back to me by Sable in eight months. Every week after that, Sable and I were able to clear ten thousand dollars apiece. We agreed we wouldn't buy new cars, jewelry, or anything that would bring attention to us. Instead, we purchased guns, rifles, bulletproof vests, and semi-automatic weapons to protect ourselves if need be.

Unfortunately, money had a way of turning people against each other. After eight months in business, our first encounter with this fact was from one of our own people. Terry kept trying to turn Sable and me against each other. As our lieutenant, Terry knew where all the dope houses were because he went to pick up the money. One day, two of our houses got robbed.

When he was alone with me, Terry said, "I think it was an inside job." He got a look on his face like he regretted having to say the next part. "I think Sable set it up."

When he went to talk to Sable, he changed it to "I think Krystal set it up."

Luckily, we were too smart to fall for his act. Sable and I talked about it in private and agreed we would keep an eye on him. We went with two of our enforcers to one of the houses that got robbed to talk to the dope fiend that ran it. We always used dope fiends in the houses because we paid them in drugs and kept a roof over their heads. They were usually loyal.

We drove up the street in an all-black, four-door old school belonging to one of the guys with us. I noticed the expressions on people's faces when we passed them. It was as if, seeing this big black car, they knew there was going to be trouble. It was then I got the idea that that would be our calling card when we had a beef: You would see black cars riding the blocks.

When we arrived at the house, the dope fiend first didn't seem to take it seriously. He said lamely, "Somebody caught me off guard and took the money."

I guess he thought it was a joke, looking at two women holding guns on him. One enforcer watched the door, while the other one watched the people in the house.

"You got two sawed-off shotguns and a pistol, and they caught you off guard?" I yelled at him. Before he could manage to respond, I shot him in the side of his left foot. His shrieks rang throughout the house, and everybody got quiet. "Negro, I'm only going to ask you once. If you know, tell me. If you don't know, the next bullet is for your balls." I stuck the gun between his legs.

Tears were running down his face as he tried to balance on one leg because his injured foot was bleeding all over the place. "Krystal—"

Before he got another word out, Sable had hit him in the face with her gun. "Don't lie," she warned with fever.

Blood ran down his face from the gash in his head, and pain flowed up his leg from the gunshot. "Okay, okay, okay! Terry told me to give him the money. He gave me an extra package for myself. I'm sorry, Krystal. He said he was going to put me out the house."

I thought for a moment. Sable and the guys were looking at me to give a nod so they could kill him. I told him, "I'm going to give you a pass on this, but if I come up a cent short on any package, it's a done deal. You feel me?"

Pete nodded his head nervously, showing me that he understood my terms.

"Now, I want you to do something." I looked over at one of our enforcers. "Lloyd, gimme some bags."

Lloyd threw me a package of dope.

"Pete, this is yours. I want you to call me when Terry comes. And don't tell him I was here. You keep him here until I get here any damn way you can. Then call me. You understand that?" I mean mugged around at everybody, "Nobody better not say nothing to nobody."

The guys with me walked around and looked at everybody eye to eye, their pistols out. Most of the dope fiends lost their high. They were terrified of getting hurt themselves for being in the wrong place at the wrong time.

"Pete, you got dope in the house?" I asked, visibly tired of the bullshit.

"Yes," Pete replied, teary-eyed.

"Well, give everybody two dime bags on the house. I'll have Lloyd bring the replacement package back. Now, are we cool, Pete? You got the plan?"

With fear in his eyes and blood still running from the hole in his foot, Pete nodded his head in agreement.

We showed no mercy for him or anyone in there. We were prepared to kill everybody if necessary. On the way home, we talked about the situation and our next step.

"We'll let Terry think he's getting away with it," I said. "But when we get the call that he's at the house, we'll catch up with his ass."

They all agreed with the plan.

Terry was supposed to make a pickup that night, so we prepared. I got two nine millimeters and put them in my coat. I put on the bulletproof vest.

"Sable, you stay back and watch the fort in case something happens to us."

"Nah, fuck that," she said, putting on her vest and grabbing a gun.

I took her in the office so we could talk without anyone else ear hustling.

"Look," I said, "We decided I would handle all the enforcement and you'd handle the cash," I reminded her. "I trust you with my money, right? So you should trust me."

"I do trust you," she said, "but Terry came for both of us, so I wanna be there with you to take care of his ass."

I appreciated her loyalty, but it wouldn't be a smart move, I explained. "If something happened to both of us, all we've accomplished would be for nothing."

It took her a minute to think about it, but finally she agreed to stay behind.

Before I left, we sat and talked with Ms. Lady to tell her what was up.

"Well, you know that as a mother, I still worry about you. But I know what you have to do," she told me. "Ya know, I can go with you and put in work."

I shook my head. "No, Ms. Lady, you stay here. I gotta handle this part of the business myself."

We waited a couple hours until the phone rang. It was Pete, saying he and his halfwit brother were holding Terry at gunpoint in the bedroom. I came out of the office. Not a word spoken as I headed straight for the door, followed by seven guys—three of my enforcers and four runners. We got in Lloyd's whip and Hakim's Malibu.

We arrived at the house in four minutes and were let in by the doorman. He had a sawed-off shotgun in his hand. The joint was crowded with dope fiends getting their high on. When the group of us walked in, everything became silent.

We went straight to the room. Terry was there on the bed with his hands tied. Pete's brother had a shotgun close to his chest. Pete was at the door with his pistol cocked, pointing it at Terry. My once loyal soldier didn't know what was going on until he saw my face and then saw my enforcers. I never let anyone see my enforcers until they were needed. They were part of the Bottom Barrel community, but deadly and loyal to me. I paid them well.

"Krystal, I swear I didn't do nothing. I don't know what Pete has told you. He's a dope fiend," Terry yelled in anticipation of what he knew was going to happen.

Pete's brother hit him with the butt of the rifle.

"Pete didn't tell me nothing," I said, shaking my head at his pitiful attempt to fend off what was coming for him. "Someone untie this nigga," I ordered.

All my guys had their guns out, ready for any command I'd give. I walked casually over to him, my gun out, and placed it to his head. "I'm only going to ask you this one time. Where is my fucking money?"

"I didn't have nothing—"

Before he could finish the sentence, Lloyd had hit him with some brass knuckles. Blood poured out the open wound on his head.

"It's in my car," Terry blurted out in fear of being hit once more.

"Gimme me the keys!" I demanded.

He reached in his pocket, happy to oblige my firm request.

Lloyd hit him again on principle. "Just in case you thought about reaching for something else."

Terry gave me the keys, and I threw them to Hakim. "Go get my money." I then turned to evil-eye Terry. "Every penny better be there from both houses."

"Walter got the other shit," Terry quickly confessed, recklessly spitting blood on my clothes.

"Walter from the number streets?" I questioned.

All my enforcers looked at me to see the next move. Walter was a killer from back in the day rumored to have murdered two undercover officers. To me, this only meant we had to come correct to get my money back.

Hakim returned with a bag full of money. He counted four thousand dollars.

"Where's my other two thousand, Terry?" I yelled.

"I spent it. I'll get it back, Krystal, by tomorrow." Terry was in tears.

My mind was racing. I had to set an example, or I would be tried again and again. "You two get him and bring him in the living room," I commanded.

Lloyd and Hakim grabbed Terry. Lloyd put duct tape around Terry's mouth.

"No, put the tape around his chest. I want his mouth free," I said.

We walked into the living room. All eyes were on us. Lloyd and Hakim pushed Terry to the middle of the floor.

"Listen up!" I yelled to the dope fiends all around. "I will give fifty dollars cash to any man in here that is willing to let ole Terry here suck his dick."

The fear in Terry's face became evident as he tried to search my eyes for pity. An old man with big arms stepped to the middle of the floor. His legs were big, too, swollen from the years of shooting drugs in his veins.

"Excuse me, Ms. Krystal, but you said if I let him suck my dick, you gonna just give me fifty dollars? No lie?"

"Yes. Hakim, give him fifty dollars." I smirked with satisfaction. The old man unzipped his pants and found his little penis and stuck it in Terry's face.

"If you bite anybody, it ends right here," Lloyd promised with authority, eager to pull the trigger.

"Open your fucking mouth, turncoat-ass nigga," Hakim hissed as he nudged Terry, who had tears and snot running down his face. He pissed on himself, and I thought I smelled some shit as his pride was taken. This went on for two or three minutes before the big dude finished.

"Next! Who's next to get this cash?"

The rest of the male dope fiends in the house saw that this was some easy money and a free high, so they got in line.

I walked to the door, and Lloyd followed me. He was always two steps behind me wherever I went. I really wanted to give him some, but then I'd have to kill him, because he would try to take advantage of me. I stopped near the men who were guarding the door.

"Lloyd, tell Hakim to put him in his car. I don't want no body found." I put my pistol away as Lloyd went to whisper in Hakim's ear.

Lloyd told the others to stay with Hakim, and we left. On the way back to the greasy spoon, we spoke about what the consequences of our actions would be. Whatever they were, we would be prepared. We also talked about Walter and decided we would pay his disloyal ass a visit the next day. If he heard about Terry, he would be looking for us. So, we would strike first.

CHAPTER EIGHT

When we pulled up on the block, I saw police cars everywhere, marked and unmarked. As we got closer to the greasy spoon, we noticed they were going in and out. Lloyd looked at me and I looked at him, concern in our eyes.

"Keep going, Lloyd. Go around the block." I thought about my mother and Sable.

I hope nothing happened to them. Maybe somebody stuck us up. Sable would never call the police without calling me first.

"Lloyd, stop the car."

He pulled over, and we took off our vests and put all the guns in the trunk. We left the car around the block and walked back to the greasy spoon.

"I don't like this," Lloyd said. "I feel like we're unprotected."

"Relax. It's gonna be a'ight," I assured him.

When we arrived at the greasy spoon, the police asked me, "Who are you?"

"I'm the owner," I told him, then pointed to Lloyd. "And this is my husband."

He let us pass by, and we rushed inside. "Where's Ms. Lady?" I yelled in a panic, noticing all the solemn faces. Lloyd held me as Sable came running from the office at the sound of my voice.

"Krystal, Auntie got shot! She got shot in the leg, but she's all right. They rushed her to the hospital."

I looked around and saw bullet holes everywhere. The police were taking fingerprints and looking around. "What happened? You all right?" I was shaking as I leaned on Sable.

"Somebody tried to stick us up, and Auntie was forced to shoot him to save our lives." Sable gave me that look, like "don't ask no more questions." She tightly hugged me and whispered in my ear, "I'll tell you later."

I hadn't really noticed, but all the police officers were coming from the office.

Did they find our guns and drugs? No, if that was the case, we would be in handcuffs.

Sable pulled me into the office, with Lloyd following right behind. A few police officers were bending over something. As we got closer, I saw it was a male's body. The face was almost blown off. I couldn't see his nose or ears. It looked like his pants were pulled down.

Lloyd tapped me on the back to get my attention. "Yooo, that's Walter's good thieving ass."

I couldn't wait to hear this story.

The police tried to talk to us, but I told them, "My mother just got shot. I can't think straight to talk to y'all right now."

The morgue finally came and got the body, and then most of the officers left. One stayed and tried to get Sable to go out with him. She begrudgingly agreed, and he finally left as well.

Ms. Lady returned from the hospital with a bandage wrapped around her leg. She took one look at my face and saw how concerned I was. "Relax," she told me. "It's only a flesh wound. God was on my side today."

I hugged her tight, relieved that she wasn't hurt worse. Then I turned to Sable.

"So, yo, what really popped off?" I asked.

"I was coming out the office when this guy comes in. He said he wanted to make a purchase. Auntie knew him, so I went to hook him up. When I came back, he had a gun on her. He asked where you were."

"He asked for me?"

"Yeah, you. Then Auntie came up blasting from her hip after hearing your name. But she was so high, she kept missing his ass. He messed around and shot her in the leg. Then he asked where we kept the money and the drugs.

"I had my gun on me, and he saw it and took it. He shoved me in the office, all the time looking at my ass. 'You are a pretty young thing,' he mumbled and then he started rubbing his nuts.

"I went to get the house money we keep for this kind of occasion, and I gave it to him. He was so busy looking at me, he dropped the damn money," Sable explained all in one breath.

She paused for a minute and then continued her story.

"He yells at me, 'You pick it up, little bitch!' I started thinking that all this fool wanted was some pussy. So, I bent down to pick up the money."

I could already tell where this story was going, and when she continued, she confirmed what I thought.

"Of course, you know I don't wear no panties, and I had on this mini skirt. So, he saw my bald private parts staring him in the face. I opened my legs more and pretended to be scared. *Please don't hurt me.*" She said that last part in a little girl voice. She had played her part well.

"And then I looked up in his eyes and gave him the money. I could see the lust written all over his face. He says, 'Don't play with me. I'm not the one,' like he was in control, but I could tell his excitement was getting the best of him.

"I started fake crying, but my mind was on Tick Tock you left in the desk drawer. When dude got on top of me and started to unfasten his pants, I told him, 'Wait, let's get on the desk. I promise I won't resist as long as you don't hurt me.' So, he let me up. I got on the desk and laid back so I could reach my left hand in the drawer.

"Girl, I opened my legs and lifted them over my head so I could pull the gun out without him seeing me. He was all like, 'Damn, that shit looks good.'" She laughed at how stupid this fool was.

"He pulled down his pants. Just then, I saw Auntie out the corner of my eye. She was close. She shot him in the fucking ear. Stupid fool turned to try to retaliate, but he had left his gun on the damn floor. Auntie shot again, and I found Tick Tock. Then I shot him dead in the face."

"That's what I'm talking about," I said, proud of both of them.

She continued, "I got up off the desk as he fell to the ground. I was pissed that he thought he could rape me like it was nothing, so I shot him two more times. To make sure he was good and dead, Auntie shot him once more in the heart. We made sure that he would never be able to come back on us."

"Well, y'all did good," I said, "and I'm relieved that no one was seriously hurt. Now, what did y'all tell the cops?"

"I told the police that he tried to stick us up and rape me, which was true. So, if we have to lawyer up later down the road behind this bullshit, then so be it."

CHAPTER NINE

The word was out, and our reputation was growing. Family First Enterprise was growing. Our name-brand product of heroin was selling throughout the state. You would see white and black folks coming from all parts to visit the greasy spoon. We had to have at least five guys on the payroll to help Ms. Lady because of the steady traffic. We had detectives visit us once a month to pick up an envelope. I had been against this all the way, but Sable insisted, and I guess she was right. We never had a police raid.

I was twenty-one, I had a six-figure bank account, and a new house in the suburbs. Here I was, making all this money, and I wasn't happy. Sable said I needed to get out more and meet different people. I agreed to hang out with her and her police officer friend, the one that was at the greasy spoon the night Ms. Lady got shot. He was also the one who picked up the envelopes.

We went to this fancy restaurant downtown. The food was decent, and I enjoyed spending time with Sable away from the greasy spoon. Seeing her happy made me a little jealous. Sable and her man were laughing and talking. I guess that was what I missed in my life. I was so focused on trying to set up my business that I missed out.

While looking away, not trying to intrude on their time together, I thought I saw someone I knew. It looked like Cedric from high school. He appeared so mature and businesslike, sitting there with a suit and tie. I tried to catch his eye, but the waiter got in my way so he couldn't see me.

"Krystal, are you enjoying yourself this evening?" asked Sable.

"Yes, girl, I—" Before I could finish my sentence, a bouquet of flowers was in my face.

"Hello there, beautiful." It was Cedric.

"Cedric, what are you doing here?" I asked while blushing and taking the flowers.

"I'm in here all the time. I'm a silent partner," he said.

I was impressed, and for a minute, I just stared at him. Sable cleared her throat to get my attention.

"Oh, I'm sorry," I said, snapping out of my trance. "This is my cousin Sable and her friend Tim. Can you join us?" I asked with my brightest smile.

"No, I'm sorry. I'm waiting on a new client."

The disappointment must have been all over my face. My whole demeanor changed.

He continued, "Not to be rude, but Krystal, would you join me for a few minutes at my table while I wait for my client? We can catch up."

I looked at Sable, and she gave me that look that we had only between us.

"Sable, Tim, I'll be back," I said.

Cedric pulled my chair out so I could get up, scoring points with Sable on his manners.

"Nice meeting you guys." Cedric smiled as he grabbed my hand and led me to his table.

We talked for hours. He said he was an investor, and he bought properties and resold them.

"I don't sell drugs no more. Everything I do is legit," he said, sounding proud of himself. "But I heard you slangin' the Bottom Barrel."

I couldn't tell if he was judging me, so I just nodded my head slightly, not sharing any details.

"I also heard you got it all sewed up down there. Good for you," he said. It felt good to know he was impressed.

A while later, Sable came over to our table and said, "Yo, we're gonna head out. You okay over here?"

"Yeah, I'm cool," I told her.

Cedric spoke up. "If you'd like, I can bring you home later."

I thought about it for a minute and decided I didn't want the night to end yet, so I said, "Yeah, you can take me home later."

Sable looked in my eyes to make sure I really meant it. I could tell she wasn't sure about this dude yet. She looked out for me like that.

"Okay," she said, "but you got Tick Tock, right?"

"Sure do."

Once she was satisfied that I was okay, she left.

"Tick Tock, huh?" Cedric said, laughing as he watched her and Tim leave the restaurant.

"Yeah," I said. "A sister can't be too careful out here."

"I hear that."

We stayed until everyone else had left and the crew was cleaning up the restaurant. I had Cedric take me over Sable's house because I didn't want him to know where I lived so soon.

We sat in front of Sable's house talking. It was raining outside, but the temperature was warm. The light rain on the windshield was so romantic. I was getting this funny feeling, like when you are happy to be somewhere, but you don't know where you're going. We let the seats back and talked until the sun came up. It seemed like we had so much in common. He was where I wanted to be in the next five years.

"I gotta go. Look at what time it is," I finally said.

He looked into my eyes. "I enjoyed the time we spent together. I'm sorry we never had the opportunity to get together in high school."

As I got out of the car, he followed me, to my surprise. *I hope he don't think he's getting some.*

As a true gentleman, he walked me to my door, gave me his card, and asked me to call him. Cedric kissed me on the cheek and walked back to his car and left. My past was about to be my future.

CHAPTER TEN

Three hours later, the smell of bacon and eggs awoke me from my sleep. In the kitchen, Sable was cooking breakfast.

"Good morning, Krystal. How was your night? You must have gotten in pretty late," she said.

"Yeah, I got in late," I responded briefly, knowing she wanted to hear details about Cedric and my night with him. I washed my hands and got a plate to eat.

"Okay, Krystal," she said when she figured out that I was not giving up the details easily. "Who was he, and what did you do last night?"

I started gushing like a schoolgirl with a crush. "I had the most beautiful night. We just had a good time talking, laughing, and getting to know each other. We stayed in the restaurant until after it closed. And I had Cedric bring me over here so he wouldn't know where I stay."

"Uh-huh. That's how we do it. Smart move," she said. We laughed, and she gave me a high five.

"But it felt good being around someone that you can identify with, someone who looks at you and doesn't just see money or a profit. You know what I mean?"

"Yes, but guys always want something. You just haven't figured out what." She was skeptical.

"Girl, I don't think he's like that. I've known him since high school, even though we never had the chance to hook up because he was with some crazy ho. Anyway, we laughed and talked until the sun came up."

Sable looked at me with her eyebrows raised like she was surprised. She'd never heard me talking like this about no dude.

"Shit, I better stop thinking like that," I said, coming back to reality. "We got work to put in. I ain't got time to fall in love."

"Krystal, trust, there is no right time. When it hits you, it hits you. Ain't jack shit you can do about it but deal with it. Now, go on and eat this breakfast while I go upstairs and get dressed," Sable said.

A half hour later, Sable came downstairs dressed to the nines. She had on a sexy hat tilted to the side and a black business pants suit with a fluffy blouse that she accented with a red tie, which matched the color of her lipstick.

"Girl, where are you going?" I smiled, seeing how fresh she was.

"You better get dressed too. You forgot we supposed to meet a big supplier today?"

"Damn, yeah. Give me ten minutes." I went upstairs and got dressed in a blue jean outfit with a big shirt that hid the holsters of my guns. Then I put on some flat shoes. I always dressed the opposite of Sable. My logic was that somebody had to be prepared in case something gangster jumped off.

When I came downstairs, Sable was already in the car on the phone.

We arrived at our destination and soon realized the two men didn't have much in the way of security. I assume they felt we were women, so they could handle us if need be.

The Ridgeway brothers let us know what their offer was. "We want you to sell crack in the greasy spoon. We'll give you fifty thousand dollars' worth of drugs, and you give us thirty thousand back." This meant that we would have to give them eighty thousand dollars.

Sable, the businesswoman that she was, objected. "That's not a deal for us. You're making profit on our hard work."

Desmond Ridgeway grinned. "You ladies are getting a steal, a real bargain. We're letting you in the business."

"You letting us in? Is that right? We're letting you in, 'cause you can't sell nothing in the Bottom Barrel without coming through our camp." Sable's voice was filled with contempt. She looked at me, letting me know to get ready for anything.

John Ridgeway jumped up, irate. He was obviously the hothead of the siblings. "Make these bitches take the deal or else!"

Both of my hands found the triggers of my guns. I was ready to come up firing at any sign of trouble.

Sable grabbed her purse and remained calm. "Come on, Krystal. These guys ain't ready for us."

I got up with both hands inside my shirt. Sable looked Desmond eye to eye. "Mr. Ridgeway, I'll give you fifty thousand cash for your drugs, and we'll be even. But you have to deliver it to the Bottom Barrel. So, let's see if you really got balls. Here's my card if you wish to make that happen."

John Ridgeway's tone was arrogant. "So, you people got fifty large?"

"*We people*, whatever that's supposed to mean, got a hundred large. That's if you got the balls to deliver. If not, then don't call us no more. We good doing what we do, making money moves." Sable headed to the door with me backing out behind her.

When we got to the car, we sighed with relief. Any more dealings, we'd always have backup. The game was getting elevated.

CHAPTER ELEVEN

When we reached the greasy spoon, Lloyd met us at the door. He had this stupid look plastered on his face as if he didn't know what was what.

"Dawg, what's wrong? What done happened now?" I asked, dreading what he was going to say.

"Hakim done messed around and OD'd," Lloyd finally blurted out.

"What? I didn't know he used," Sable fired back, shocked.

"Where the hell is he now?" I rushed Lloyd for the answer.

We were led back to the bathroom, where Hakim was laying on the floor with a needle plunged into his arm. Ms. Lady was trying to wake him up by slapping him repeatedly. Although I'd sold drugs for years now, I had never seen anybody like this. Hakim's eyes had rolled to the rear of his skull. He was turning blue. His mouth was wide open, and his tongue was to the side.

Sable, however, was not stunned. She sprang into action. "Get him up, Lloyd," she feverishly demanded, taking control. "Put him in the shower, turn on the cold water. Krystal, go get some ice, lots of it. Auntie Charday, get some towels. Lloyd, you take his clothes off."

Lloyd barked, "No homo, I ain't taking his clothes off."

"Then move, nigga! I'll take them off." Sable had no time to squabble or stand on formalities.

While Lloyd held Hakim up, Sable jumped in the shower with him. She took off his pants, then his underwear.

"Let him down in the water, Lloyd," Sable ordered, not caring that she was soaking wet. Her focus was on saving Hakim's life.

I returned with the ice, and Ms. Lady got the towels. Sable sat in the tub with Hakim, on her knees, facing him. She took the ice and shoved it under his nuts. Wetting the towels, she put them on his face.

"Go get a spoon so he won't swallow his tongue," she said to Ms. Lady. She kept rubbing the ice on his nuts as the water continued to run on his head and on her.

She put the spoon in his mouth. "Krystal, you hold the spoon and the towel on his forehead."

I did what she told me to do.

"Hakim! Hakim! Hakim, wake up!" Sable repeatedly shouted as we all stood around.

"I had a friend name Chuckie that used to OD from time to time before you were born," Ms. Lady told me. "But I ain't never seen no one do all this."

Seeing Sable take control made me confident and glad she was there. Lloyd was terrified, to say the least. A big man like that couldn't watch his friend and crime partner so close to death.

Sable was soaked from head to toe. Her nice black suit was clinging to her body, and one of her black pumps was floating in the water.

After what seemed like a lifetime, Hakim began to cough. His eyes weren't rolled back in his head anymore, so we could see his pupils, and he was regaining his color. Still, Sable sat there putting ice underneath his nuts until he came around fully. She'd saved his life, and Hakim would be forever grateful to her for the rest of his drug-filled days.

CHAPTER TWELVE

It had been a week since Cedric and I had sat in the car talking all night. I hadn't called him yet, but he was most definitely on my mind. My days were busy handling day to day operations, and my nights were spent thinking about Cedric. I decided I would call him the next day. My birthday was coming up the next week, so maybe we could go out and celebrate together. The thought of Cedric lured me off to sleep. Maybe he would be the one to settle down with.

The birds were chirping and the parade of squirrels playing on my roof woke me up. On my way to the bathroom, the phone rang. I knew it was Sable or Ms. Lady. They were the only ones who had my second cell phone number.

It was Sable. It seemed the Ridgeway brothers had called to accept our deal, and they set up a meeting for two o'clock. We both needed cash on hand to make the deal happen.

"I gotta go the bank for some money. We got last week's cut of twenty thousand and the five thousand safe money. What you got, Krystal?"

"I got about forty thousand in the house. I haven't made a deposit in a couple of months."

"Krystal, I told you about having all that money laying around."

"Look Sable, don't lecture me. You handle the business at hand and let me worry about my money," I shot back at her.

"Okay, so are we doing this today, or should I call and reschedule?"

"We good, worry wart. I'll handle the security and will meet you at the greasy spoon. Its eight thirty. I'll be there at eleven. Tell Ms. Lady to close up and only let in our people. Tell them to stay put."

I got dressed and snatched up my big purse so I could hold my two guns and the forty thousand dollars.

As I made my way to the greasy spoon, I went over the plan in my mind. I called all my runners and all the house sitters. Usually, we had two people in each house. That was so someone was always awake and they could watch each other's backs when they opened the door. Today, I pulled one person from each of the six houses we now had. I had two lieutenants and four enforcers. So, I had twelve guys to set up a front for the Ridgeway brothers. I called each person and told them to drive their own car. I wanted a lot of cars parked around the greasy spoon.

When I arrived, all twelve guys were there with Ms. Lady and Sable. I sat on the counter and told everybody what my plan was. "I want four guys outside, two on each side of the street in your cars. I want to hear horns when they arrive, and not again unless the police are coming or there's trouble. The two lieutenants and two other house sitters will be chilling."

Everybody nodded to show they understood their orders.

"I want all guns visible. Everybody should have holsters. If not, put them in your front pants belt, visible. Ms. Lady, I want you on the shoeshine stand. I'll give you an AK assault rifle." I was in my hustle zone, wanting everything to go off without any issues.

"Hakim, you and Tank will be at the front door. Y'all search them crackers good. I only want them to have a briefcase, no guns. Tank, you stay at the door after they are searched. Don't let anyone in. Hakim, you lead them to me, and all the time, you are behind them."

"Got you." Tank checked the bullets in his clip.

"Lloyd, you and your boy will be at the office door with your guns out. You bring them in and lock the door behind you. I don't want any interruptions. Everybody be relaxed, but I want you to look your usual mean-ass selves." I cracked a halfway smile but was dead-ass serious.

"So, it's eleven forty-five, and I want everybody in place at one o'clock. No one getting ghost until three o'clock. I done ordered some steak dinners. They on the way. And oh yeah, Hakim, no getting high." I singled him out because he was always getting teased about his overdose.

"What am I supposed to do, Krystal?" Sable asked.

"You the businessperson in this company, so handle our business, Sis."

After a brief time, our food arrived. We ate and talked shit as a family for the next hour. By 1:15, everybody was in place ready for business.

I took Sable in the office, and we waited.

"If this dope is as good as the Ridgeway brothers say it is, we gonna make a lot of money," Sable said, and I agreed.

We had upgraded our security system since the incident with Walter. We had cameras installed, and we could see the whole block from our office.

My cell phone rang, making Sable and me both jump. It was one of the lieutenants on the outside.

"We got a little problem," he said.

I looked at the monitor to the front door, and I saw six white men surrounded by ten black men. So much for a good plan.

"Don't nobody move!" I yelled through the speaker system.

Sable and I went to the front door, closely followed by Lloyd and Tank. Everybody else was outside. When I got to the door, John Ridgeway, the brother with the big mouth was on ten.

"So, is this how you people treat your guests? Seriously, no home training! This must be a joke!"

"You may think this is funny, but does it look like anyone out here is laughing or playing? You breathe wrong, and they will never find your white ass again. Why you thought you could bring six white guys with guns to my business is beyond me."

The faces of the white guys turned beet red, but neither side moved a muscle.

Sable broke the stalemate. "Okay look. We'll let two of your guys inside, but no guns. The other four guys will be escorted out the perimeter of the Bottom Barrel until our transaction is complete."

"Okay then," Desmond Ridgeway agreed, wanting to keep the peace and just get down to business.

There was fear in the eyes of the four other men, not knowing if this meant their last day on earth.

As Sable led the way back in the greasy spoon, Desmond and John came inside, followed by the two other white men. They were each searched and stripped of their guns. Desmond and John Ridgeway came into the rear office. The other two white men were sat at the bar, facing the shoeshine stand and Ms. Lady with the AK trained on them.

I motioned to Lloyd to come over and open the briefcase. We didn't want or need any more surprises. Lloyd opened the briefcase, which had nothing but kilos in them.

"Shall we get down to business, gentlemen?" Sable opened her own briefcase and took out a testing tool. She also had the money in it.

She opened one of the bags in the brothers' brief-case. Cutting the bag, she dug out some of the product. She put it in a bottle and put in a few drops of liquid, then shook it up.

She smiled at the sight of the color. "Yeah. Hell yeah! This looks like some good stuff," she affirmed. Sable, being the thorough businesswoman that she was, tested each bag to the annoyance of John Ridgeway.

"What do you people think we are, stupid?" he asked.

"You stupid enough to bring six white men to a black neighborhood with guns. What do you think?" I fired back with attitude.

Before I could say another word, Lloyd was behind John, his pistol to his head.

"Hey, hold up! Just relax!" Desmond gave John a de-manding look. "Like, you are going to get us killed."

"Yeah, relax," Lloyd mumbled, ready to end John's life on my word.

"Look, ladies, we'll finish our business at hand, and then we are gone. You got the cash we agreed upon?" Desmond asked.

Sable threw the money from her briefcase on the desk. I reached in my bag and threw out four bundles of ten thousand each. John got up and started counting the money, but Desmond stopped his brother.

"No need. I trust you girls. I think we'll be back again, and we will have a good working relationship down the line." Desmond got up and put the money in his briefcase. He closed it and headed for the exit.

When they reached the door, he looked at Lloyd to let them out. Lloyd was in a trance. He had never seen that much money or dope before at one time. Lloyd's eyes showed dollar signs of greed as he finally opened the door. Right then and there, I made a mental note to watch Lloyd very closely. I think Sable was thinking the same thing, as she gave me that look.

When the door opened, the greasy spoon fell silent. The two white men were still sitting in the chairs, sweat running down their faces.

When the men came out of the greasy spoon, all they could see was black faces, black cars, and men dressed in black. It was clear to them that we were definitely in control of the Bottom Barrel drug game.

CHAPTER THIRTEEN

After the Ridgeway brothers left, we had to keep the greasy spoon closed while Sable and I tried to figure out our game plan for selling the drugs. I called Ms. Lady in the office to get her advice.

"The fastest way to get rid of that much is to sell weight, which means selling to dealers. The downfall is the dealers might try you more, knowing that you have gotten bigger than them. The other way is to continue selling at street level. It may take longer, and you will have more traffic, but you can stay a little bit more in the background. You'll make lots of money," she told us.

We talked and re-bagged the drugs into smaller portions. Then Sable and I left to stash most of what we bought. We didn't allow anymore drugs to be sold at the greasy spoon. It was our headquarters where we hung out and held meetings. The only rule was no drugs sold. We had three money stashes—Sable's house, my house, and a safe deposit box. Could you believe that? I wouldn't trust money in a bank, but we put our drugs in a safe deposit box in the bank. I told Sable we had to find another place. It would be a federal case if we got caught.

Pretty soon, we had everybody wanting our name-brand drugs. Our brand name for crack was N.O.D.D. This identified us from other dealers. We split up the narcotics and divided them amongst the lieutenants. We had sworn that we would never use any drugs, smoke any weed, or drink alcohol. We wanted our minds to be totally focused on making this money. We were already at a disadvantage being females in a male-driven game.

***

It was around 9:30 before Sable and I actually had time to sit down. The greasy spoon always closed at 9:00.

Overall, it had been a good day. I just wanted to go home and relax. Sable was meeting Tim, and she asked me if I wanted to come. I declined, but my mind immediately turned to Cedric. I didn't want to be alone, so I called him.

"Hey, Cedric, this is Krystal. You busy?"

"What's up, Krystal? I know your voice, and I was praying you called me. I really enjoyed the last time we were together. I just can't stop thinking about you. I hope you don't think I'm too blunt, but I'd like to see you tonight."

"Cedric, I've been thinking about you too. But it's been a long day, and I just wanted to relax." I had changed my mind about being with him or anyone else for the night.

"I just wanted to take you to get something to eat and talk to you. I don't know what you've done to me. I just want to be around you. Can you blame a brother for that?" he said in a convincing voice.

"Look, I'm not at home yet. It's late."

"I tell you what. You go home and shower, and if you are hungry or you want to see me, you call me. I couldn't call you since you didn't give me your number. It's good you didn't, because I would have called you every day just to hear your voice."

"That's so sweet, Cedric. Did you really mean that?" I asked.

"Would I lie to a beautiful woman like you?" he remarked.

I told him to call me in an hour, then hung up the phone and looked at it for a minute. A smile broke out on my face, and again I got this tingly feeling in my stomach.

I went home and showered. I usually wore big clothes that didn't show my body lines, but tonight I wanted to look pretty. I looked in the mirror. I couldn't remember dressing up like this since I was nine. My body was slim-thick in all the right places, making my outfit fit like it was made for me.

After speaking to Cedric, I got in my car and headed downtown where he wanted to meet. Of course, you know I had to be fashionably late to go inside. I sat in the car and thought about my mother. She would love to see me now. Every time she saw me, I was dressed for work, with my hardcore look on. If you didn't know me, you would think I was a dyke.

It was time to make my entrance. Cedric was sitting toward the door, and the waitress was talking to him. Our eyes met, and I could swear it felt like something out of a movie. He looked at me while the waitress was still talking to him. He smiled as I started my long walk to his table. I hadn't worn high heels in five years. I had to take it slow, which made it look like I was a movie star entering a restaurant with ordinary people waiting for the camera flashing to stop.

He pulled my seat out and gently pushed it in before I sat. A real gentleman. That was a point for him.

"You look good. I knew you had potential when we were in high school, but I could have never imagined you'd grow up to be this beautiful," he said.

"Thanks. You are making me blush with all these compliments."

"I'm sorry. I'm just feeling good tonight. Krystal, have you ever wanted something so bad, but because of the timing, you couldn't get it? Then later on in life, you have another chance. That's how I feel. But this time, I'm not going to let you slip away."

"The only thing you wanted was that smart-ass girl and to be with your homies."

"I wanted you then, but you weren't ready," he confessed.

"Am I ready now?" I grinned.

He couldn't stop staring at me. He looked deep in my eyes as though he were thinking of our high school days.

"You are more than ready. I want to beat the pavement of the world with you by my side."

The band played soft jazz, and the atmosphere was romantic. We talked a lot, getting to really know each other. I was shocked to find out that Cedric had graduated from college. Divorced, he had two sons. As a broker and investor, the man had good deals on property. He asked me what I wanted out of life. I had to actually think about it. He asked me where I wanted to be in ten years. Again, I couldn't answer. Cedric's conversation was out of my league. The guys I dated were more of hit-it-and-quit-it types. Never had I come across someone so confident.

When he received a call from a client, the night took a turn. Once Cedric ended the conversation, he filled me in. "I just closed a deal for a lot of money, but I have to fax the purchase offer to my client before he changes his mind."

"That's okay. It's late, and I need to go home anyway."

"I don't want to end this. I'm really enjoying you. Please don't let this business stop our evening. I just need to fax this form. If you don't mind, I live five minutes away. Ride with me, and I will bring you back to your car after I fax this form."

"That's fine with me," came out my mouth. *Did I say that? I know the games men play. He wants to take me to his house and seduce me. The feelings I have had the last couple of hours, though. Hell, let's roll with it.*

Cedric paid the check, and we left. The valet brought his car, a new BMW different than the first vehicle he'd taken me home in. We drove along the river road until we reached a complex that I had never seen. The homes looked like mini mansions. We stopped and pulled in the circle driveway. I noticed four or five cars on the side of the house before we went inside.

"I have to go upstairs to my office and fax these papers. Make yourself at home. It's some juice or water in the refrigerator. The kitchen is to the left," he announced as he ran upstairs and disappeared in a room.

I was glad he gave me directions. The rooms were so big, but they were clean. No evidence of a woman. No plants, not a lot of pictures. Neutral colors. This was impressive. I got some water and one for Cedric and went to look at every room.

I was ready to get naked and lay on the floor in the family room. The furniture was white with a beautiful white rug close to the fireplace. I imagined making love right there on that rug. I began to get wet between my legs. It had been a while since I'd had sex. It was not one of my priorities. Ms. Lady and Daddy Duane always said, "Get that money and you can have anyone you want. Instead of them picking you, you pick who you want."

Cedric startled me when he came in the room. "You ready to go?" he asked.

"Can I use the restroom first?" I asked, trying to see the upstairs, being the nosy woman that I was.

"It's one down the hall to the left," he said.

"Which way?" I asked as if I hadn't looked around downstairs.

"Let me take you to the bathroom upstairs. When you finish, I'll show you the rest of the house."

He led me upstairs, passing pictures of better places in life. The art looked expensive. The floors were made of light oak, shining like a bald head. He pointed to the bathroom. Everything was made of silver with blue trim. The bathroom was as large as my kitchen. Towels were matching, and the shower was made of block glass. There were two sets of mirrors and two sinks and two toilets, one smaller than the other. I thought that was for a baby but didn't want to ask Cedric.

I didn't want to come out of the bathroom. It smelled so good in there. I really wanted to jump in the Jacuzzi tub and relax, then get out and put on one of those big robes I saw folded on the table with the towels and wash cloths. Then I would go lay in Cedric's arms by the fireplace.

"Cedric," I called when I came out of the bathroom.

"I'm in here." I followed the sound of his voice to his office.

He was behind a big desk with a big picture window looking out to the landscape and pool. There were diplomas on the wall and files neatly stacked on his desk. His office looked like one that would be in a high rise in New York overlooking the city.

"This is my office. Let me show you the rest of the house, then we can leave." He got up and showed me two other bedrooms, which were nice and clean but weren't really decorated. Then he showed me his bedroom.

When he opened the door, I stepped into the plush white carpet. The room was large. It had a couch and a love seat, with a chaise couch close to the fireplace that was burning and crackling softly. All the furniture was white, and the walls were a soft neutral color. On the other side of the room was the bed, a large king size with what looked like ten pillows on it. The satin sheets made the bed look as though you were in heaven. The room had four walk-in closets. Two were empty, and two were full of suits and shoes belonging to Cedric.

"That's it. This is my world. Are you ready to go?" Cedric asked, heading toward the door.

"Not just yet. If it's all right with you, can we sit by the fireplace?"

Needless to say, we ended up making passionate love all night long.

CHAPTER FOURTEEN

The next morning, I awoke to the wonderful smell of breakfast. I had to gather my thoughts. *How did I get in this bed? What time is it?* I looked at the clock on the nightstand. It was eleven o'clock. I couldn't believe I had slept this long.

I lay in the afterglow of the good lovemaking the night before and began to get excited. I jumped up and took a shower in the adjoining bathroom and then put on one of those big robes that were hanging on the rear of the door and went downstairs to the kitchen. Cedric was preparing breakfast.

"Good morning, beautiful. Did you sleep good?" he asked.

"Good morning. How did I get in the bed?" I asked, knowing he must have put me there.

"The angels lifted you up and put you in the bed," he said.

"Cedric you are crazy, but I got to go. Are you going to take me to my car?"

"Right after you eat. I prepared this lovely omelet for you, with turkey bacon, juice, and some green tea. You must eat. It's our first breakfast together. I'm hoping we have plenty more," he said with a bright, wide smile.

"Me too." We sat by the fireplace and ate breakfast. Then I got dressed and went home to change into my natural work clothes.

I had just changed and started heading for the greasy spoon when my phone rang.

"Girl, you all right? I got the guys together. We was getting ready to come look for you!" Sable yelled.

"I'm fine."

"Well, I haven't talked to you since last night. That's not your usual. You are supposed to be here be ten o'clock." Sable expressed her worried nature.

"I'll be there in five. I'll talk to you then," I said and hung up the phone.

When I arrived at the greasy spoon, there were four black cars in front, our signal for trouble. When I walked in, two of the counters were full of guns. Everybody looked at me wide eyed.

Ms. Lady came over and hugged me. "I told them you was all right. They wouldn't listen," she hissed.

I hugged Ms. Lady and told everybody, "Look, never start a war before you know the facts. By not thinking, you can get us all killed. Think before you react."

Everybody looked down.

"Fuck all of that! We was worried. Worried!" Sable came and gave me a hug. "Okay, y'all, let's put this stuff away and take it back to where it belongs."

Within ten minutes, the greasy spoon was empty except Sable, Ms. Lady, and me. I began to tell them about the romantic evening I'd had with Cedric.

"Is this the same boy I rescued you from in high school?" Ms. Lady said with a laugh.

"Girl, we're just happy you finally met someone," Sable joked. "Just don't run him away."

The next couple of weeks were uneventful. I talked to Cedric a lot. We spent some time together, but I wanted to fulfill my goal. I wanted to stay focused. The drugs we bought had begun to turn a profit. We got our investment out and still had a lot left. The only problem we were having was where to keep all the money we were getting. I think for the first time, we both began to get nervous. We started accumulating garbage bags full of money. We had to count it because we didn't trust anyone.

It seemed the bigger we got, the more noticeable we became. The payment for the police got higher. We paid our enforcers and lieutenants more. Everybody was making money.

I bought a small house from Cedric and used it to mix drugs. Sable and I were never supposed to be at the house. One morning, the house was stuck up by some masked gunmen. They shot and killed two of our workers. This brought more attention than we needed.

I got my enforcers together, along with my lieutenants, and went to the house. Everybody who was at the house the night of the robbery was there. I talked to each person by themselves. Nobody remembered anything, even after being told of the five racks they could have if they remembered something.

The last interview was with one of the baggers. "I saw a tattoo on the right arm of the person who took the drugs I was bagging," she claimed.

"What kind of tattoo?" I asked.

"I couldn't see the whole tattoo because he had on gloves, but I saw what looked like a skeleton right where his wrist starts."

"Above his hand?" I pointed to the part on my hand.

"Yes." she nodded.

In my mind, I knew who it was. Only one person on my crew had a tattoo like that. I was so glad that I had decided to talk to these people by myself. I had everybody wait outside.

"Okay, girl, you listen to me, and you do exactly what I tell you."

"Okay," she quickly agreed.

I reached in my coat and counted out seven thousand dollars. "Here, I want you to take the money put it in your bra or your panties. Don't ever tell anybody you got this or told me anything. You tell them you didn't say anything. You understand?"

"Hell yeah!" She smiled while she was counting the money.

"Listen up," I told her as I grabbed my gun. I had her attention now. "You take that money, go home, pack, and leave town. You go somewhere, because if I see you again, I'll think you snitched, and I'll kill you dead!"

"Okay, Miss Krystal. No problem. Thank you. I'll be gone tonight," she vowed.

"Not a word. And act like you crying when you leave. We understand each other?"

"Yes, Miss Krystal. I'm sorry." She started crying. Truth be told, she must have been crying because she got some money. She really had the tears flowing.

I opened the door and walked out to the living room. "I don't believe nobody saw a damn thing! What am I paying you guys for to keep your eyes open, or just to bag drugs? You all fucking fired. I want this place closed down as of today! You hear that, Lloyd? Now, come on, guys." I motioned to my enforcers and lieutenants.

As we got back in the black cars, I offered ten thousand to anyone who led me to my money. Everybody was quiet. Nobody knew how I would react. I guess they thought I would shoot everybody until I got some answers, but I'd learned a lot in the last few years. Now I thought before I reacted.

"Drop me off at the greasy spoon. I'll see you guys tomorrow at ten at that house. It better be closed and cleaned out."

No more words were spoken before I got dropped off at the greasy spoon. Sable and Ms. Lady were sitting at the door with AK assault rifles.

"What's going on?" I asked when I came in.

"We got caught the first time with our panties off. Not no more. Somebody else was going to drop this time," Sable swore with a vengeance.

"Listen, y'all, we need to talk," I told them.

"What's wrong, baby?" Ms. Lady spoke up.

"I got some information on the robbery. It's somebody on our crew."

"What the fuck? Who is it?" Sable leaped to her feet, full of questions.

"It's Lloyd," I said, waiting for them to react. I knew they would be as shocked as I was.

"What? Are you playing? Girl, he our most loyal worker."

"He was. But now he ain't. So, Sable, how you wanna handle this? We gotta be very careful. What do you guys think?"

"If Lloyd was in on it, so was Hakim," Sable interjected.

"Yeah, I know. We have to get them together. If not, a lot of people are gonna die."

"Can I say something, girls?" Ms. Lady exclaimed. "You ladies must realize you have the best hand in most situations. You are females, and men think they are stronger than you, so that makes them weaker. Use what you got whenever you get in a bind. Now, I have a plan," my mother continued. "My only interest is to make sure you girls are all right. I don't care about the money or the drugs. I want to protect you two."

We sat there until the wee hours of the morning, working out our plan. We left the greasy spoon and agreed to meet the next morning at the house.

CHAPTER FIFTEEN

The next morning, Ms. Lady and I arrived at the house at eight o'clock. We couldn't decide if we wanted to call Hakim and have him come first, but then he might call Lloyd if they were in on it together. The only thing we had going for us was the element of surprise. They didn't know we knew, so we had an advantage.

Sable had an idea that she would call in her favor from Hakim for saving his life. She called him and asked him to help her move some stuff out of the house now that it was closed. Hakim never expected anything because to him, Sable was not a threat.

Hakim picked up Sable at the greasy spoon to bring her to the house. When they arrived, Hakim seemed a little bit nervous. We had put all the cars in the garage so he wouldn't see them, but he still kept his hand on his gun.

Sable took out the keys to open the door. Hakim pulled his gun out and put it to his side. When Sable opened the door, she walked in and dropped the keys. When she bent down to get the keys, Hakim looked down too. Before he could look up, Ms. Lady and I had our guns on him.

"Drop the gun, Hakim," I firmly ordered.

He looked at both of us with our guns at his head. Then he looked down and saw Sable holding a gun to his nuts.

"Yeah, drop it, Hakim," she giggled.

He dropped the gun, and we pushed him to sit on the floor while we asked questions. I let Sable talk, trying to play on his emotions.

"Hakim, all we want is our drugs and money. If you did this after I saved your life, you straight scum. So why, Hakim?"

"I didn't rob y'all," he lied through his teeth.

As Sable and Ms. Lady talked to Hakim, I started cooking up some drugs. Hakim watched me out of the corner of his eyes. "You wanna get high, Hakim?"

"Krystal, you don't scare me with that." Hakim shrugged his shoulders.

"Well, this here is pure cocaine. You about to get this shit in your veins." I walked up to Hakim and jabbed the needle in his upper arm. The potent drug took effect right away. I didn't want to kill him. I just wanted him to feel good and give me some information. Hakim started smiling as the drug entered his bloodstream.

"Hakim," Sable asked with attitude, "who stuck us up? You gonna die anyway. I saved your life once. You owe me that much."

I put some more drugs in the needle and walked back over to Hakim. "Okay, motherfucker, who was in this with you?" I asked, ready to give him another hot shot fix.

"You bitches crazy as hell! I ain't telling you shit!"

Sable, still holding the gun on him, pulled the trigger and shot him in the nuts. Hakim's bloodcurdling screams rang through the house.

"Shit! You done shot my nuts off." Hakim panted, trying to catch his breath.

Sable moved in for the emotional kill. "I sat in a tub and saved your black ass from dying, and this is how you repay me?"

Blood poured down his leg as he began to drift. "I'm sorry, Sable. Lloyd and Tank set it up," he mumbled as his eyes started to roll to the back of his head.

After hearing this, I plunged the needle in his pupil and pushed the drugs out. Hakim fell to the ground and was gone.

We had to move him to the bedroom before any-body came for the meeting. We pulled Hakim's body with the rug and put it in the bedroom. We then cleaned up the house and placed all the furniture by the door like we were waiting for the movers, hiding the spot where Hakim had died. Each one of us went on with this serious business like our life depended on it. We didn't talk; we didn't second guess each other. We were ready to die if necessary. We had to set another example because there were some who didn't believe.

I called three of the dope houses and asked the runners to meet me at the house as soon as possible. It was 9:30 when the last one showed up. I told them that I had a proposition for them. I would give them two grand each for having my back, just holding their guns to be ready for whatever might happen. I didn't tell them who or what might happen; I just asked for their loyalty. I also told them I would give them more each week if we didn't have a problem. They were all dope fiends, but they han-dled their houses. They all agreed, and I gave them the money up front. I also told them not to say a word, just have our backs if needed.

It was ten o'clock when Tank and the other lieutenants showed up. Ms. Lady stayed close to where Tank was, always making sure she was no more than inches away from him. Ten minutes later, in comes Lloyd,

"You late." I frowned.

"I'm only a couple minutes late." Lloyd returned the same energy.

"Well, when I call a meeting, I expect everybody to be on time. You understand me?" I made my feelings known.

"Wait a fucking minute," he raged. "I'm not some little punk, Krystal!"

He must have smelled trouble because he reached for his gun. I came up firing mine. I hit him in the stomach.

Everybody reached for their guns as well. Ms. Lady shot Tank in the foot before he could reach for his gun. Sable, Ms. Lady, and the runners who were placed by the door so no one could leave, had their guns out.

"Don't nobody move." Everything was silent for a minute. "This is between Tank, Lloyd, and us," I proclaimed. "Everybody else put your guns on the floor. The rest of y'all better be cool unless you wanna be down with them."

Sable put the gun to Tank's head. "Nigga, move over to the middle of the floor with Lloyd."

"Lloyd, why did you rob me, man?" I fumed.

Lloyd, lying in a puddle of blood, holding his stomach with his hand, was shocked. He had no idea I knew. I shot him in the hand. Lloyd grimaced in pain.

"Lloyd, where is my shit? That's all I want to know."

The room was silent. Fear was in every man without a gun. That's when Tank spoke up. "We didn't do it. It was Hakim."

Lloyd, bleeding and trying to think his way out of the situation, said, "Yeah, Hakim did it. He's the only one not here." He tried to run game.

I laughed. "Negro, Hakim is in the room. He sold both y'all out."

The fear finally began to take its toll on Tank and Lloyd. They both lay in the middle of the floor with seven guns on them, watching them bleed to death.

"Lloyd, I want my drugs and money. I'll let you live if I get me stuff back. You my boy. We go way back."

Lloyd, losing a lot of blood, saw his life pass before him. "It's buried in my back yard by the tree," he blurted out, trying to bargain to see another day. "Let me go, Krystal. You will never see me again."

"Krystal, it was Lloyd's idea," Tank yelled, searching for his own way to live.

"Fool, you just said it was Hakim's idea," Sable said.

I motioned to the runners. "Get Hakim out the bed-room."

The runners went in the bedroom and returned. They threw the rug on the floor, and it unrolled with Hakim laying there dead. "Shit!" I heard from one of the lieuten-ants.

The room fell silent. Fear of the unknown was on the face of all the other guys.

"I don't want nobody fucking with our shit. Nobody!" I said as I waved the gun in the air.

Ms. Lady and Sable had their guns moving from one man to another. The runners had their guns out, ready for the command to kill everybody in the room. This is the ultimate fear for any person in the streets—to be in the wrong place at the wrong time.

I called Ms. Lady and whispered in her ear. She dis-appeared to the back room for a few moments, then she came back with barbecue lighter fluid. I put my gun to Lloyd's head and told him and Tank to undress. They hesitated, so Ms. Lady shot Tank in his other foot.

"Undress, she said." Ms. Lady's voice was hard and strong. There was no doubt she meant it. Both men struggled to take off their clothes.

"Get on top of Hakim," I told Tank.

While Sable held her gun to his head, he obeyed, crying and pleading to Sable.

"And you lay on top of Tank," I told Lloyd.

"No way," Lloyd said, so I shot him again, and his limp body hit the floor.

"Put him on top of Tank," I told the runners. The room was so silent you could hear a piece of thread hit the floor. I again repeated, "I don't want nobody to fuck with our money." If I could read the minds of the guys there, I would think they were praying they could leave this nightmare.

I poured the lighter fluid on the three naked men as I looked at everybody in the room. "Did anybody see this?" I asked. All these so-called hardcore men were looking like a bunch of pussies getting ready to be fucked.

"Let's go," I said, and everybody started leaving the house. The runners, Ms. Lady, and Sable were the last to leave before me.

As we were gathering up the guns, I saw a death look on the face of Tank. "Please don't do it, Krystal," he begged quietly.

I struck the match and threw it. The flames engulfed the room. From outside, everyone leaving took a glance at the flames shooting out the windows. They jumped in their cars and got out of the neighborhood. You could hear screams and you could smell the burning of human flesh. I thought I saw one of the windows burst open and something came out flying, but I didn't care. We were on our way to retrieve the items that were stolen from us. Again, we had sent the message: don't fuck with Family First Enterprise.

CHAPTER SIXTEEN

I pulled up to Lloyd's house with Sable, Ms. Lady, and the runners, where we searched the back yard for the drugs and money. We found a big army bag under a tree as Lloyd had said we would. There was about six thousand dollars' worth of drugs and some hundreds in cash. It was such a small amount to lose your life for, but to me, it was the principal. I couldn't have anybody thinking we were a bunch of pushovers. I let the runners take what they wanted from the house, then I gave them the dope to sell and five hundred dollars apiece. That brought us loyalty and advertising by word of mouth. Then we went back to the greasy spoon and went on with our daily chores, making sure our operation was running smooth.

When Cedric called me, I told him, "I want to see you later." I wanted to spend some more time in that heavenly house of his. It was kind of ironic that I killed somebody during the day, and then I thought I was supposed to go to heaven when I was at Cedric's house.

Laying in his white bedroom and heavenly atmosphere, I saw Cedric, and he just looked so good to me. I guess it was because I hadn't seen him in a week. I just needed him to hold me.

After a few hours of talking, we both fell asleep. I was awakened by a call from Sable.

"Look at the news. We got a problem."

"I'm not at home. What's going on?" I asked.

"Krystal, they found the bodies at the house."

"That's okay. The house was not in my name. It was in a dummy corporation," I explained.

"Naw, Krystal, they only found two bodies."

"Huh? Where was the other one?" I asked.

"They never said anything about another one. They never found it. What do you think happened?" She was out of sorts.

"Not on the phone. I'll see you at work at ten." I hung up before she responded. I had to think.

I thought I had seen something fly out the window as the house burst into flames, but I couldn't be sure. If Tank had jumped out the window, he could've been alive. He could go to the police, or he could come looking for us. I knew Tank had a lot of brothers because he grew up with me. We'd have to watch our backs even more.

I got up, brushed my teeth, showered, and got dressed and left Cedric's house. I arrived at the greasy spoon at 9:45, but Sable wasn't there. Neither was Ms. Lady. I began to get a little concerned. Ms. Lady was always in by nine o'clock. I called her cell phone and got no answer. So, I called Sable.

"You heard from Ms. Lady? She ain't here at the greasy spoon," I said to Sable.

"She's with me," she revealed. "She had to drop her car off to get it fixed. We'll be there in ten."

When they arrived, we talked about the consequences of last night's events. We agreed on stronger security in the greasy spoon and that we shouldn't go anywhere alone and without a gun.

After getting some crew to post up at the greasy spoon, we went and started our everyday jobs, running our operation. I had to promote three lieutenants because of what had happened at the house. Things were beginning to unravel. The pressure was mounting. The more money we made, the harder things got.

***

Months passed after the house incident, and we let down our guard.

After distributing product and counting the money, Sable and I left to put the money in our stash. I decided to go over Cedric's to watch television. A lot of times, I would go over Cedric's during the day just to get away and think.

At the same time, three men entered the greasy spoon, acting strange. After a while, they started arguing. When our enforcer approached them, they turned around, and two guys shot him. Ms. Lady, hearing the commotion, came out of the office just as the enforcer was shot. She unloaded her automatic weapon, instantly killing one of the men. The other two kept shooting, and Ms. Lady ducked in the office.

While the guys continued shooting at the door, Ms. Lady got the AK automatic and began spraying the greasy spoon, wounding another perpetrator. They ran outside as the police were coming, and they began shooting at the police. The police returned fire, killing the wounded guy. One got away, and the other one lay inside, dead from Ms. Lady's gunfire. Ms. Lady was hit three times and collapsed.

I learned about the attack while watching television. I saw a breaking news report scroll on the screen.

A shootout at a local greasy spoon. Three people confirmed dead.

The sight of my business on the screen made my heart skip a beat. I nervously called Ms. Lady but got no answer. Then I called Sable. She was on her way back to the greasy spoon because she had gotten a call from Tim, who was at the scene.

I asked Cedric to take me there because I was too in my feelings, and I didn't think I could drive. Police had the area blocked off. As we arrived, Tim let us through the army of police officers, some still with their guns out, looking for more suspects.

My heart was in my stomach as I ran in, screaming, "Where is my mother?" Assuming the worst, I started crying when I saw the tears in Sable's eyes. "No, no, not Ms. Lady!" I was out of my mind. Sable grabbed me and held me.

"Auntie was shot three times. She is in intensive care." Sable gave me the needed update.

The police wanted to interview us. They wouldn't let us leave. Sable asked Tim to see if we could come down to the station after we saw that Ms. Lady was all right. The detective agreed, and we went to see about my mother.

Ms. Lady was an emergency case. She was in surgery, and we had to stay put in the waiting room. Sable and I were crying like the true females we were. The doctor came out and called Ms. Lady's government name.

"Charday Davenport. Anyone here for Charday Davenport?"

"I'm her daughter, and this is her niece." I didn't want to ask the doctor if she was dead. I gave in to all my fears, and tears poured. I fell to the ground and pounded the floor hard, crying like a baby, expecting the worst.

"Wait, stop, please. She's going to make it," the doctor said as he helped me up off the floor.

Sable inquired of the doctor, "Can we see her, please?"

"She is heavily sedated. However, I'll give you a few minutes with her." He led us to the room my mother was in. A policeman was outside the door in a chair.

"What do they think, she's going to get up and leave?" I yelled so the cop could hear me. He jumped up to respond, but the doctor stopped him.

"She's a little upset," the doctor stated. The policeman sat back down, and the three of us went into the room.

"She was shot three times. We're lucky the bullets didn't hit a main artery, or the outcome would have been very different," the doctor said.

From where I was standing, the outcome was fucked up enough. Ms. Lady had tubes running out of her mouth. She had IVs in her arm, and she wasn't moving. She was breathing with the help of a machine. Sable and I held each other, looking at Ms. Lady lying there helplessly. It made me sad to think that this was the first time I remembered seeing Ms. Lady in years when she wasn't high. I vowed to myself that she would not return to the greasy spoon.

"Okay, ladies, you have to leave and let her get some rest. Give the receptionist your number, and I'll call you if there is any change. She will be out at least until the morning." The doctor gave a faint, encouraging smile.

"All right." Sable returned his smile. "But can I get your card to call you personally to see how my auntie is doing?" Sable never missed an opportunity.

"So, Sable, I'm going to wait in the lobby a while," I said.

After the initial shock of seeing my mother lying there looking like a vegetable started to wear off, I began to get angry. One hour ago, I was crying like a spoiled child, like a daughter would when seeing her mother like that. Now I felt like a killer, and all I wanted was revenge. I thought about who could have done this. I thought about why it happened. I blamed everybody but myself.

When Sable came to the lobby, we went over what happened at the greasy spoon. "It had to be Tank's brothers. But nobody knows but Ms. Lady. Our enforcer was killed, and Ms. Lady killed one of the suspects, the other one the police killed, and one got away. We have to find out who did this to Ms. Lady," I said.

Sable's voice had a serious tone. "Krystal, I think it's time we got out the game. It's getting too hard. It's beginning to hit home."

"Say what?"

"Krystal, we got more money than we could ever spend. I got one hundred seventy-five thousand dollars, and we still got a hundred thousand in the streets. It's time to go."

"You getting scared, Sable?"

"No, I'm getting cautious," she responded.

"Sable with you or without you, I have to get revenge for Ms. Lady."

"I'm not saying not to. I'm just saying think about getting out so we can really enjoy life."

"Girl, I can't think about anything but my mother right now, and I know she would want me to find the person that did this to her."

"You know I'm down with you all the way. But after we do what we have to do, I want us to enjoy our life, okay, Krystal?"

We left the hospital, and I had Sable drop me off at Cedric's since I had left my car there.

"I'm tired. I'll call you in the morning."

"Think about what I said," Sable reaffirmed as she drove off.

Cedric wasn't home, so I looked under the plant to find the spare key and let myself in. I took a long, hot shower, rubbed some lotion on my body, and climbed into the bed, or the pure gates of heaven, as I called it. I needed to rest my mind.

Tears began to form in my eyes as I thought about my beloved mother. *Lord, I know I'm not worthy of anything because of all my sins, but could you please make sure my mother is okay? She is all I have.*

I cried myself to sleep.

CHAPTER SEVENTEEN

Cedric woke me up around seven o'clock. "Your phone has been ringing. I didn't want to wake you, but it might be something about your mother."

I jumped up to grab my phone. It was Sable. "What's wrong? Is Ms. Lady all right?" I asked, my voice shaking, thinking the worst.

"Auntie is still the same, but the police is charging her with murder, Krystal."

"What! Murder? I can't believe that."

Cedric put his arms around me to comfort me.

"We have to be downtown by nine o'clock. You want me to come get you?" Sable brought my full attention back to the phone.

"No, that's okay. I have to go home and change clothes. I will see you downtown. I need to get a good lawyer."

We hung up. I asked Cedric, "You know any good lawyers? Ms. Lady's gonna need one."

He gave me the number for Paulette McKenzie and told me, "I'll call for you, and someone from the law firm can meet you downtown."

I was thankful for having Cedric in my chaotic life.

When we arrived downtown, the detectives were waiting on us. They took us in separate rooms and interrogated us. We were in there for three hours, until a young lady came in and informed the detective that she was my lawyer. She was dressed in a business suit with her long hair tied up in a hair clip. I could tell she was known by the detectives, because they gave her a lot of respect.

"My client will not answer any more questions. If you are not charging my client, we are leaving." She opened the door to the room without waiting on a response. "Goodbye, gentlemen. If you have any questions for any of my clients, Charday Davenport, Sable Thomas, or Krystal Davenport, please call me." She gave each detective her card, and we left.

Outside, Sable was waiting. When she joined us, the attorney made her formal introductions. "I'm Paulette McKenzie. Cedric had me come down. You ladies have any problems, call me. They are going to arraign Charday Davenport tomorrow in her hospital room. I need you girls to be there. Nine o'clock sharp." She shook our hands and left.

We didn't even get a word in. She was good. I liked her style. She commanded respect.

Sable and I left to go see Ms. Lady at the hospital. She still looked the same, not responding, with tubes coming out of her mouth. I really couldn't take it. I began to get so much hatred in my mind. I wanted to find out who did this.

"Sable, I can't stay no longer. I got things to do. We must still take care of our business." I kissed Ms. Lady and touched her hand. "I'll be back, Ms. Lady."

Out in the parking lot, I told Sable, "I have to put on my working clothes. I'll meet you at the greasy spoon in a hour and a half."

She nodded.

"But don't inside till I get there. We will go in together."

I called a couple of my lieutenants, and we met back at the greasy spoon in an hour. I wanted to talk to them before Sable got there to see if I could get some information. People will talk more by themselves than with someone around.

Leon was waiting for me when I arrived. He was a young lieutenant with a deadly crew, and he wanted to get his own game. He was honest and told me that when I hired him, but he said if I put him down, he would always be loyal to me. That meant a lot. He didn't have to tell me.

"Leon, what's going on with you?" He had two of his boys with him. They waited outside in the car, but I could tell they were strapped. This made me feel good because I was going to need someone I could count on.

"Hey now, Krystal, you all right? Sorry about your moms. Whatever you need, I'm down."

"Thanks, Leon. So what you hear on the streets? Who did this?"

"I heard that it was Walter's cousin, along with Tank's two brothers. You know two of his brothers got killed?"

"Yeah, dig that, but who you think put them up to do it?"

"Krystal, you know I'm not a snitch. If you did something, you wouldn't want me to snitch," he said.

"I feel you," I said then looked him in his eyes to make my point. "You know I was getting ready to give you your own package on consignment. But if you aren't all the way down with me, I'm going to wait a while until I trust you more."

"Krystal, you can trust me, but you got to understand, talking could get you dead," he said. "But I want to be down with you, girl. So, look, they got a contract out on you. The only fool that's not on your side was Walter's people and Tank and his people."

"Wait a minute. Tank, is he around?" I was shocked. I didn't want to ask if he was alive. Then Leon would know I tried to kill him.

"Yes, he works for Harden-Bey."

"Harden-Bey?"

"Yeah, Harden-Bey. He put the contract on you. He even asked me to take it."

My senses kicked in, and my hand touched the gun in my waist. I turned my back to Leon while watching him in the mirror over my shoulder. "Well, did you take it?" I asked.

It was a gamble. If he did take it, I would be dead. He could shoot me in the back. I pulled my gun out in front of me so he couldn't see it.

"Krystal, I wanna learn from you. I told him I worked for you and I'm loyal," he said.

My gun went back to my waist as I turned around. "Leon, how many in your crew?"

"Six I can seriously count on. I have been building for years. All of us got heart."

"Well, I got a special deal for you. It will get you what you want if I get what I want. Are you down?" I asked.

"Hell yeah! Whatever you need." He was hyped.

"Suppose it means you might lose some of your crew or you yourself get killed."

"Then it wasn't meant to be. I am ready to do or die. Krystal, whatever you need," he said with pure honesty.

I looked at him for a few minutes as if I were pondering something. "I'll give you five thousand a week. I want your crew to watch my back and my cousin Sable's as well. That means one of your crew will always be with us. But the catch is, I don't want you to be seen. I want you in the background. No one will know. If something goes down, you come in blasting and ask questions later. You feel me? Can you handle that?" I asked.

"Let me see. That's twenty thousand a month. How many months I got to do this?"

"Three months for both of us. Then I'll hook you up with a package."

Leon's mind was racing. I could see him figuring his plan in his head. "Shit, Krystal, in three months, I'd be able to buy from you, and all I'll need is a connect. Hell yes, I got your back," he said with enthusiasm.

We shook on it. I told him, "This is between us. No one must know, not even Sable."

"Did I hear my name?" Sable asked as she entered the greasy spoon. "Krystal, I thought you was going to call someone to help us clean up all this blood and shit." She turned her nose up.

"I did." I winked at Leon.

"Oh yeah, let me go get the fellas," he said.

He went outside, and after a few minutes, we had six guys in there, scrubbing and cleaning. I couldn't believe I had set myself up for a shadow, but I had to protect Sable and myself until we got to the bottom of this.

CHAPTER EIGHTEEN

We arrived at the hospital at 8:30. I visited Ms. Lady while Sable talked to the doctor. I wasn't sure if she was finding out about my mother, or she was trying to get to know the doctor.

Paulette McKenzie arrived and told us, "Your mother's arraignment was postponed. I told the court that my client obviously can't understand the charges. Therefore, she can't be charged."

"Thank you so much," I said. I would always keep her number. She was a good attorney.

Every day I visited Ms. Lady. Sometimes I stayed long, while other times I stayed for a few minutes. After a few weeks, Ms. Lady started getting better. Our attorney got her arraignment done without her being present. Her bond was set at fifty thousand dollars, and she would have to go to court as soon as she got out of the hospital. I guess the court had decided it was too costly to have a policeman there every day.

Business was as usual. We continued to make money. However, we had lost three of our own in the last couple of months, which took a toll on me and Sable. We had to do more and look over our shoulders more. We never used to worry about looking back because Lloyd was always there. Now we had to be more careful about what we did and when we did it.

Even though I now always looked over my shoulder, when I looked down the block, I always saw Leon. He was becoming a good soldier. I had given Leon a little more responsibility to test his loyalty. I let him lock up the greasy spoon every night and open it in the morning. His day of protection would start when Sable and I arrived at the greasy spoon.

One particular day, after Sable and I arrived, we took care of some business, and we were getting ready to leave. Two of Leon's boys were there, but I didn't see Leon. This was unusual. He always personally had my back after I left the pool room.

I cautiously got in my car and headed over to Cedric's house. Before I arrived, I got a phone call from Leon.

"Me and my boys cornered Harden-Bey in some girl's house, and he was alone," he said, then gave me the address. "But I'll pick you up. I don't want your car being seen in the area."

I agreed, so he picked me up at the greasy spoon. We drove about eight blocks. As he got out, my antennas went up.

This could be a set up, I thought.

Leon, seeing me hesitate before I got out of the car with my gun in my hand, said, "Krystal, be cool. I got you. Stop worrying. You got to trust me."

"Leon, at this point I don't trust nobody." I put my gun back in my purse, but I kept my hand on it.

He led me through the alley into the back of this house. When we entered, I heard a lot of loud talking.

"You faggots ain't going to do nothing. I raised all of y'all. I know you ain't got the heart to kill nobody. You might as well let me go and forget about this." Harden-Bey was in his feelings.

When Leon entered the room, Harden-Bey said, "You punk." Before he said another word, he saw me. His eyes got big, and for the first time, he was scared.

Leon told all his boys, "Go outside and watch the back and the front."

"Look, Krystal, it was nothing personal. Just business," Harden-Bey said.

"Did you put my mother in the hospital?" I asked as I thought about my mother telling me to always be cool and calm.

"I didn't tell them to do that. The contract was for you. Tank told them to do that. He wanted to kill Ms. Lady too."

Leon hit him with the back of his pistol. "Where is Tank hiding?"

"I don't know," Harden-Bey answered, and Leon hit him again. Blood started flowing from the back of his head, staining the front of his shirt. At the sight of his own blood, he changed his tune.

"Krystal, if I tell you where he's at, you going to let me live?" he asked for mercy. I guess since he thought I was so calm that I wasn't angry and hurt by what he did to my mother.

I gave him a look like I might.

Then he said, "Check it out, Krystal. He's at his girl Mae Mae's, around the way. He can't move. He's burnt bad. All he does is get high."

I took out my gun and looked him straight in the eye. "Why you put a contract out on me?" I asked as I put the gun to his left eye.

"Krystal, you getting too big. Everybody wants to see you fall so they can take your turf."

I looked at Leon, who was in back of him, and motioned my head for him to come in front.

"Why you wanna kill Ms. Lady, Harden-Bey?"

At this point, he knew he was going to die. He knew my reputation. "Your dope fiend mother is already dead as far as I'm concerned!"

Before he got another word in, I shot him in his left eye, then his right. Leon jumped, gun up, aiming in case someone heard the shots. He peeked out the door to make sure nobody was looking.

"Come on, Krystal. We got to get out of here."

I turned around and spit on Harden-Bey's body. "I'll meet you in another life."

Leon told his boys to follow us as we headed back to the Bottom Barrel.

"Krystal, we got to find Tank tonight. If not, he will go into hiding, and he might go to the police for protection."

"We gotta have a plan," I said. "We can't just go blasting our way in. We don't know what he's got inside."

Leon thought for a moment, and then he said, "A'ight. I got a plan."

I was really beginning to trust Leon. *I hope he doesn't cross me. I'd like to see him take over when Sable and I leave the business.*

"What kind of idea do you have?" I asked.

Leon pulled over to the gas station, and the two cars with his boys in it followed. We got out, and they came to Leon's car.

"Tank is around the way," he said. "He's with his girl. We need to catch him by surprise, so we won't have a shootout," he said. "Louis, you got any dope on you?"

"I was on my way to drop this package off when you called me," Louis said, pulling out a brown paper bag. In it, he had four packs of drugs. Each pack had twenty bags in it. He gave it to Leon.

"Is this enough?" Louis asked.

"That's more than enough. Biff, I want you to knock on the door and give one of these packs to Tank. You tell him that Harden-Bey told you to drop it off. When he sees the dope, he's gonna open the door. Then we all go in and catch him off guard." Leon ran down the plan. "Look, I want you to be careful. The only chance we got is if he hasn't heard about Harden-Bey yet. We know how fast word gets around the hood. Be on point and alert."

"I can handle it, Leon." Biff was trained to go.

I was impressed with these young guys. They were serious, and they were all business.

Leon and five of his guys stood with me on the side of the house when Biff walked up the stairs and rang the bell. No one answered. He looked at Leon, who motioned for him to ring it again. Biff rang the bell and knocked on the door.

After a few minutes, someone peeked out the window. He saw Biff and came to the door. Without opening, he asked, "Who is it?"

Biff responded, "Harden-Bey sent me over here to deliver this to you."

"What is it?" Tank asked.

"Look, fool, if you don't want it, I'll take it back to Harden-Bey. I'm not no fucking delivery man!" Biff yelled.

"Hold on a minute," Tank said.

Inside, Tank had his gun in his hand, but he put it down because he thought that Harden-Bey had sent somebody he could trust. He slowly opened the door. Biff walked in and looked around to make sure no one else was in the apartment. Then he looked at Tank and almost threw up. Tank still had open burns on his face and hands. He hadn't been to a doctor for fear the doctor would call the police.

Tank had bolted the door back, and Leon told everybody, "Be cool. We'll wait for Biff."

After getting his stomach to hold down his lunch, Biff threw Tank the dope. "Harden-Bey said this is your last one. Make it last."

Biff looked around to see if Tank had a gun. He noticed it back on the cocktail table in the next room. It didn't matter, though. Tank was so excited to get high off the drugs he didn't notice Biff pulling out his snub-nose .380 automatic.

"Don't move." Biff smirked.

"What the fuck is this? Harden-Bey set me up?" Tank asked.

"Anybody else in the house?" Biff searched the room with his eyes.

"Just my girl. She's sleeping." Tank noticed the hardness of Biff's face. "What's this about, man?"

"Just open the door. Now," Biff demanded.

Tank went to the door slowly, eyes staying on Biff. When he got the locks and the bolts off, he looked at Biff again, telling himself he could outrun him. Tank decided to make a move. He opened the door fast, went out, and slammed the door behind him. He them jumped off the porch and started to run down the street. Then he saw three guns pointed at him.

"Hold up, guys. I didn't do nothing," he said while backing up. When he turned around and saw me, his heart jumped a beat.

"Yeah, Tank. So we meet again."

"Naw, naw, Krystal. I didn't do it."

"Take him in the house off the street 'fore someone sees us." Leon muffled his voice.

Everybody went inside. By this time, Biff had gone in the bedroom and woken up his sleeping girlfriend. She must have thought she was dreaming because she kept rubbing her eyes. She probably hoped that these seven guys in there with guns were a bad nightmare.

She didn't see me until they tied her up in a chair. She knew me from high school. I recognized Mae Mae as the girl that kicked me down because of Cedric. Although she was now a drug addict, I'm sure she knew this couldn't be good for her, even though she wasn't involved.

"Hey, Krystal." She tried to act as though we were friends.

I didn't say a word. My attention was on Tank.

"You look terrible, fool." I turned my nose up at the sight of him.

Tank began to shake as though he needed a fix—or else the chills were because he feared that his chances for life had finally run out. He lowered his head and didn't respond.

"Tank, why you send your brothers to kill my mother? Your beef is with me. You not man enough to handle a woman like me? So, the big man had to go after my mother?" I was heated.

"I'm sorry."

"You sorry, but you can't tell me why?" I asked once more.

The tension in the house was thick. The eyes of the girl in the chair got big, and she started to cry.

Biff walked over to her. "Shut up unless you want some." He tried to sound hard and strong but came across to me like he really wanted to give her some. Although this girl was using drugs, she still looked decent. She had a nice body, and her chest was sticking out from the gown she had on. She didn't have any underwear on, and the way she was sitting, every guy in the room could see her hairy pussy. It was enticing Leon's boys.

"Do what you want to me, but please leave my girl alone. She doesn't have anything to do with this." He begged for leniency.

The sores on his face from the night he got burned were making me feel sick. "You need to worry about you." I turned to Leon. "This is your plan. You work it."

I had to see how far Leon and his crew would go. I didn't want them to witness me kill someone that might haunt me later on.

Leon took control as I would have liked my successor to do. His crew looked at him, each holding their nuts in one hand and their guns in the other. I wondered if this was a sign. Had they gang raped somebody before?

While I was in my thoughts, Biff hit the girl with his pistol. "Lay down and take that gown off." By then, two of the other guys were standing over her and grabbed her arms so she couldn't move. The girl began to cry and scream. Biff socked her. "If you scream again, you won't make it out of here."

The girl just lay there with tears streaming down her face and her eyes closed. Before Biff could get up, the others were yelling, "Let me get some! Is it good?"

Biff was acting like he was fucking his own woman. "Damn, this shit is good." He let his juices flow into her, then he got up, and the next guy started.

"Leon, she got some good pussy. You going get some?" Biff asked.

"Naw, I'ma pass," Leon said.

My gun was out, and I was feeling a little uneasy because it was obvious these guys had done this before. They were in sync. My hand was sweating, and my fingers were itching. They didn't talk, just took care of business.

I noticed Leon didn't move from my side. He looked at me. "You good, Krystal?"

"I'm cool," I said, and I meant it, as long as they don't come my way.

I think we both were testing each other. He wanted to see if I was hard enough to take the way they were treating the girl. I wanted to see if he could handle the situation.

"I got your back, Krystal, for life," he whispered to me.

From that day on, he would be like my little brother.

Tank was crying and screaming. I don't know if it was because he knew it was his end or he was feeling sorry for his girl, who was at the wrong place at the wrong time. The raping lasted for thirty minutes or so.

"Leon, you tight?" Biff asked. Then he threw the bag of dope to the girl. "Go cook some up for Tank. If you do it right, I might let you live," he said.

The thought of her getting hurt left her mind for a few minutes. She went and fixed the dope and brought Biff a needle full of drugs. I watched to see how Leon would handle this. Tank was begging for mercy, not a true gangster like he claimed he was.

Leon took the needle and stuck it in his arm without a word. In unison, all his guys squeezed the drugs in Tank's arm, each taking their turn. As the drugs took effect, Tank's eyes rolled to the back of his head. His head slumped down between his legs.

I was really gaining a lot of respect for Leon that day. They were a team. I believed if one died, they all would.

"What about the girl?" Louis wondered.

Everybody looked at Leon, then the girl, who was pushing a needle in her arm. The girl didn't cry. I guess the drugs were telling her, *if you die, you at least die high.* She just looked at Leon, waiting on his decision.

"Biff," he said. There was a moment of silence. "Don't you need another person to sit at your spot?"

Biff, thinking about all the good pussy he could have at his beck and call, said, "Hell, yeah. Baby, you want to work for me?"

"If you will have me." The drug-addicted girl smiled as if she had not just been gang raped.

Louis laughed. "If you want to be down with us, you got to give your boy another hit of drugs."

Without hesitation, she started cooking up some drugs. This time, she put a lot on the spoon and melted it down. She retrieved the needle from Tank's arm and put the whole spoonful in the needle. Everybody in the room watched closely. No doubt she knew if she didn't do it, she would be killed. She was the only witness who was not part of the crew.

With precision moves, the girl went over to Tank, who was still nodding. She held his head up and asked, "You want some more, baby?" She carefully took his belt off and placed it around his arm. She waited patiently for the vein to come up. She stuck the needle in his vein, and when the blood came up the needle, she pushed all the contents of the needle in his arm.

Tank's eyes disappeared behind his eyelids, his face turned blue, and his tongue stuck out of his mouth. She looked at him, and then she surprised us all. She got up went and got all her belongings.

"We should leave him like this. He just overdosed. Now, let's get out of here."

Without thinking, I opened the door and we all left. On the ride home, I asked Leon, "What you going to do with her? You think you can trust her?"

Leon broke his logic down. "Sometimes you give people a break, and they are more loyal alive than dead. If we killed her, there would be too many unanswered questions."

I thought to myself, *This guy is smart. I think I will keep him close to me. I'd rather have him as an ally than an enemy.*

CHAPTER NINETEEN

Ms. Lady had gotten much better. She had regained all her strength back, and she was doing fine except for a limp when she walked, so they started her trial. It lasted about two weeks. A jury of her supposed peers, an all-white jury, convicted her of involuntary manslaughter and she was sentenced to three to five years. I was really upset with the justice system. How could they convict someone for trying to protect themselves?

Paulette McKenzie told me, "You have to just accept it and keep quiet. The police know what's really going on at the greasy spoon, so if you don't want them coming after you, you're going to have to make sacrifices." In other words, they had to convict somebody to take the heat off of them taking bribes. That meant we had to watch what we were doing at the greasy spoon.

Sable was upset about Ms. Lady's conviction, but also because she and Tim broke up. She still talked about wanting to get out, so I set her up with Cedric, and she begun to purchase properties. "You should invest, too, Krystal," she said. "If we ever got busted, they will find the cash. You need to place some money in legit investments, so you don't end up broke." She set up another corporation and ran all her investments through the company.

We continued to sell and supply drugs, handling only large weight. Leon had moved up the ladder of our organization fast, so he did most of the selling and collecting. I never had any problems with him. We were making around sixty or seventy thousand a month. My goal of more than two hundred thousand was met and exceeded.

I had all this money, and I still wasn't happy. Cedric and I were cool. I think he loved me, and I loved him, but something was missing. I missed Ms. Lady more each week she was gone, but I wouldn't admit it.

On Ms. Lady's birthday, I was feeling a little down. Ms. Lady had been away for three years, and she was coming out in one year. I needed to be with someone, so I called Cedric and didn't get an answer. I decided to go by his house. I got the spare key from the safe spot and entered his house.

I heard him talking in the family room, so I went upstairs to greet him. When I opened the door, I was absolutely floored when I saw him by the fireplace with Sable.

"What the fuck is going on?" I screamed at the top of my lungs.

Cedric was so surprised to see me that guilt was written all over his face. "It's not what you think, baby."

Sable jumped up. "Krystal, we were just talking about you."

"I bet you were. Cedric, you fucking her? And I know you was fucking Paulette McKenzie!"

The shock on Sable's face was unbelievable. "He is not fucking me, Krystal!"

By this time, my hand was on my gun. I pulled it out of my purse with one motion and pointed it at Cedric. "You motherfucker!"

"Krystal, this is all a misunderstanding. We weren't doing anything. Just handling some business," Sable claimed.

"So, did you fuck Paulette McKenzie, Cedric? And what about Mae Mae? Did she do your crew in high school or what?"

Cedric was at a loss for words. He couldn't do anything but stutter.

"Answer me," I said, pointing the gun at him.

Cedric was really scared. He had always avoided violence. That's why he never sold drugs after high school.

"Yes," he said with his voice cracking. "Paulette and I were married, and Mae Mae has a two-year-old boy that's mine."

"Two years old! You have been seeing me for four years! I can't believe you would hurt me like this—then with my cousin, too!"

"We haven't done a thing, Krystal," Sable pleaded.

"Shut up 'fore I blow your head off too!" I turned my gun toward Sable only to be met with the barrel of her gun. Behind my back, Sable had pulled out her gun, so she was ready for me. I should have been watching her sneaky ass, but I was still in shock from finding out she had betrayed me.

"Krystal, don't do this. Think. I would never hurt you," Sable cried.

We both kept our guns pointed at each other for about three minutes. Neither one of us spoke, lost in our own thoughts. I couldn't believe she would hurt me like this. But maybe she was telling the truth and Cedric was the culprit here. Sable was so beautiful that any man would want her.

Sable finally spoke. "Damn. All the money we made never made us go against each other, and now you gonna let a man come between us? Look, you might not trust Cedric, but there's no reason for you to be so insecure about me. I don't want Cedric."

I stared her down, thinking about what she had said.

"Krystal, think about what you are doing. Think before you react." She looked me straight in my eyes, pleading with me.

Her words got to me. We had been through so much in the past twelve years. It couldn't end like this. It was all Cedric's fault, I decided. He couldn't escape her beauty. Before I knew it, I had pulled the trigger.

It was a total surprise to Sable. She wasn't expecting it. The bullet hit her in her right chest, just above her heart. The look on her face was so unbearable. She had an unbelievable questioning look on her face.

"Why, Krystal? How could you?" Sable clutched her chest and fell to the ground.

I turned the gun on Cedric, who was now begging for his life. "Baby, you got this all wrong! Please—"

I shot Cedric two times and left the house. I didn't even look back once to see if they were dead.

On the ride back to my house, tears started running down my face. This was the first time since I had killed that guy hurting my Ms. Lady that I felt guilty. I was hurt and confused. I killed the only relative I had, my partner, my friend, and my cousin. I felt so alone. I couldn't talk to Ms. Lady about this because she was locked up.

I had no outlet. All the money I had didn't make me feel any better. I had built an organization, but I didn't make friends. All I made was money and enemies. People trying to claw their way to where I was and take over my business. That was the only consistent thing in my life. I now had to look over my shoulder all the time.

I thought I saw Uncle Nardo following me one day not too long after that. Leon told me I was paranoid with Sable not watching my back. Running the business and collecting the money, I had too much to do.

I really missed Sable. Something inside me died when Sable departed my life. The funny thing is that I didn't hear anything about the shootings on the news. I felt again like I was alone. Ms. Lady would be coming out in six more months. Then I would have some help. Hopefully she wouldn't start using drugs again. I needed her support. Things were unraveling in my life.

CHAPTER TWENTY

Four months later

The day started like all the others. It seemed like I was looking for something to happen to make my meager existence feel alive.

Leon called me. "I'm gonna be at the greasy spoon. I need to talk to you." From the sound of his voice, I knew something was wrong.

We met at the greasy spoon, which had been closed for business ever since Ms. Lady got shot. It was used for business and meetings only.

When I got there, Leon told me, "One of my guys just gave me some information that I want to go and check out. I want you to stay here in case something goes down."

He left, and minutes later, Biff was at the door with Louis. I opened the door and saw that Mae Mae was behind them.

"What is she doing here?" I asked. "I don't do business with anyone who's not in our organization."

"Come on, Krystal. We just want to shoot a little pool," Louis said.

My mind began to race. I was getting a gut feeling, so I eased to the office to get my automatic weapon. Before I got there, I felt a crushing blow to the side of my head. I hit the floor. I turned around to find Biff standing over me with his gun in his hand.

"What's this about, Biff? You know I don't keep no money or drugs in here," I said, spitting of blood out my mouth.

"Shut up, bitch. This ain't about money," he said.

I turned and looked at the faces of Louis and Mae Mae. They were smiling. Mae Mae was looking like she had in high school when she had her girls with her.

Biff hit me in the head again. "Just do what we ask, and we won't hurt you," he said.

"Get on with it," Mae Mae said.

I looked deep in her eyes. She looked confident, like she had total control. Then it hit me. She done pussy whipped both of these fools. She was trying to get revenge. I wasn't sure if it was over something from high school or from Tank's house. While I was trying to figure out why they were doing this, I should have been trying to figure out what they were going to do. Deep in my mind, I didn't want to believe this could happen to me.

I stared up at Biff's big gun in my face.

Louis jumped on top of me while I was laying on the ground. "I wanna be first," he said. He ripped off my blouse, exposing my little titties. I tried reaching my hand down my leg to get my piece.

"Don't move, you bad-ass killer, 'cause I'm going to fuck the shit out of you," he said. He started laughing as he pulled down my pants. Then he saw the gun at my ankle, and he hit me again.

"Were you gon' shoot me, Krystal?" He took the gun.

The look on Mae Mae's face was enjoyment. I think she was getting excited. The sound of my panties being torn off brought me to a fighting mode. I kicked and screamed, "Get off me, motherfucker! I'm going kill your ass!"

"What makes you think you going to get that chance?" Biff asked.

I stopped kicking when the butt of the gun hit my head again. I think I must have passed out for a minute. I woke up and felt penetration in my vagina. I screamed in pain.

"Make her enjoy it, Louis," Mae Mae said.

"Hurry up, Louis. I want some of this powerful bitch," Biff said.

I let my mind wander, trying to forget what was going on. *A woman will always be a bitch no matter how much money she has or how much power she has,* I thought.

Louis was shaking and looking in my eyes, and I knew he was about to finish. I tried to move my butt so he wouldn't release his fluid in me. But he put it in deeper, and I just cried.

Then the front door opened. Leon was the only one who had the key.

"What the fuck's going on in here?" Leon said. His gun was out.

"Leon, we been boys for a while. I know you down with us. You want some?" Louis had jumped up and pointed his gun on me, then back to Leon.

Biff's gun was on Leon. I didn't know if Leon was in on this, or if he didn't know. I assumed it was over for me because these guys had been together since grade school. My tears rolled down uncontrollably.

Leon looked at Mae Mae. "What is she doing here? She put you guys up to this?"

"Can't no bitch make me do anything," Louis said.

"So what is she doing here? She going to fuck her too?" Leon asked.

"Yeah, I wanna taste her pussy juices after you guys finish polishing her up," Mae Mae said.

All this time, I was almost unconscious. I convinced my mind and body that this was the end. You reap what you sow. I tried to close my legs, and I sat up.

Leon said, "Hold up. I wanna test this shit myself."

I couldn't believe what I was hearing. He wouldn't touch Mae Mae when they raped her, but he wanted a piece of his friend and business partner. Money will make you do funny things.

"Yeah, Leon, I knew you would hit it," Biff said.

Leon approached me and put his gun in his coat pocket. Then he opened his coat to undo his pants. He looked me in my eyes and looked down at his waist, trying to unzip his pants. A gun was in his waistband. He unzipped his pants and pulled his dick out.

Everybody's eyes were on Leon in anticipation of unity. They always stuck together. Then he got on top of me pushed my legs apart. He whispered to me, "I got your back for life." He stared deep into my eyes, making sure I was getting his message. "My coat is in the way. They can't see shit. Just take it slowly," he whispered.

I took the gun from his belt and put it on my side. Once it was where it needed to be, Leon jumped up with his dick in his hand and his other hand in his coat pocket.

"That shit is whack. She ain't wet, and she hurting me. I couldn't get hard," he said. For a split second, everybody looked at his limp dick in his hand, not paying attention to me.

Biff was near Mae Mae, with his pussy whipped ass. Louis was on my left side. He took a step to look at Leon's dick. At that moment, Leon pulled his gun from his pocket and shot Biff in the head. Before he dropped to the floor, I shot Louis in the back of the head. I kept shooting, emptying the gun into his lifeless body.

Mae Mae couldn't believe the turn of events. She tried to run, but the door was locked. Leon's bullet caught her in her shoulder. By this time, I was up on my feet and right behind Leon. I keep pulling the trigger with blinding tears until my gun was empty.

She turned around just in time to look me in my eyes when Leon raised his gun to end her life. The bullet went straight through the middle of her forehead. She dropped to the ground dead.

I was zoned out. I kept pulling the trigger as I looked at her body on the floor. Tears were flowing and sweat was pouring from my face.

Leon grabbed the gun and said, "I'm sorry, Krystal."

I let out all my built-up tension and cried for at least twenty minutes, holding Leon tight. Leon and I had never had any physical touching. We just bonded together.

The greasy spoon was closed. I let him decide what to do with the bodies. I went to the office to take a shower. I was in the shower for over an hour or more. I couldn't wash the dirt off my body just like I couldn't wash the dirt out of my life. I didn't care. This had all come full circle. I had almost lost my life. No money could have saved me.

When I got out of the shower, all the bodies were gone. No blood was evident.

"Leon, what just happened? Were we set up?" I asked.

He shook his head like he still couldn't believe everything that had happened. "They tried to kill me and you and take over the business. Louis, Biff, Nick, and Carl. They were hired by a white man downtown. They were promised they could run the Bottom Barrel," Leon said.

"Leon, I really want to thank you. I thought I was gone," I said.

"Nick and Carl called me to this house. The other two guys in my crew are my cousins, and they hipped me to what was going on, so we caught them. I didn't know of their plans, Leon said. "That girl made their plans. I think she wanted to get even."

"Leon, never let nobody go again to come back at you," I said. I hugged him again, and we left.

Leon wanted to go get something to eat. Although I didn't feel like eating, I didn't want to be alone either. I asked Leon if we could do something different. We went to the movies in the suburbs. I don't even know what movie we watched because I couldn't get the image of Louis out of my mind.

I didn't want to go home. So after the movie, we went to a bar until two o'clock in the morning.

"You wanna come to my house?" I asked Leon after the bar closed.

He was hesitant at first because we always had a brother-sister relationship.

"It's not like that. I just don't want to be alone. You get the couch," I said, and he laughed. Little did he know that I was starting to think of him as something more than just a partner.

I had never looked at Leon in any romantic way. Now I noticed that he was really nice looking. He had a dimple on one side of his cheek and a set of beautiful white teeth. He didn't dress like a hood. He dressed more like a worker going to a nine to five. My whole outlook on Leon changed that day. According to my rules, I never mixed business with pleasure, but Leon was beginning to look inviting to me. I don't know if it was because he never approached me in any disrespectful way or because he always had my back, but there was something about him that had me intrigued.

After that night, we spent a lot of time together. He was fulfilling my loneliness. We would conduct business together in the day, and he would come by at night to keep me company. My heart began to get attached to Leon, and I knew he was feeling me.

After three months of him sleeping on the couch, I thought it was time we took our friendship to another level. I cooked him dinner that night—fried chicken, rice, and string beans. I called him into the kitchen to eat, and when he came in, I was standing there with only a little white apron on my body.

He looked at me, then at the food.

"Undecided?" I asked.

"Not really. I just want to enjoy the best first," he said. He walked over to the plate to take a bite, and then he looked at me. He took me in his arms and kissed me deeply. His mouth tasted like a cool, fresh breeze. His warm mouth had my body hot with desire.

We kissed for a long time. The sounds of our hard breathing made the moment of anticipation seem long. I could feel the pulsating vibes of his manhood hitting between my legs through his pants. He took his time as though it might be his last and he wanted to remember every moment of it.

He was fully dressed as he lifted me on the kitchen countertop. He began to kiss me slow and hard. My juices begin to flow as his kisses started to erupt the inside of my body. He kissed my chest down my side. His tongue rolled around my navel. He gently caressed my chest while his mouth wreaked havoc on my begging body. This man was doing things to me that I hadn't felt. He was pulling feelings from my body that I didn't know existed.

He let me simmer as he took a drink from the juice I made for him. With my legs dangling from the countertop, he started kissing my inner thighs. I felt this cold sensation going up and down my legs. He was kissing me with the ice from the glass. This cold and hot mixture was taking me to another place.

He then hit the magical spot. His hot tongue and the cold ice had me climbing the walls. All of a sudden, I felt his warm mouth on my hot pussy. His tongue probed my insides like a mad scientist. The juices in my body spoke the language of ecstasy. I shook as I climaxed like I never had before.

He didn't let me off that easy. He continued licking and plunging his tongue into my hot body. Just like a dope fiend trying to get that first high again, I knew I would always want to repeat this feeling.

I felt the inside of my body come to a boil. I came again, and Leon sucked my juices up like a vacuum. Damn, this guy was good.

He then dropped his pants and inserted all his manhood inside my wanting body. He moved ever so slowly. As I was about to explode again, he stopped and pulled me to the floor. He pushed my legs to the back of my head then inserted himself in me, and I felt the feeling of true womanhood.

He moved like a master artist finishing the last touches on work he had been doing for years. Leon finally reached the heat of his passion.

We lay there on the floor in the afterglow of our first sexual experience for what seemed like hours. The floor was hard and cold, but our hearts were warm, and for the first time in my life, I felt loved and not alone.

The night was blissful, but the next morning, all hell broke loose.

CHAPTER TWENTY-ONE

I received a phone call at 7:30 a.m., telling me that there had been a break-in at the greasy spoon. Leon and I got dressed and went down there. The place had been ransacked. Everything was broken. The pool table was cut up and the legs broken off. My office was overturned like someone was looking for something. Fortunately, I never kept a lot of money there, usually only a thousand dollars or less for mad money in case of an emergency.

Leon and I called everybody in to help clean up. "What's the word on the street about who did this?" I asked them. No one had heard anything. We put out a five-thousand-dollar reward for any information.

While trying to reorganize the greasy spoon, Leon got a call. He stepped away to take it. When he came back, he said, "Someone heard the Ridgeway brothers are trying to take over our territory by any means necessary."

I was heated. I still bought from them, but I bought in such large quantities that they had to hook me up to their connection, therefore cutting them out of the picture. We had paid them a hefty fifty thousand for the connection.

I took Leon in the office to discuss the problems ahead of us.

"We should play it cool and tighten up security," Leon suggested.

"No. I want immediate results," I said.

We were interrupted by a phone call from my alarm company. I couldn't believe what they told me. My house was on fire, and the fire and police departments were at the house.

"No, this can't be happening!" I shouted.

Leon, seeing the look on my face, asked, "What wrong, Krystal?"

"My house is burning!"

We rushed out of there like a bat out of hell with the guys following us, sensing trouble. Leon held them at bay.

"Everything is cool," he told them. "Krystal got some problems at home, but we can handle it. If I need you, I'll call." He then followed me to my house.

By the time we arrived at the house, the fire was blazing. There were fire trucks everywhere. I jumped out the car and tried to run in the house, but I was stopped by two firemen.

"Miss, you can't go in there," a fireman said.

I started crying, screaming like a baby. Leon came over to try to comfort me. I stood there in denial. I couldn't believe it. I cried and screamed for thirty minutes. Everybody thought I was a little overdramatic, but they just didn't understand. My whole life was in that house. The house was paid for, and I had over four hundred thousand dollars in that house.

Questions began to pop up in my head. *Did somebody set me up? Did the money burn in the house? Did someone take the money and set the house on fire? Did the Ridgeway brothers have something to do with this?* All these unanswered questions. I did know that somebody close to me had to know that there was money in there.

I looked at Leon at that moment. He looked so caring and understanding. It couldn't be him. But who, then? I felt so sad and alone again. I wished I had listened to Sable when she told me to use safe deposit boxes.

Sable? She was the only other person who had a set of keys to my house. *Naw, Sable wouldn't hurt me like*

*that. Besides she is dead. Maybe Uncle Nardo found
the keys and is trying to get his revenge by stealing my
money and burning down the house,* I thought.

I was not thinking logically. I looked at Leon. He held
me gently in his arms and told me everything would be
all right. But how could everything be all right when my
life had been shattered? I had nowhere to go.

Then I thought about Ms. Lady's house, the house I
grew up in—the house where I stored a hundred thousand dollars just in case of an emergency. I wiped the
tears away and tried to pull the little ounce of dignity out
of a bad situation.

"Leon, I got to get away from here."

"You want to go to my house?" Leon asked.

"No. I just want to be alone for a little while. I'll call you
later and we can get together."

"You sure you all right? A lot has happened to you this
week. I just want to be there for you," he said.

"I'm cool. Just need some me time. I'll call you if I need
you," I said as I pulled away from him and walked away.

"Call me later," Leon said as I got in my car and drove
off.

My thoughts were somehow on my daddy. He had
always told me to be prepared for the worst.

"Life changes," he had said. "You can be up one day and
down the next. Always have a plan B."

My plan B was at Ms. Lady's house. I began to drive
faster in anticipation of what was ahead. I would know if
someone close to me was causing all these problems. Ms.
Lady and Sable were the only ones who knew about the
cash at Ms. Lady's.

When I arrived at Ms. Lady's, everything was okay.
I went to the basement and found my money. Then I
looked around. I couldn't believe how my mother lived.
The house had the same furniture that my daddy had

bought, and most of the furniture was broken. Two tables had only three legs. The sofa table had books under it as the fourth leg. The dining room table was propped up against the wall with a bat under it for support. There was no stove or refrigerator. All the paint was dirty and old. There were holes in the walls.

This had been a beautiful house when I was young. The lives that shared this house were gone, but the memories were still there. Tears formed in my eyes as I thought about Daddy, Ms. Lady, Uncle Nardo, Aunt Rose, and Sable. This house was warm with love and family. Now it looked like an abandoned home.

Even with the time Ms. Lady had been locked up, it still looked like the house really died when my daddy got killed. I couldn't see this until now, almost fifteen years later. I knew at that moment I was going to live in the house and transform it before Ms. Lady got home in a couple of months.

My tears became uncontrollable as I thought of Sable, Cedric, and Ms. Lady. It seemed like I always lost the ones I loved. I thought about Leon. If I was to have a relationship with him, I would give it my all.

I sat on the dirty floor for the rest of the day, and I must have fallen asleep. I was in a deep sleep, too, because when I woke up, I had to get my bearings of where I was. I felt so content lying in the home I had grown up in. I knew that inside this house I had no worries, just like when I was young and didn't have to worry about anything.

I spent the night cleaning and scrubbing. Before I knew it, daylight was beginning to come through the windows. I thought about Leon and raced to my cell phone. The ringer was off, and I had twenty-four messages. I called Leon to let him know I was OK.

"We have some business to take care of," he informed me.
"Can you handle it on your own?" I asked him.

"Not a problem," he said.

I took the rest of the day off and went to visit Ms. Lady,
who told me that she was getting out in thirty days. They
were letting her off before her release date for good
behavior. That was the best news I'd had in a long time.

I didn't have the nerve to tell Ms. Lady what was going
on with me. She looked good. She was smiling, and her
voice was strong and confident. We talked for as long as
they let us.

I felt rejuvenated when I left. I made plans to have the
house remodeled to surprise Ms. Lady when she got out.
For the next couple of weeks, I bought new furniture and
had the house painted and the kitchen remodeled.

I communicated with Leon every day, and he ran the
business. One day, he called me and said he needed to
see me.

"Is it any problems?" I asked.

"No, but I need to see you as soon as possible," he said.
This, to me, meant he couldn't talk over the phone.

I met Leon at a restaurant, and he couldn't wait to tell
me what he had found out.

"The Ridgeway brothers had the greasy spoon broken
in to, so they made sure you were out the house so they
could rob you," Leon said. "The dope fiend that set you
up called my cousin."

"I knew it was them," I said, shaking my head.

"What do you want to do, Krystal?" Leon asked.

The last couple of weeks had been carefree for me. I
didn't worry about anything. I was focused on the house.
Now, the game was pulling me back because I had some
unfinished business.

"Leon, we got to think about this. We can't go downtown in the white area and start blowing people's heads
off," I said.

"I got some running to do. I'm collecting all the money off the street as you asked. Are we going to re-up?" he asked.

"Keep collecting the money," I answered. "I need to know how many good, dependable guys we got. I want an army together if we going downtown. Don't tell them where we going. Just tell them to be ready, just in case."

"Okay. What about you?" he asked. "Why you been MIA lately?"

"I'm trying to get Ms. Lady's house together. I just got a lot on my mind. We'll meet tomorrow, and then we will talk more."

"All right, Krystal. Take care until tomorrow," Leon said as he got up and left.

I sat there to gather my thoughts. I wanted to start my business back and make the money that I had lost. I also wanted to build my life and spend time with my mother. As always, thinking about what my daddy would do led me to make a decision.

The next time I spoke to Leon, I told him to offer a ten thousand–dollar reward for good information about the Ridgeway brothers' organization.

"I want to take care of this before Ms. Lady gets home. We got one week," I told him.

"I'll have some info in a couple of days. Ten K is ten K. I'll call you," Leon said as he left.

I was so happy when I stayed focused on the house. It seemed like I had a purpose. For once, I didn't have to prove anything. I think I was finally beginning to under-stand this thing called life. I told myself after I got my money back that I would stop the business selling drugs and let Leon take full control. I would take any money I had and move Ms. Lady to Florida.

Over the next few days, Leon and I talked and planned our moves. We were getting a lot of information—some good, some bad. We heard that one of the brothers went to the doctor's office once a month. His other brother always went with him. Someone who worked at the office had called one of Leon's boys to give him the info. It's crazy what some people will do for money.

We had our plan together. I wanted to get this over with so I could start the new life with Ms. Lady. It was a Wednesday morning. I had Leon and the entire crew meet me at the greasy spoon.

Leon was in the office when I arrived. Everybody else was playing pool.

"Krystal," he said, sounding serious. "I'm not trying to tell you what to do. I only want to suggest something."

I nodded to let him know I was listening.

"We don't need to go downtown with a lot of guys. We are going in the heart of the city. We will get stopped before we even reach downtown if we go with eight carloads of black men. The more guys we have, the more people know what we doing, you know what I mean? I just want you and me to go. We can handle them," Leon said.

"That may be true, but we still need some backup. We take two guys with us. We don't know what we might run into," I said.

"That's cool. I'm gonna let these other guys leave."

I pulled out my bulletproof vest and put it on with my shoulder holster that held my two guns. I put on my long black coat with the inside pocket that held the AK assault rifle. I was ready to do battle.

The doctor's office was on the outskirts of downtown. We sat on the other side of the office building, waiting for the Ridgeway brothers to arrive. One car was at the other end of the block.

It brought a smile to my face when I thought of the time my daddy and Uncle Nardo did this same thing. I was beginning to see my daddy in myself, but I didn't want the end result to be like my daddy, killed in the streets. I wanted to see the other side of life through my daddy and Ms. Lady's life's faults. I just didn't know how to read between the lines.

While deep in my thoughts, a car came up the block, moving slowly. Leon called his boys in the car up the street. We wanted to catch them before they got to the doctor's office. Leon pulled his car out of the parking space, burning rubber as he swirled out in front of the oncoming car.

The other car with the other guys in it pulled behind them. We had them boxed in. Leon put the car in park and jumped out. His two henchmen were out, guns drawn, before Leon. I opened my door so I could come around the car, since my side was on the outside of the two cars.

All of a sudden, gunshots rang out. The people in the car started pumping round after round. I ducked behind the car and came up blazing with my two 9 mm.

I heard Tyrell, one of Leon's boys, say, "It's a setup. Leon, get back!"

Before Leon could respond, he was hit in the shoulder and stomach. He fell to the ground. Tyrell and his partner were ducking and shooting. It looked like a scene out of a Wild West movie. The two guys in the car were shooting automatic weapons, so their bullets were continuous.

Out of instinct, I came around to where Leon was slumped in between two parked cars. I shot until my gun emptied, trying to protect Leon in case they got out of the car. I dropped the two 9 mm and pulled out the AK automatic.

At the same time, the car we had boxed in must have run out of bullets. They rammed the car I had been riding in and tried to pull off.

Tyrell and the other guy stood up and fired round after round at the car. Our bullets were flying off the car. It must have been bulletproof. The only damage we were making was little dents on the body. The windows were rolled up, and the guys inside were trying to get away. I stood up and unloaded my automatic weapon, putting my body in front of Leon in case they rolled down the window and started shooting again.

The car went back and forth, ramming each car a little, until it had knocked the car out of the way so it could get by. Then the car sped away.

This whole incident had taken about three minutes, but it seemed like forever. My adrenalin was pumping.

I asked Tyrell, "Are you hurt?"

He looked at his partner and said, "We fine."

"Let's get Leon out of here," I said.

Leon was moaning and losing a lot of blood. We got him in the car with Tyrell's help.

I told his partner, "Take the other car to the Bottom Barrel and hide it." I jumped in the car and put Leon's head on my lap.

He looked up and smiled at me. "For life, Krystal," he said.

Tears formed in my eyes. "Hold on, Leon," I said. I had to think of what to do.

Tyrell was driving. "Where you want me to go, Krystal? You know the hospitals will be asking questions," he said.

"Just drive and let me think," I said. Then suddenly, I had an idea. "Turn around. We going back to the doctor's office."

"Where we just left? Police will be around there," he said.

"Just drop me and Leon off if you want, but I'm going back to get Leon some help," I said.

Tyrell turned around and pulled up to the back of the building. I struggled to pull Leon out of the car.

"Come on, Leon. We going to get you fixed up," I assured him.

Tyrell's thoughts had been to drop us and leave, but he couldn't leave when he saw how determined I was. He got out and put Leon's arm around his shoulders and dragged him in the office.

I had retrieved and reloaded my 9 millimeters in the car. We burst in the doctor's office, shocking the secretary. Luckily, no one was in the office but the doctor and his unfortunate secretary. The look on the secretary's face told me that she was the one who had collected the ten thousand dollars for the information. I know she wished she had stayed home on this day.

"Get the doctor," I yelled with my gun swinging.

The doctor came out. "What's all the commotion out here?" he said. He was startled when he saw Leon bleeding and on the verge of passing out. "I can't take care of this man," he said.

I hit him with the pistol before he got another word out. "You will take care of him now, or you will need a doctor," I said. My heart was beating fast. My thoughts were clear, and I was willing to die with everybody in here before I let Leon die without being treated.

The fear of death was in the eyes of the doctor as I told him this. At this point, I didn't care.

"Get him in the room," the doctor blurted out.

The secretary held the door open, and we took Leon to the back room.

I whispered to Tyrell, "Make sure no blood trails lead to the doctor's office. Take the car back and get another. When you come back, bring me some money from the stash."

The secretary must have thought she was going to die since she was the one who gave us the information. She tried to help us in any way she could.

The doctor was still a little hesitant, so I let off a couple of shots in his direction. "I don't want to kill you, Doc, but I want my friend to leave hear alive. If not, I will kill you. So, if it takes a week, then we will be here until he can leave. I suggest you get busy," I said.

The doctor told the secretary to get some towels and other things I didn't understand. He worked on Leon for an hour. Then we heard the buzzer in the front.

The secretary looked out and said, "It's the police."

The doctor looked as if he was going to yell for help. I put my gun to his head while he was bent over Leon. "Don't say a damn word," I threatened.

The secretary convinced the doctor to cooperate. I guess she thought if she survived, she would get some more money. By being raised on the Bottom Barrel, survival was in her blood.

"I'll take care of this," she said to me. She walked out to the office area.

I could hear every word. My fingers were getting itchy, but I had a firm grip on the 9 mm at the doctor's head.

"Can I help you, officer?" the secretary said.

"There was a shootout on the street. I want to know if you heard or saw anything strange, the officer said.

"No, officer, I been in here waiting on the doctor doing some paperwork. Did anybody get hurt?" she asked.

"We don't know yet, but there was blood at the scene. If you hear anything, give me a call," the officer said and gave the secretary his card. The officer left and went to the next office.

The secretary was closing the door when Tyrell came back. He came in the back room and gave me a bag of money.

"Is he gonna be all right?" he asked the doctor.

"He had a bullet in his shoulder, and one grazed his side. He'll be all right in a couple of months," the doctor said.

I removed the gun from the doctor's head. Leon was beginning to gain consciousness. He looked up at me, holding the gun at the doctor, and smiled.

I said, "Doc, give him some medicine that will last a while."

"You need to have some X-rays and go to the hospital," the doctor said.

"You need to make sure he can make it out of here so you can go home," I said.

That was the first positive thing the doctor had heard since we came in. I think he thought he would be killed because he could identify us. I was just trying to make sure Leon was all right. I still believed money can buy everything.

The doctor gave us a lot of painkillers and told Leon to take them twice a day.

"Give me your driver's license," I demanded.

"What?" the doctor said.

Tyrell hit him in the face with his fists.

"Give me your license," I said.

He reached in his pocket and gave me his driver's license. I looked at it, and then I gave it to Tyrell. "If I get locked up for this, he will visit your family. Do we understand each other?" I asked.

The doctor nodded his head nervously.

I took three packs of money out of the bag. Each pack had ten thousand dollars in it. I gave them to the doctor. I gave the secretary one pack, and we left, but not before Tyrell said a few words to the secretary and got her number.

Tyrell had one of Leon's BMWs. Leon was awake but in a lot of pain. We drove back to the Bottom Barrel. I dropped Tyrell off and drove Leon to his house.

I knew where Leon lived, but I had never been in his house. He had a beautiful house in the suburbs of Bloomfield Township, with tree-lined streets with expensive cars in the driveways of all the houses.

I helped Leon get out of the car after we pulled into his attached garage. I struggled with him because he was so weak. The medicine had also started to take effect.

Once in the house, I noticed how clean and organized it was. He must have a maid, I thought. I found my way to his bedroom, where I laid him down. I took his blood-soaked clothes off and used a towel to clean off the dried blood. I found a robe hanging on the door and put it on Leon. He looked so peaceful, so I didn't want to disturb him.

I went downstairs and gathered my thoughts to try to understand why we had been set up. I knew that the Ridgeway brothers were really trying to take over our territory. They must have been paying a lot of people in the neighborhood to set us up like that. My first thoughts went to the secretary at the doctor's office, but she had helped us out. Then I thought about Tyrell. With all that shooting, Leon was the only one who was shot.

My mind needed to rest, so I went and took a shower and lay down next to Leon and fell asleep. It would be a long time before I got a full night's sleep again.

CHAPTER TWENTY-TWO

The next morning, I made sure Leon had some breakfast. Although he didn't eat much, I made him try, telling him he had to eat to regain his strength.

"I have to go check on the house and the work being done there. Call me if you need something," I told him and put the phone close to him. "I have to take your car. I left mine across town."

"Okay, Krystal. Thanks for everything," he said.

I looked at him then kissed him softly on his lips. "For life, Leon."

He tried to smile, but I could see he was in pain. So, I waved and left.

On the drive, I thought about the Ridgeway brothers. I was not raised to run from anyone. I had to face the situation. I tried to focus on Ms. Lady and spending some time with her. She would be out in a week. I was excited. She was going to be so surprised by the way the house looked. I felt good to be doing something good for Ms. Lady.

The phone rang, startling me. It was Leon. "What's wrong? You all right?" I asked.

"I'm fine. Hold on a minute," he said.

The next voice I heard on the phone was Tyrell. "I got some information for you," he said.

"What is it, Tyrell? Can it wait?" I asked.

"Well, you know the secretary?" he asked, not trying to say too much over the phone.

"Yes," I said.

"She wants to talk to you."

"Why me? Can't she talk to you?" I asked.

"She won't give me the information. She said she would only talk to you, and today is her last day. She's leaving the city," he said.

"Okay, have Leon give you my cell number to give her. This better be on the up, Tyrell," I blasted.

"Krystal, everything's cool. I been talking to her," he said.

"Tell her to call me. And you meet me at the greasy spoon in an hour," I said and hung up before I got a response.

I checked on the house quickly and cleaned myself up. After I got out of the shower, the phone rang.

"Hi," the female voice began. "The appointment you requested is for tomorrow at ten a.m. They both usually arrive before the doctor. I will not be in, but I will leave the door open for you at nine a.m. when I pick up my things. If you would like to pay for your appointment afterward, you can reach me at the number on your caller ID. Thank you very much." She then hung up.

It took me a moment to realize what had just happened. The secretary told me the Ridgeway bothers would be in the doctor's office the next day, and no one would be there. She was giving me an opportunity. It always amazes me what people will do for money.

Will I be set up again? I wondered. I had to end this one way or another.

I packed a bag and met Tyrell at the greasy spoon, and I told him about the information. He said, "I knew, but I didn't want to say nothing in front of Leon, 'cause he woulda got out his bed and tried to go."

"I have a plan," I said. "I'm going by myself."

"Krystal, what if it's a set up? I'm going with you," he said.

I liked his directness, telling me what he was going to do, but that didn't change my mind. "I already got my plan, and it don't involve you," I said, being a little nasty with my attitude.

"I'm not trying to be hard or nothing," he said. "My cousin told me to keep an eye on you and help you if you need it. Shit, those bastards shot my cousin. I got to get revenge."

He was very convincing, and I did need someone to watch my back.

"Okay," I finally said. "Meet me at eight a.m. Get some sleep. I need you to be sharp."

"A'ight. I'll be here in the morning."

I left the greasy spoon and went to do some shopping before I went over Leon's house. I made sure he took his medicine and ate when I arrived. I also washed him and brushed his teeth. Then I lay down next to him to tried to sleep.

My night was restless. My mind was going in too many different directions. For the first time, I thought about what would happen if I got killed. What would Ms. Lady do? What would Leon do? I thought about my plan, tossing and turning all night long. I really needed my sleep.

I looked at Leon. I wanted to make love to him, but he was too drugged off the medicine to notice that I couldn't sleep. I held him and let my imagination take control until I feel asleep.

The next morning, I woke up at six a.m. I had purchased a nurse's outfit and a wig. I showered and got myself together. As I looked in the mirror, I had to smile at myself. I looked totally different. My nurse's uniform, wig, and the heavy makeup I put on made me look like an older woman. I wore a long white doctor's jacket to hide my bulging guns. I made sure Leon took his medicine and I had some breakfast ready when he woke.

Leon looked at me in my outfit and closed his eyes. I guess he thought he was dreaming.

I called Tyrell at 7:30 and told him to meet at the doctor's office at 8:30. I didn't want any surprises again.

While Tyrell and I were waiting in separate cars, we noticed the secretary leave at about 8:45 with a box full of stuff. *She must really be leaving,* I thought. After her car left the block, I went inside. The door was open like she said it would be, and I made my way back to the office, which was separate from the waiting room.

I went over my plan again, then called Tyrell. "If anybody comes in, wait two minutes, and come in after they do. Be prepared for whatever goes down," I said.

Ten minutes passed, and my phone rang. "One guy coming to you," Tyrell said then hung up the phone.

Within a few minutes, the office door opened, and Desmond Ridgeway walked in, smoking a cigar. The smell made me choke as I went out to greet him. I had a chart that I had picked up from the back in one hand, and my right hand was in my pocket, holding a .380 automatic. It was smaller than my 9 millimeters but just as powerful.

Without looking up, Desmond said, "I have a nine o'clock appointment."

"Yes, Mr. Ridgeway. I thought it was for two people," I said.

"My brother couldn't make it," he said as he looked up from the magazine in his hand.

I tightened the grip on my gun. Tyrell came in the door and sat across from Mr. Ridgeway, not looking at him at all. He didn't notice me, or else he forgot how I looked.

"So, your brother won't be making it, sir?" I said.

"I said he wasn't coming. Where is the damn doctor?" he asked as he bent over to put his cigar in the ashtray.

I seized the opportunity. Before he rose his head up, he felt the coldness of my .380 barrel at his temple.

"What the fuck is this?" he asked.

Tyrell followed suit and locked the door and pulled the blinds down. His big .45-caliber gun was pointed at Desmond Ridgeway's head.

"You black people don't know what you are doing," Desmond said as he looked deep in my eyes. I took my wig off, and he squinted his eyes, trying to focus on me.

"I think we know what we doing, Mr. Ridgeway," I said.

He started to turn red. "You're Sable's cousin," he said.

"Why you try to kill me? Why you burn my house down?" I asked.

"I didn't," he said.

Tyrell walked up on him and hit him in the face with some brass knuckles. Blood shot out of his mouth like a cannon. One of his teeth hit me on my arm before it splattered on the carpet.

"We just want to ask you a few questions. Where the fuck is my money?" I asked. My adrenalin started to peak. I picked up the cigar and waited for an answer.

"What money? I don't know what you're talking about," he said.

I looked at the cigar and put it on his forehead. I held it there, despite his yelling from the pain. Tyrell looked out the door to make sure no one was coming.

As Desmond screamed, I yelled at him, "Where is my money?"

"I don't know about no money," he said.

I pulled the cigar off and put it on a different spot of his forehead. "Why did you set me up?" I asked.

His screams were very loud, so I pulled the cigar off. "Look, Desmond, I want my money and some answers. The next time, I will put this in your left eye, then your right eye. Then we going to leave and let you enjoy your blind life."

"My brother wanted to control your turf on the Bottom Barrel. We burned your house, but we didn't find any money," he said.

"Where's your brother?" Tyrell asked.

Just like I took the opportunity, so did Desmond. When I was putting the cigar back in the ashtray, Desmond acted like he was reaching for it. He pushed my hand, and before I could raise my gun and shoot, Desmond jumped out the window. I started to shoot, but I realized we were on the third floor, and I knew he wouldn't survive going headfirst.

Tyrell and I looked at each other and started moving fast. I made sure I took anything I had touched with me. I wiped down the counters and desk. We were out of there almost before Desmond hit the pavement.

We closed the door and were going down the stairs, walking slowly, not trying to get noticed, when I heard some screams. Then I heard a large bang like a car accident. We both made it to our cars with no one seeing us. They were all too busy looking at the guy who seemed to fall from the sky.

I drove straight to the greasy spoon, and Tyrell took another route. After an hour, Tyrell knocked on the greasy spoon door.

"You all right?" he asked.

"Yeah, I'm cool. What happened?" I asked.

"A guy jumped out a window downtown and a car hit him. I saw the body. It was flat like a dead squirrel after cars run over it on a highway," he said.

"That is awful. I'm going to check on my house, then I'll be over Leon's. You coming by?" I asked.

"Krystal, I still have to run your business. I'll check on Leon, but then I got to hit the streets to collect money," he said.

"I feel you. See you."

We both left and went our separate ways. I tried to understand what had happened to the money. Maybe it was still in the house. Maybe the vandals got it. The house was boarded up, and I hadn't been there since the night it caught on fire. When Leon got well, I would have him go with me to look.

I turned up the car radio and let the music ease my mind. I wanted to clear my head, so I drove around for thirty minutes with no destination. When I arrived at Leon's house, I was surprised to find he was up, walking around.

He smiled when I came in. "Hi. Is everything all right?" he asked.

"You look better. I'm glad to see you up and around," I said.

"I'm feeling better."

I hugged him, and we ate and talked about what was going on around us and what we needed to do to correct it.

Leon and I became very close after that. He soon got all his strength back, and we went back to business as usual.

CHAPTER TWENTY-THREE

I went to pick up Ms. Lady the day she got out. She looked so good—not like she was getting out of jail, but as if she had just come back from an extended vacation. Her skin color was back. Her hair had grown. Her voice was strong, and she looked like she had before my daddy died. I knew when I saw her that we had to change our lifestyles. I wanted to enjoy life, and I wanted Ms. Lady to enjoy the rest of her life.

I took her back to her house. When we pulled up, her eyes lit up. The new siding on the house was beautiful. The landscaping around the house was flawless. The grass was manicured to perfection. The trees around the house were tapered, looking like green boxes lined across the front of the house.

When we got out of the car, Ms. Lady was speechless. She put her hand over her mouth like I had just bought her a new mansion. Tears formed in the corners of her eyes. She followed me closely as I opened the front door.

The marble floors in the foyer and the sanded wood floors in the living room and dining room made the house look new. The new furniture had Ms. Lady hugging me and crying. When she looked into the kitchen and saw the remodeled kitchen with built-in stove and an island range, Ms. Lady just stopped. She didn't move or say anything.

"Ms. Lady, are you all right?" I asked.

"Yes, Krystal. Thank you so much. But what am I going to do with all this by myself?" she said. Her temperament seemed to go down a little bit.

"I'm going to stay with you," I said.

She again started to smile and cry at the same time. "You know, your daddy had a dream that the house looked like this. He told me about it the week before he got killed. He said he was going to remodel it the next year. This is just kind of weird," she said. "Had your daddy ever talked to you about doing this?"

"No, I just wanted to do this for you," I said.

I showed Ms. Lady the rest of the house. Then we sat down in her new living room and talked.

Ms. Lady told me, "I'm through with drugs."

I smiled. "And I'm gonna get out of the business." I also told her what had been going on in my life. I told her about Sable, Cedric, and my new love, Leon.

She was so happy for me. That night changed her, and it also changed me. We became closer than we ever were. I moved in with Ms. Lady.

After a couple of weeks, I asked Ms. Lady to go with me to my house to look for my money. We went, but we didn't find it where I had put it. I gave up hope.

I was running my business through Leon and Tyrell. I didn't have to do anything but collect money and hold meetings. My life was starting to go in the direction that I had hoped when I had this dream of hustling in high school. I gave myself and Ms. Lady six more months. I would retire with a cool million dollars if everything went well until then.

Leon and I spent as much time as possible together. He worked a lot, holding down security, buying, distributing, and collecting. He did much more than I could have done on my own.

My crew had grown to over two hundred strong. Our reputation was known throughout the city. No one messed with us. We always got tried by a wannabe, but after Leon's boys took care of them, the small guys stopped trying.

Time was passing, and Ms. Lady and I started looking for a new city to live in. I had three more months to go, and we were excited.

I started telling Leon of my intentions, and he said he wanted to come and spend the rest of his life with me. This made me feel so complete. That was the only piece of the puzzle I hadn't figured out yet.

One day, Leon picked me up for lunch and a little business. I still wasn't confident enough to leave home without my gun, so, as usual, when Leon picked me up, I grabbed it and was ready to go. We went to a nice Italian restaurant in the downtown area. The food was good, and the atmosphere was almost like we were in a Mob movie. We were the only non-whites there.

Leon was his usual well-mannered self, pulling out my chair and opening the door for me. "I have a surprise for you," he told me. "I've been investing in the stock market, and you are my partner."

I was shocked. "What?"

"We just made sixty thousand on some stock I invested in and then sold."

"You are amazing, Leon." I knew he was smart, but I didn't figure he knew how to make things work in the real world.

"I'm planning for our future," he said. "I want to marry you when we leave the city."

I think he was looking to see what reaction I would give him when he said that. I jumped out of my seat and gave him a kiss. I was so excited.

We sat there and ate our four-course meal. We had been at the restaurant for four hours when Leon looked at his watch and said, "We have to go. Time flies when you're with someone you enjoy being with."

Leon went to pay the bill, and I went to the restroom. He waited for me at the front door, then we walked hand in hand to his car that was parked at a meter down the block. When we were walking, I noticed someone following us.

As I turned around to see if he was getting closer, I heard a blast. I turned my head back as Leon fell against me. I pulled out my gun and turned around as the guy following us was pulling out his gun. I shot two times, hitting him in the top of his head.

I noticed John Ridgeway coming toward us, his gun spitting bullets. He looked like a zombie. He wanted us to see him. He wanted us to know who killed us. Leon was hitting John in the chest with shots from his .45 Magnum, but he kept coming. I shot at John's legs, hitting him in his calf. He fell to the ground right before he reached us. While falling, he shot Leon at point blank range. I pulled the trigger and hit him on the left side of his forehead. His torso was dead before his head hit the pavement.

I suddenly felt a sting in my back. Then I felt some wetness run down my clothes. My attention was on Leon. I grabbed his head as he begin to fade in and out. I heard the police sirens racing down the street.

"Give me your gun," Leon said, gasping for air.

I put the gun in his hand, and he tried to pull the trigger at the body of John Ridgeway. I didn't want to tell him he was already dead. I knew he was still trying to protect me. Blood was coming out of the corners of Leon's mouth. He looked in my eyes as though he was trying to tell me something, and then he took his last breath. His eyes remained open while tears poured out of mine.

"Put the gun down!" I heard the police say.

I looked up and saw six police officers standing over us with their guns drawn.

"Put the gun down or we will shoot," a female police officer said.

"He's dead already," I said. A part of my heart lay dead in my arms. I just wanted to join him.

CHAPTER TWENTY-FOUR

I passed out, and the next time I woke up, I was in the hospital with handcuffs on my wrists. My vision was blurry, but I focused in on Ms. Lady. She was asleep in a chair beside my bed.

"Ms. Lady," I whispered. She turned in her sleep as though she thought she was dreaming. "Ms. Lady," I said, getting a little more strength in my voice.

Ms. Lady pulled the blanket off herself and rushed to my bedside. She started to cry. "Baby, it's so good to hear your voice," she said between tears.

"How long have I been in here?" I asked.

"Two months. You were in a coma. They didn't think you were going to make it. You had been shot in the back, and a bullet hit your lung," she said.

"I'll be all right, Ms. Lady. Stop worrying," I said, trying to convince her and also myself. I moved my left hand and felt the tension of the handcuffs. "What's this?"

"You are under arrest. They're trying to indict you for Mr. Ridgeway's death," Ms. Lady said.

My thoughts went back to the night of the shooting. All I could remember was Leon lying there, looking at me. He died content.

Ms. Lady held my hand, as she could see I was in deep thought. Everything about the shooting was vague. I couldn't remember anything but Leon dying in my arms. Tears engulfed my pupils. I closed my eyes as the tears rolled down my cheeks.

I guess the medicine and my state of mind took me back in a hole where nothing mattered, and I drifted off to a sleeping darkness. Every time I woke up, Ms. Lady was there.

I began to gain my strength and get up a little more. They took the handcuffs off, but there was a policeman outside my door twenty-four seven.

One day when I woke up, Ms. Lady informed me, "An attorney is coming to see you."

"Who?" I asked.

"Paulette McKenzie."

"I don't want her to represent me," I said.

"Krystal, she's the best. If you want to get off on this charge, then you better put your differences aside. She is the best, and she is going to represent you," Ms. Lady said in a no-nonsense tone.

"All right. When do I get out of here?" I asked.

"Paulette is trying to get you bonded out. That's why she wants to talk to you."

When my attorney came, she informed me, "You can beat this case. The fact that you didn't have the gun in your hand helps you. But be aware that they are going to try and hang you. Three people are dead— two white— and they want to put it on you."

I was bonded out the next week. I was still recovering from being shot, but I was so happy to be home. My business had fallen off, but I really didn't care. I gave Tyrell complete control even though, truthfully, I didn't think he could handle it long term. I hooked him up with my connection, and I had Tyrell collect all the outstanding money. I gave him money to set up his business.

I told him, "I'm out the business. Don't call me, and don't contact me anymore."

Tyrell agreed with my terms. He kissed me on the cheek and said, "My cousin was crazy about you. He was planning to give up the life to be with you. Take care of yourself, Krystal. If you ever need anybody to watch your back, you know where to find me."

It made me feel good to hear Leon's thoughts, but I was sad we couldn't fulfill them together.

"Bye, Tyrell," I said.

He walked out the door and never called me again.

I sold my house to an investor for much less than it was worth. I was trying to get money together for my trial, but it wasn't nearly enough. Paulette McKenzie said that she could pull some strings, but it would cost me.

My trial was coming up, and I began to worry. Ms. Lady tried to calm me down, but the closer it got to the trial date, the more nervous I got.

My jury was picked in one day. A jury of my peers was two blacks and six white jurors. Paulette told me not to worry about it. She suggested I wear a business suit every day to trial.

"Look at the jury during the entire trial, and always look confident," she advised.

The trial went on for four weeks. I didn't know where the money was coming from to pay for my attorney. After the fourth week, the prosecutor asked that my bail be revoked. She thought I would be a flight risk. My attorney was livid. She argued that I cooperated with the investigation and with the prosecutors. The judge ruled against me, and I was locked up.

I had a lot of time to think and soul search to see what direction my life was going. I was locked up and might lose my case and spend more time in jail. I thought about what Ms. Lady would do without me. Would she start using drugs again? I thought about Sable. I missed her so much, and I was very sorry that I had killed her.

Then Cedric came to mind. I was still angry at him, but I did love him. When I thought about Leon, the tears started. I cried, and I cried hard.

The officer on duty at the jail came to see if I was okay. I still couldn't stop crying. My life was not what I wanted. It was what I thought I wanted—a lot of money, lots of power in the neighborhood, and a lot of kids looking up to me for what I had. I never knew the negatives that came along with it. I didn't believe I would be caught up in it. All the hundreds of thousands of dollars I had made couldn't buy my independence back. I was locked up in a dirty, four-by-eight jail cell with white women trying to make me their bitch. Didn't they know I was a killer? But I guess everybody in there was a killer.

I told myself, *I will survive the weekend until my trial date on Monday.* I must admit, for the second time in my life, I was truly scared. The first time was when I had to face the girls I knew would beat me up.

I tossed and turned every night. When I finally did go to sleep, it was Sunday night, and I woke up in a cold sweat. I knew I had to pay the piper.

My attorney was at my jail cell at seven a.m. She wanted to prep me for the trial. Paulette McKenzie seemed so confident that it bothered me. I began to snap at her for any reason I could.

"Krystal, you have to relax and let me do my job," she said.

"I know I'm going to jail, and I'm feeling alone," I said. I couldn't tell her I was scared, but I think she picked up on it.

"You have to trust me. I got this covered. I don't expect you to do any jail time. They don't have any evidence. You didn't have the gun. The police saw Leon with the gun in his hand. They want you to confess so they can close the case and look good downtown. Two white men dead, they want to put it on somebody," she said.

"I trust you to handle my case, but I don't trust you." There it was. I'd said it.

"What?" she said, confused by my statement.

"Why didn't you tell me you and Cedric was married?" I asked.

"Cedric and I have been divorced for ten years. It didn't matter. He wanted me to represent you. I didn't want to at first because he told me he was going to marry you. He talked me into it. Since then, I began to like you, and I think you are a nice person. I gave you one hundred percent in the first trial, and I will do the same in this one," she said. "So stop worrying and let me handle this. I got an inside track, and I'm going to win this case. That prosecutor can't beat me." Paulette stood up and fixed her three-piece suit.

She looked at me and asked, "We all right, Krystal Love Davenport?"

I knew when she called my full name that she was putting her game face on and getting her mind mentally ready to win this case. I went to her and hugged her. "We cool, Paulette McKenzie. Please get me out of here," I said.

She just smiled and yelled, "Guard! We're ready."

When we entered the courtroom, I looked around for a familiar face. The only folks I recognized were Ms. Lady and Tyrell. I thought I saw Uncle Nardo and Aunt Rose, but I knew it couldn't be them. If it was, they were probably there hoping I got life for killing Sable.

My mind started to wander. I thought about all the lives I had taken and all the people I had hurt. The people I loved that were not around because of me. I began to think the worst. I thought about going out like a killer. I looked at the deputy with his gun on his side. I could take him if I caught him off guard.

Tears filled my eyes, and for one more time, I put on my killer face.

"Everybody please rise," the deputy said.

Paulette grabbed my arm and brought me back to reality. She pulled me from the chair to stand up.

After the judge sat down, the deputy said, "Everybody please be seated."

The case was called, and we resumed from last week. The prosecutor had rested, and Paulette had the jury's attention. She told them, "The police department just wants to close the case and hold someone accountable. That someone is my client." She went on to say, "Don't forget that the man my client was supposed to marry is also dead." I guess she thought that would make them have sympathy for me. After a while, she rested her case.

The prosecutor looked so confident as she delivered her closing remarks. She almost had me believing that I killed everyone by myself. I looked at the jury, and I convinced myself that they would find me guilty. I would spend the rest of my life in jail.

I felt a little better when Paulette presented her closing arguments, But I still had a gut feeling my life in the outside world was done.

The judge warned the jury, "If you convict, there must not be a shadow of doubt. If there is doubt, you cannot convict."

As the judge was talking, I thought about Leon. I wondered how our life would have been in another place, another time.

When the deputy announced, "All rise," I looked at Ms. Lady. She had tears running down her face. I was sure it was Aunt Rose by her side consoling her.

The deputy led me back to the holding cell. I saw Uncle Nardo, Tyrell, and a lot of people from the neighborhood. I saw Tim that I used to date, Sable, and a few more familiar faces. I held my head up and walked with confidence, seeing the support I had.

Paulette McKenzie came back and said, "The jury is deliberating. They might be done before the day is over."

"What time is it?" I asked.

"It's twelve thirty," she answered. "Krystal, I know this is rough, but we only got a little more to go. I need you to be strong and hang in there."

"I am, Paulette," I said, but then I broke down and cried.

She held me real tight and whispered, "Trust me, Krystal." The tears stopped, and she looked at me like a concerned mother. "I'll be back when the jury reaches a verdict," she said and knocked on the holding cell window so the deputy could let her out.

After she left, I contemplated suicide when I got back to the jail cell. Then I thought about Sable. She didn't go out like a sucker, even when I had the gun pointed at her. I missed her, Cedric, and Leon. My thoughts wandered with questions I couldn't answer. Would I ever again be with a man? Would I ever see daylight or a streetlight? Would I see green grass on the house I remodeled for Ms. Lady? But the most hurtful thing was that I wouldn't get a chance to bear children and take care of my mother when she got old.

I lay down on the cot, my mind spinning with negative thoughts. I tried to block out everything. The images of all the people that were dead because of me, directly or indirectly, jumped back and forth in my mind. Was I going crazy? I closed my eyes, trying to force myself to sleep.

I whispered, "I'm sorry, God," and soon, I was asleep.

CHAPTER TWENTY-FIVE

"Krystal Davenport, Krystal Davenport!"

I awoke when I heard the deputy shouting my name.

"I'm Krystal," I said.

"The jury is back in the courtroom," the deputy said.

My heart started to race, and my stomach had butter-flies flying around inside like it was a hot summer day. I was truly scared. I thought about how I was never scared in the street. I was willing to die, not afraid of anything in front of me. Now, faced with a life in jail, I was scared to death.

As I was led back in the courtroom, I tried to see the expressions on the face of the jurors. Their faces were stone. I knew my life was now in the hands of this jury and judge. I hadn't paid too much attention to them before. Now I noticed that almost everybody was female. The prosecutor, most of the jurors, and the judge were all females.

The judge was a young black woman. She couldn't be more than thirty-five. I admired her for taking the right steps in her life to achieve her dream. I had once thought the dream I wanted was fulfilled. This was the part I hadn't counted on.

"All rise," the deputy said, interrupting my thoughts.

When the judge sat, we all took our seats. The judge asked the jury, "Have you reached a verdict?"

My heart wanted to stop. Paulette McKenzie must have heard me thinking. She held my hand under the table.

The foreman stood up. "Yes, we have, Your Honor." She gave the deputy a piece of paper that represented my fate. The judge read the verdict, then she asked the foreman to read it.

My legs shook uncontrollably. Facing my fate, I clutched Paulette's hand hard.

"We, the jury, find the defendant guilty." The roar of the people in the court drowned the rest of her sentence.

The judge banged on her gavel. "Order in the court! Order in this court!" she said, and the crowd quieted down. "I will not have any more outbursts or I'll clear this courtroom," she said with confidence. I think she scared everybody in there.

"Now, can the foreman read the verdicts without any interruptions?"

The foreman stood up again and read off the verdict. My heart would not stop pounding. I thought I was going to have a heart attack. I didn't let go of Paulette's hand, and she held her grip on mine.

"We, the jury, find the defendant guilty of involuntary manslaughter. We find the defendant not guilty of first degree murder."

The crowd went crazy. I sat there in a daze, thinking about how I could end this all. I didn't understand what had happened. Paulette stood up and held me. The look in my eyes told her I didn't understand.

"We won, Krystal," she said.

I looked around the room as if I had just woken up from a coma. Everybody was smiling and talking. I saw Ms. Lady, surrounded by cameras, and she was crying tears of joy.

"What happened?" I asked Paulette.

"You won the case."

"Order in the court," the judge said. Everybody sat down. "Counselors, please approach the bench," the judge ordered.

The judge and both lawyers talked for ten minutes, sometimes raising their voices. When they finished, the look on the prosecutor's face was not happy. Paulette McKenzie, however, looked like she had won the lottery. She walked back to the table, back straight head up in the air, looking very confident.

"Quiet down," the judge ordered. "Krystal Davenport, would you stand please."

I looked bewildered. Paulette pulled me out of my chair with a big smile and looked me in my eyes. "Let me do the talking. Just agree," she said.

I shook my head to acknowledge I understood.

"Ms. Davenport, the court is willing to sentence you now for the charge that you were convicted on. Do you understand?" she asked.

Before I could respond, Paulette said, "She does, Your Honor. She is willing to accept her sentence now rather than waste any more of the court's valuable time."

The judge gave Paulette a look, and then she looked at me and the prosecutor. "Ms. Davenport, the evidence presented against you was not enough to warrant an indictment. Therefore, the waste of court's time caused by the prosecutor and the waste of time you sat in a jail cell contradicts the meaning of justice. I am sentencing you to time served and releasing you immediately and dismissing the other case with prejudice," she said.

The courtroom erupted. I didn't really know what was going on. Later in life, Ms. Lady would tell me the trial was about yet another black person being tried for killing a white person, when the white man gets off for killing a black person. The shock was incredible. Paulette had to pinch me hard for me to realize I was free.

"Krystal, you can go home. You are free," she said. It didn't hit me until I felt the warm, secure arms of Ms. Lady holding on to me, crying, that I understood that I was free. Her tears met mine as we were locked cheek to cheek for a very long time.

By the time Ms. Lady let me go, the courtroom was empty. Paulette McKenzie, Ms. Lady, and I stood there talking. Paulette wanted us to come with her to finalize the final payment. I was so happy to be out that I just followed like a puppy.

I noticed everything in the streets: the noise, the cars, the people, the houses, the grass, the stores, the sounds of life. I vowed I would never be locked up again.

"Thank you for all your support," I said to Paulette. "And sorry for the conversation we had in the cell."

Ms. Lady held my hand on the ride to our destination. We pulled up into this gated community. We had to be let in by a button on the intercom.

"Whose home is this?" I asked Paulette.

"It belongs to my firm," she said.

It was their office. I was impressed. She was a strong, independent Black woman who worked for herself and called all the shots in her life.

We got out and walked into the foyer.

"Surprise!" People started coming out of nowhere. I was so taken aback that I just stood there. I saw Uncle Nardo and Aunt Rose. Then I looked to my left, and I almost fainted. It was Sable.

She looked at me and smiled. "You can't get rid of me that easy," she said.

Tears of happiness came so easily as we embraced. "I'm sorry, Sable," I said. "I'm so, so sorry."

She rubbed my head and said, "It's okay, Krystal. I forgive you."

I thought I was dreaming. This was too good to be true. All my family was there with me. I got hugs from Uncle Nardo, and Aunt Rose talked to me for an hour. We ate and talked, then the door opened, and a woman came in. The room got silent. There was some high authority feeling in the air. It was like royalty was arriving.

When the woman came in, Sable, who was sitting next to me, got up and greeted her. Then she brought her over to me. I recognized her face, but I couldn't put it together. Then, when Paulette McKenzie came back into the room, everybody shouted.

Sable said, "Krystal, this is my sister, Cathy. You remember her."

I couldn't move. I looked up at her, and it all became so clear. This was the ace that Paulette McKenzie had talked about. This was why she was so confident.

"Krystal, you all right?" Sable said. "This is Judge C. Thomas."

I really passed out this time. I woke up lying on a bed, with Sable sitting next to me. I had so many questions, so much to say. I just sat there and looked at Sable as if I were dreaming all along.

"Krystal, I know you been through a lot in the past few months. I want you to know I have always been there with you," Sable said.

"Sable, I am so sorry. I thought you were dead," I said. "Is Cedric dead? Where have you been? I'm so confused. I need some answers."

"One question at a time, Krystal. First, when you shot me, you were not trying to kill me. If you were, you would have shot me in the head like you've done before when you wanted someone dead. You shot me in the chest. I had on my vest. Since we were having so many problems, I always wore it. Your bullet knocked me out, and when I came to, you were gone.

"Cedric was dead. I realized what had happened, and I made it look like he was robbed. I would never let any man come between us, Krystal. It was only business with Cedric and me. I called Paulette and told her I hadn't heard from him, and she went to his house and found the body.

"I'm sorry, Krystal. My sister convinced me to take this opportunity to get out the life. I moved to California, close to my parents, invested all the money I had. My only hope was that you would wake up before it was too late and get out the game," Sable said.

"I can't believe your sister Cathy is a judge. She did always stay in the books," I said as I felt my stomach gurgle. I had to throw up.

"Where's the bathroom?" I asked Sable.

She pointed. I barely made it into the bathroom before I couldn't hold it anymore. I was in there for ten minutes.

Sable knocked on the door. "You all right, Krystal?" she asked.

"I'm okay," I said while washing out my mouth.

When I came out from the bathroom, Sable was standing there, laughing.

"What's so damn funny?" I asked.

"Girl, you are pregnant," Sable said.

I was shocked just to hear that. "No, I'm not," I said.

"When was the last time you was on?" she asked.

I was at trial for four weeks. I was in a coma for two months. Shit, I couldn't remember. "Sable, it's been at least four months," I said. The thought of me being pregnant floored me. I needed time to think. Too much was going on.

"Look, Krystal, you got a lot going through your mind. Let's go back out and enjoy your homecoming. Then I want you and Auntie Lo to come back to my house. Is that okay?" she asked.

I couldn't do anything but shake my head. We went back out with everybody else. Ms. Lady looked so happy to see her friends Aunt Rose and Uncle Nardo.

The judge and I talked privately for a while. She told me, "You need to get your life straight. You got a break this time, but next time, you may not."

I knew she was right. "Yeah, I never want to go back in that jail," I said.

"I revoked your bail to cut down on suspicion. I knew all along you would get off."

We hugged and joined the others. Everyone was just enjoying each other's company. I looked around and thought to myself, *This is my family. No money or power could buy this.*

CHAPTER TWENTY-SIX

On the ride to Sable's house, I told Ms. Lady I was pregnant. She was so excited. She couldn't believe it. Neither could I. I knew it was Leon's child, and I decided I would keep it. Ms. Lady was going to be a grandmother.

When we got to Sable's house, I was flabbergasted. She lived in a mini mansion. After she showed us around, we sat in the kitchen and talked.

Sable said, "This is my East Coast house. I have a big house on the West Coast in California. I want you both to come live with me."

It felt like old times again. Sable, Ms. Lady, and I were talking and planning like we were back at the greasy spoon. For the next two weeks, Ms. Lady and I packed. We sold everything we could. Ms. Lady put the house up for sale, and I had an offer to sell the greasy spoon. Most of my money went to my attorney and the trial, so we wanted to get all the cash we could before we left.

Everything was all set. We would be moving in a week. I set up a meeting with someone from the neighborhood who wanted to buy the greasy spoon. The meeting went well at the greasy spoon. The money would be paid to my attorney, and the buyer could pick up the deed the next day when he brought the cashier's check.

After he left, I took my last look at the greasy spoon, reminiscing about all that had happened there—the good times and the bad times. This place would always make me have goosebumps when I thought of it.

Just then, the door burst open and two white men rushed in. Both had their guns spitting bullets, and one had a wine bottle filled with a liquid. He lit the bottle and threw it toward me.

I ran and closed the office door as the flame hit it. I felt some blood on my side, and I must have passed out. I woke up smelling smoke. I looked around me and saw the greasy spoon was engulfed in flames.

I stumbled trying to get up. The blaze hit me in the face. The smoke was unbearable. I couldn't breathe as the smoke started to fill my lungs. Through the smoke, I could see all the faces of the people whose lives I had taken. They had smiles on their faces, waiting anxiously for me to join them. Leon was by my side, guns blazing, but no one was falling. He looked at me and said, "I got your back for life. Go back, Krystal. Go back." The last thing I thought I saw before I passed out was Satan himself coming to get me with horns and a red suit.

CHAPTER TWENTY-SEVEN

The hot July temperature made the funeral procession seem longer than it was. Cars were lined up for miles. People from all walks of life were there. The hearse was the last car in the procession. It was open, with lots of flowers covering the top of the casket. The casket was made of my favorite color, gold with black trim on the outside, laced with black satin on the inside. The sides of the hearse had an open glass box so you could see the casket.

As the procession came to the burned-down greasy spoon, it stopped to pay homage to the life of a killer. Lines had formed for blocks around the building. The crowd raised their right hands wearing white gloves, a neighborhood tradition that signified cleansing in hope that in the next life, all sins of the person in the casket would be forgiven.

I stood in the background and watched the hundreds of people paying their respects. I didn't know my life had reached so many people. I watched as the tears flowed from friends and Ms. Lady received constant hugs. I got the notion to cry myself, seeing such an outpouring of love coming from a community that hated what I did.

I thought back to the day the greasy spoon burned down. I remembered seeing Satan coming toward me before I passed out. It turned out that it was really Tyrell, Leon's cousin, wearing a red shirt. He had seen my car outside the greasy spoon, and when he saw the flames, he came in to rescue me. He dragged me outside and gave me mouth to mouth. The firemen took over when they got there.

I woke up in the hospital. I had been shot in my side, but the bullet went in and out. When I got out of the hospital, Sable, Ms. Lady, and I decided that we should continue with the story that I had died in the blaze. So, here I sat, wearing a disguise, mourning over a casket that was supposed to have me in it.

At the church, the preacher hit home, talking about selling drugs and how drugs were killing our community. He also said good things about me and how I tried to help the people in the neighborhood by loaning money to those in need. Ms. Lady must have paid him good for the kind words. I was beginning to believe his words myself.

Then, shots rang out. People were screaming, and guys were shooting back. I ducked in an aisle, and the next thing I knew, I was being trampled near the emergency exit where I was hiding.

I felt Ms. Lady pulling me up to leave. We went out the side door, where two men ran past us with their guns out. While Ms. Lady and I walked back to the car, we talked about our need to escape from the Bottom Barrel, our way out of the drugs, violence, death, and the envy I received from people because of the the power that being a drug dealer gave me.

That night, we left town on our way to California, hoping to change our lives forever. Uncle Nardo and Aunt Rose gave us directions from the airport. The day was beautiful. It was about 2:30, the sun was shining, and the warm autumn air was blowing slightly. The smell in the air was unlike the smell of the Bottom Barrel. The poverty, the death, and destruction were not evident in the air in California.

The smell and the people made me realize what I had been missing in my life. I had thought I was on top of the world, above most people in the old neighborhood. I had money and the power to control people's lives. In California, everybody had money. I was just a person. I was looked at like everyone else. No one knew me or my past. I could finally put my gun down and start carrying a small purse.

Ms. Lady and I got settled in at Sable's house. It was a beautiful house off the beach, with a terrace where we could sit and watch the sun rise and listen to the waves beat against the marina while the boats swayed back and forth in the distance. It was so pleasant and serene. I woke up early every morning to catch the sunrise.

I had Leon's child in April, a beautiful eight-pound, four-ounce baby girl. I named her Leethia after Leon. She looked just like him, and I vowed to keep her away from the fast life.

This was a good time in my life. It was the first time since my daddy was alive that I felt secure. I was away from the fast life. I just enjoyed being with family. Sable, Ms. Lady, Uncle Nardo, Aunt Rose, and I were inseparable. Raising Leethia was a full-time job, and I didn't have time to even think about a man. I was really happy.

On Leethia's third birthday, we were having a party. Sable and I went to the mall to pick up a cake and some gold earrings. I wanted to have her ears pierced. I remember looking at my watch and getting a little dizzy.

"What's wrong, Krystal?" Sable asked.

"I don't know. I feel a little dizzy," I said. "It's one o'clock. We got to get home. The party starts at four," I managed to say.

She grabbed my arm. "Girl, you look sick, but you can't be pregnant. You ain't had a man since you been in California." She started laughing.

"That's not funny, Sable, and believe me, that's my choice," I said.

We left the mall. As we approached the house, I felt dizzy again. "Sable, something is wrong. I feel something inside my stomach."

"That's probably that sexual tension trying to escape," she said, and we both laughed.

We parked the car and went to the front door, which was slightly open. We looked at each other.

"Daddy!" Sable yelled. "Ms. Lady!"

At that moment, she was probably thinking what I was: *I wish I had my gun.* But we had traded them in for the good life.

I slowly pushed the door open and eased inside. There was no sound.

"Ms. Lady!" I yelled. "Where are the party decorations?"

"We're getting played. They're just fooling around," Sable said, but she didn't look like she believed it.

"All right, Ms. Lady and Daddy, this ain't funny no more. Where are you?" Sable said.

We slowly walked up the stairs. Nothing was out of order. Sable walked into her parents' bedroom and fell to her knees, screaming and crying.

I went in behind her and saw her mother lying in a pool of blood on the bed, hands tied to the bed, and one foot tied to the post. She was naked, with blood running down between her legs. Her father was tied in a chair. His mouth was duct-taped, and his eyes were duct-taped at the eyebrows so that he couldn't shut them. He had had to witness the violation of his wife. Even as he sat there dead, bleeding from the gunshot wound in the middle of his forehead, his eyes were focused on his wife. I could still see tears in his eyes.

Everything was moving so slow. What seemed like minutes were just seconds.

"My baby!" I screamed. "Where is my baby?" I ran from room to room, looking for my child. I was done. I didn't want to believe what was happening. "Leethia, where are you? Ms. Lady! Ms. Lady, where are you?"

My heart raced as I approached the room I stayed in. I saw blood trailing from under the door. There were bullet holes in the door. Fear entered my heart. I didn't want to open the door, afraid of what was on the other side.

I was moving in slow motion. I opened the door and screamed until there was nothing left. Ms. Lady was sitting in a pool of blood with a gun in her hands and a bullet hole in her head. Her lifeless body was up against the opened bathroom door.

I was frozen. I couldn't move. Time must have stood still for a couple of seconds. I couldn't stop yelling and screaming. Then, I remembered my baby.

"Where is my baby? Leethia, Leethia?" I saw the blood trailing from the bathroom. My knees were weak, but I rushed into the bathroom and saw my baby in the tub, cold and blue.

For the first time in my life, I lost control. The next thing I remembered was a lot of men with guns holding me, trying to pry me away from my baby. I was in the tub, holding her. She had duct tape on her mouth and around her legs and arms.

I thought she was dead because she was not moving. I held her and rocked her as if she were an infant. I tried to believe there was nothing I could have done to deserve this, but in my mind, I knew. You reap what you sow.

I had nightmares for the next six months as I bounced from one mental institution to the next. After two years, they decided that I wasn't a threat to myself or anyone else in society, so they let me leave. They had told me my child was alive, and the strength to get well came from wanting to see her again.

I had heard Sable was also in an institution. She had gotten released and later turned to drugs and alcohol.

After my release, I didn't have anywhere to go. My money was gone, and I was in California, where I didn't know anyone, so I went back to the house where we used to live. It was now the parking lot of a condominium for seniors.

I walked around the parking lot to the beach side, trying to get the thoughts of the past out of my head. I looked at what I thought was a cardboard tent hidden close to the marina. It was boxes tied up with string and sheets, and it looked like someone lived there.

As I passed, I noticed a body. I could see a person's hands covering their face so the sun wouldn't come through. I stopped in my tracks when I noticed Aunt Rose's wedding band on her dirty hand. I was upset. My instincts told me to grab the brick lying on the fence and beat the shit out of the person until they told me where they got the ring.

I grabbed the brick, but the person moved. She sat up. It was a woman. I couldn't believe my eyes. I moved in closer to get a better look. It was Sable.

"Sable!" I yelled.

The girl looked up at me with a blank look. She was dirty and smelled like she had been drinking for weeks.

"Who the fuck are you?" she asked.

"It's me, Sable. Krystal. You know who I am?"

"You ain't Krystal. She's dead. They all dead," she said, lowering her head as if she were talking to the ground. "Ms. Lady and Daddy are dead. Krystal, Aunt Charday, and Leethia are dead. I don't know why I'm not dead."

"Sable, it's me. I'm not dead, and Leethia is not dead. I need you to help me find her," I told her.

"She's dead. Ms. Lady's dead. Daddy's dead. Aunt Charday is dead." Sable was out of her mind. She started crying, and I started crying also.

I tried to calm her down. "Sable, you remember how we used to run the Bottom Barrel? How we were on top, had everything we wanted? Sable, remember when I shot you because I thought you were fucking Cedric? Come on, Sable. I know you remember."

I sat down in her tent, and we hugged each other so tight. She wouldn't let me go. She looked up at me with tears running down her face, leaving a trail like a train track on her dirty face.

"They're dead, Krystal. Everybody's dead," Sable repeated.

"We are not, Sable. We have to pull our family back together. I don't like seeing you like this. We have to get you help," I said. "But I can't help you unless you want to get help. You have to want to help yourself. Are you ready?"

She lowered her head. "I don't like what I've become. I need help, Krystal. I had no one to turn to except the streets. My sister blames me for my parents' murder, and she hasn't talked to me. The streets are eating me alive. I never thought I would end up like this."

"We've always helped each other and had each other's back. That hasn't changed. We have to fight to get our life back," I said as I helped her up and out from her cardboard tent. I hugged her and told her I loved her.

The smell of her body was nauseating. The dirt caked up on her yellow skin made her look two shades darker, her clothes were dirty, and the jeans she wore had brown stains on them as though she had shitted on herself. Her jeans had dirt spots at the knees. I assumed she had to suck and fuck to survive. Tears rolled down my face as I remembered how beautiful she once was and how I had looked up to her.

She hugged me tighter and said, "Krystal, please help me. I feel so lost and alone."

"You are not alone I'm here. I will help you, but you must be committed to getting straight," I said.

We held each other, both crying and both deep in thought. I didn't mind the nauseating smell and her foul breath.

Then she asked, "Krystal, is Leethia alive?"

"Yes. Your sister keeps in contact with her. You got to get well so you can help me get her back." I pulled back from her and said, "Now you need some hot water."

She looked at me and managed a faint smile. I thought I saw the old Sable somewhere in those eyes.

CHAPTER TWENTY-EIGHT

I found a job at a temp service, and Sable went to a 90-day inpatient treatment center. I think she needed more counseling because of the murders. I found out that my daughter was with Judge Thomas, Sable's sister. Although I wanted to go get her, I had nowhere to raise her. Plus, I had to get myself together first. Sable and I planned to stay in California while we tried to pull our lives back together. We both knew in our hearts we had to find the killers of our family.

While Sable was in treatment, I spent my nights at the library, looking up old newspapers. I found out that one of the suspects was shot by Ms. Lady and later caught. It seems it was a Mob hit, so the papers said. The suspect's name was Mark Ridgeway. They couldn't find any Mob ties to Uncle Nardo or Aunt Rose, so they convicted Mark Ridgeway and closed the case.

I was speechless. *Their family is still looking for me out here in California?*

My mind raced back to the first time I met the Ridgeway brothers, John and Desmond. We started out selling their drugs for them, but then we became too big, and they had to introduce us to their connect. It was their jealousy of my success that brought us all to this point.

I remembered when they shot my mother while having some of their workers stick up the greasy spoon. I remembered when I caught Desmond Ridgeway at his doctor's office. I could still see the look in his eyes when I put the cold gun to his head. I could still hear the thump of his body hitting the ground when he jumped out the window, fearing for his life.

Tears began to form in my eyes when I remembered holding Leon's body as he died from shots fired by John Ridgeway. Even though John also lost his life, it still felt unfair that he had taken the only man that I ever loved. Giving his life wasn't enough, even though I had put three bullets in his head.

Now, the Ridgeway brothers had again taken the people I loved. My anger turned to rage. Revenge would guide my life until I settled the score or died trying.

I didn't go to work the next day. I had to think. Was the Ridgeway family still looking for me? I had to be careful. I had to find the killers before they found me.

I knew I had to tell Sable. If she was down with me, then fine. If not, I still had to have closure.

I couldn't get my daughter with this hanging over me. I talked to my daughter once a week because I didn't want her to forget about me. When I called her that night, I spoke to Judge Thomas and told her that her sister was doing fine. I promised her that Sable would be with me when I could finally pick up Leethia.

She told me something I didn't expect. "Your mother had a life insurance policy, and the company has been looking for you to pay you off."

"Wow. How much?" I asked.

"A hundred thousand," she said. "You just need to get the death certificate."

I had a lot of unfinished business, and the money would help us. I went down to the city clerk and got Ms. Lady's death certificate, and soon after, I got the check from the insurance company and deposited it. Then I went to see Sable and told her what was going on. She had two more weeks before she would be released, so she would have time to think about what she wanted to do.

I found us a small house to rent and bought a few things—not much furniture, in case we had to leave in a hurry. Over the next two weeks, I did a lot of research. I spent days at the library on the internet, trying to trace the Ridgeway family. In the evening, I dressed down and started buying drugs in Compton.

After a few days, I had a steady runner who would cop for me. Claython, my runner, liked me. He thought I was a user, and I led him to believe no different. I started letting him get high when I bought drugs. When he wanted to know why I wasn't getting high with him, I told him that I only got high with my man, who worked and wanted his drugs when he got home. I couldn't believe he went for that one.

After a while, I gained his trust, and he started telling me about who ran the drugs in Compton. It was the Ridgeway family, through cousins and uncles. I checked my list and found the names of three of the Ridgeway relatives the dope fiend told me about. Now I had a place to start.

It was four days before Sable got out, and I had Claython buy some drugs for me. Only this time, he took me with him because he wanted to get high right away. He was sick. His body needed some drugs to function normally.

We went to a nice house a few blocks away. When the door was opened, I was surprised to see a young white boy and two black men. The focus was on me, even though I was dressed down.

"Who is this, Claython?" the white man asked.

"This is a friend of mine, Key—I mean Rose," Claython said. Rose was my alias that I always used when I didn't want to use my name. I got it from my aunt.

"Hey, Key, I'm Trevor," the white man said.

I didn't say a word. I just nodded because I didn't know if it was a setup.

After the transaction, we started to leave, and Trevor said, "Why don't you stay and get off here, Claython?"

"Can I?" Claython asked while sniffling and wiping his nose with his sleeve.

"You can go in the basement. Take her with you."

I spoke up. "I don't get high. I just cop for my old man. Claython wanted to hook me up to a good connect, so I brought him here to cop."

"You don't get high?" one of the black guys asked as he raised his gun and cocked it.

Everybody froze. All eyes were on Trevor. His decision would end my life. I thought it was over, and I should have known better not to be strapped going to a drug house.

"Hold up, Tommy," Trevor said. "Come have a drink with me. You do drink, don't you?"

I was really scared. I had flashbacks of me being raped by Leon's old crew. With my sexiest tone, I said, "Sure, I drink socially. I'll have a glass of wine."

Trevor was trying to hit on me. He really was nice, and we talked for about thirty minutes until Claython returned from the basement. He was ready to go and walked straight to the door.

I got up from the bar and walked over to Trevor, extended my hand, and smiled. "Thanks for the drink, Don."

"My name is Trevor, short for Trevorinique. Trevor Ridgeway, not Don."

He took offense to me calling him Don. I would have to remember that.

"Can I see you again? Take you to lunch sometime?" he asked.

I knew I had his number at that moment, but I was not into white boys. "I got a man, but thanks anyway."

When I walked out the door, I tried to shake all my curves through the big clothes I had on. I felt Trevor and his boys looking at my body.

After I left Claython, I went back to our house. The turn of events were now in my favor. I could use this way to get knowledge of the organization. When Sable came out, I could introduce her to Trevor.

CHAPTER TWENTY-NINE

For the next two weeks, I put my plan in motion. I was unaware which way Sable would go, but either way, she was still the sister that I never had.

I bought two cars—a blue Toyota Camry and an old model black Cutlass with tinted windows. I didn't drive the Cutlass at all. I just keep it in the garage.

Sable was waiting for me at the door the day she was released. I must admit she looked real good. Her color was back, her smile was beautiful, and I could tell she was getting her confidence back.

I took her to the house, and we stayed up all night, talking. We talked about the past and the future. We went over the mistakes we had made in the past and talked about our future plans. I showed her the drugs I bought and told her about Trevor Ridgeway.

Sable wanted revenge for her parents. She understood the consequences. We both were willing to do whatever we had to do, including dying, if it came to that. We again made a pact to always, no matter what, watch each other's backs.

The next morning, we went shopping, and I bought Sable a car. She wanted a red convertible Chrysler Sebring. She looked like a model in that car, and the salesman wanted to take her out.

"Some things never change," I said. "I guess you still got it."

"I never lost it, Krystal. I just smothered it for a while. Now I'm back," she said.

We went back to the mall. Sable needed a red outfit with a matching coat. After going from store to store, buying whatever Sable wanted, I heard someone calling, "Key!" as we walked down the corridor. I kept walking and talking to Sable.

Then this big black man grabbed my arm. "Hey, Rose. Trevor wants to holla at you."

I had forgotten my alias for a minute. Sable was looking at me strangely, but she went with the flow.

"Who?" I said.

The white man appeared in front of me. "Oh, you don't remember having a drink with me?"

I thought it was cool that he didn't say where I met him. He got a point for that.

"Hi, Trevor," I said.

"I'm a little hurt," he said.

"Why? 'Cause I didn't go to lunch with you?" I asked.

"Naw, because I didn't know you was this beautiful, and you wouldn't let me see you again," he said. "This must be your sister. You girls look alike. Can I buy you all lunch?"

"No thanks. This is my sister, Racquel."

He looked at Sable and spoke, then looked back at me. "I would still like to take you to lunch or a movie. Can I get your cell number to call you?"

"Trevor, thanks, but I told you I got a man," I said.

"That's cool. Here is my number just in case, or you can use it and you don't need Claython. Nice meeting you, Racquel. Let's bounce," he said as he walked off with his boys.

Sable was speechless. "You got it going on with a fine white boy and you play him?" she said. "Girl, he was all over you."

"Sable, that's Trevor Ridgeway. I told you about him. Shit, I was trying to hook you up with him. Now we got to go to plan B."

"So, I guess I'm supposed to get used to answering to Racquel?" she asked.

"That's your new name, sis." We both laughed, and then we shopped until we dropped.

CHAPTER THIRTY

Sable coming home made me happy. We sat up and talked like we used to years ago. We were both determined to find the killers of our parents.

I met Claython and gave him some of the drugs I had been buying. In turn, I needed to know where I could buy some guns. He told me his cousin had a hookup. I met his cousin and bought a small arsenal—four handguns, two nine millimeters, two Glocks, three AK automatics, and a lot of extra ammunition.

Later on that morning, I agreed to meet Trevor at a restaurant in Los Angeles. We had a nice lunch, and when I told him I had to get home, he tried to entice me not to leave yet.

"Come with me to my house. One little drink, then you can leave," he said. "I'm really enjoying your company, Key."

"I'm having a good time too, but I got to get home," I said.

"Just one drink," he asked again.

I knew this would be a good way to gain his trust, so I agreed.

As we pulled up to the house, his two bodyguards came running out as though they knew he was pulling up. By the time we parked, they were coming down the sidewalk and opening the door. From the corner of my eye, I saw a black car pulling out of the parking place across the street.

Trevor got out the car and held the door open for me. His guys had a questioning look on their faces.

"He's never done that before," Tommy said. "He must think you are special."

I walked ahead of everybody and said, "I am special."

Both the guys were standing there, looking at me, when Trevor said, "You guys never seen a pretty black woman before?"

"Not with you," Tommy said.

All three guys started laughing. Just then, the black car I had seen appeared with the window down and shots firing. The men didn't have time to react. They were caught laughing. Tommy and his partner were hit first, almost dead center in the heart.

Without thinking, I sprang into action and knocked Trevor down while pulling out my nine from my purse. I got off three shots before I was hit in the arm and went down.

The car sped off, and Trevor got up on his knees, still looking around like some little punk. He looked at me and asked, "Are you all right?"

"I'm hit, Trevor," I said, feeling the blood run down my arm.

"Come on. We got to get you inside."

As soon as we got inside, the police were pulling up. Trevor told me, "Go upstairs. I will be back."

The bullet only grazed me, even though there was a lot of blood on my clothes. I went upstairs and peered out the window blinds to see what was going on. I saw the police officers talking to Trevor. I got some towels and soaked up the blood and looked at my wound. It was superficial. I wouldn't need to go to the doctor.

When I got back to the window, I saw the coroner putting sheets over the two guys lying dead in the street. I saw them put Trevor in the car.

He looked up to the window. His eyes told me to stay put. When they finally left after four hours, I went downstairs and double locked all the doors and windows. The police were still outside doing their investigation, so I lay down on the bed upstairs and fell asleep.

I woke up feeling wet lips on my face. "What the fuck are you doing?"

"I'm sorry. I just wanted to tell you thanks. You saved my life. You took a bullet for me. I will never forget that," he said.

"You don't have to be kissing all over me for that. You can just say thanks," I said, still trying to play hard to get.

Yeah, I took a bullet for him, and he is going to pay for it with his life, I thought.

"Do you need to go to the doctor?" he asked.

I showed him the wound. "It's not that bad. I'll be all right. I need to get home. Can you take me back to my car, please?"

"Whatever you want, Key. Anything you ever need, you call me. I mean it." He looked so sincere.

"Please take me back to my car. I need to take care of this wound," I said.

"You know, Key, both of my boys got killed, and I could use someone close to me that's not scared to do work. You think you might be down with that?" he asked.

"I don't know. I watched my ex's back until he died. I'm not trying to get caught up out here in Cali. Besides, most men don't trust women to have their back."

"You saved my life. I could be dead now if you weren't around. I'd rather have you close to me. You got a lot of heart. Just think about it. I'll pay you three thousand a week," he said.

This is too good to be true. I couldn't have planned this better myself. I'll see how far he's willing to go and how bad he wants me, I thought.

"That's all cool, but I can't watch your back if no one is watching my back," I said.

"You can hire whoever you want. I'll pay them two thousand a week," he said.

"Wait a minute. Suppose I bring a woman. That means you will be around two women all the time watching your back."

"I trust you, Key. I'd rather have someone I can trust then someone I must always watch, thinking they might set me up."

"How you going to invite me out on a date and have me watch your back? What do you want from me, Trevor?"

"All I want is for you to watch my back, be there if I need you. As far as us kicking it, if it happens it happens. I'm not going to pressure you. I like being around you."

"I have to think about it. Give me a couple of days, okay?" I asked.

"Come on. Let me take you back before I get sentimental."

We left his house, and I could see how uncomfortable he was. He kept looking over his shoulders. He kept one hand on his gun in his waistband. I kind of felt sorry for him. Someone had killed his top boys, and he was worried.

"You okay?" I asked.

"Yeah, I'm okay," he said.

We didn't talk much on the ride to my car. Before I got out, I said, "Trevor, call me tomorrow. We can work something out. But I'm going to tell you up front, my sister and I cannot be controlled. If you want some puppets, you better get someone else. If we supposed to have your back, you have to listen to us. Sometimes, anyway."

"I hear you, Key. I guess it's just getting to me. I almost died today. I have to be more careful," he said.

"Here is my number. I got to go. If you need to talk to me, I'm a phone call away," I said.

"Thanks, Key," he said.

I went straight for my car and didn't look back. I felt his eyes on me all the way. When I got it my car, I saw him pulling off like someone was chasing him.

I thought to myself, *He is out of his league.*

When I got to the house, Sable was resting on the couch.

"I see you made it home in one piece," she said sarcastically.

"That is not funny, Sable, and by the way, I hope you know we are even," I said.

"Even? You shot me because you thought I was fucking your man. I shot you for business."

I thought Sable had gotten serious on me, and I was too tired to defend myself. "So, we not even?" I asked.

"Girl, I'm just messing with you. Let me look at that wound. Krystal, we sisters. In blood and death, nothing or no one will ever come between us again," Sable said while looking me straight in my eyes.

"You're right. Nothing or no one. I love you, girl," I said.

"Girl, you are a hard killer. What does love have to do with it?" she said, and we both laughed.

Sable bandaged up my wound and gave me some pain pills. I lay down and fell asleep in an instant.

The next morning, I was awakened by my cell phone. It was Trevor.

"Good morning, Key. How you doing? You ready to go to work?"

"It's only nine o'clock. What kind of business you got going on?" I asked, rubbing the sleep out of my eyes.

"I got an appointment at eleven thirty. You coming or not? I usually go by myself. I'll be all right."

"No, wait. We will be there. Where you want us to meet you?"

"I want you to come by yourself," he said.

"No, I come with my partner, or I don't come at all. She watches my back while I watch yours. We made a deal."

"It's hard for me to trust you so soon. How you think I'm going to trust someone else too?"

"I trusted you enough to save your life. Now you got to trust me. Where you want to meet me?" I asked.

"Okay, meet me where we had lunch in LA. Then you guys follow me, and don't get lost. One hour." He hung up.

I jumped up because I hadn't told Sable about our job offer. She was already dressed, looking as good as she did when we were young.

"Where you going this time of day?" I asked.

"Nowhere. It has been so long since I've felt this good about myself. I'm just trying to get back to my fine looking self."

"All that's cool, girl, but do you want to go to work with me, making two K a week for starters?" I asked.

"Who we going to work for getting that much bread?" she asked.

"Trevor Ridgeway."

She gave me a screwed-up face.

"What?" I asked.

"How we going to work for someone whose family killed our parents?"

"If we work for him, it will be easier to find the whole family and the persons responsible for our parents' death," I responded. "I have to get dressed. We have to meet him in an hour. Make sure you bring the girls."

Within an hour, we were pulling up in front of the restaurant. I noticed Trevor's car at the entrance. I decided to wait and follow him as he requested. After about twenty minutes, he came out with a young black female.

"Look at this. White boy thinks he's a pimp," I said.

"Well, as long as he's paying me two K a week, he can be whatever he want," Sable said.

Trevor looked around to see my car. He smiled and got in the car with the female. When they pulled off, two men came running out the restaurant and jumped in a car and sped off behind them. They almost hit our car pulling away from the curb.

Sable and I looked at each other and followed them a distance away. We stayed close enough so we could see the car with Trevor and the female in it, and we could still see the car with the two men.

After about fifteen minutes, the car turned onto a tree-lined street with nice cars in every driveway. All the lawns were cut and maintained with their bushes trimmed to match the landscaping of each house. Trevor and the female pulled up to a house with a circular driveway and got out.

The men following them stopped at the house next door and parked. Sable and I drove past them, pulled up the street, and parked. We could see the house and the car with the men in it through our rearview mirror. Trevor and the female got out of the car, and the female used a key to open the door.

"She must live there," I said.

Sable and I watched the situation for ten minutes. Then, to two men got out of their car and went up to the door. Before reaching the porch, they pulled out guns and cocked them. They burst through the door that must have been left open.

"It's on now. What we gonna do, Krystal?" Sable asked.

"This doesn't look good. Something is going down," I said.

Sable reached in her purse and pulled out two nine-millimeter automatic guns for me and two Glocks for herself.

"Let's do this," she said. "I miss the excitement and the rush we used to get when we were taking care of business."

"You were the one who wanted out of the business, then convinced me to get out," I said as we exited the car.

"Yeah, I know, but look what it got us. Everybody is dead anyway," she said."

"Look, Sable, stay focused and watch my back. Are you cool?" I asked.

"I'm all right. Let's do this."

"Just follow my lead. We don't know what's up in there, but make sure you have my back, and I'll have yours." I put my guns up and walked to the door and knocked. I could hear some yelling, and through the window, I could see the men with their guns out.

The knock startled the people inside. It took a couple of minutes before the female came to the door. She was a nice-looking dark girl. Her makeup was flawless. Her hair was cut short, and she had on designer clothes.

"I'm sorry to bother you, but me and my sister's car ran out of gas, and my cell phone is dead. Can I please use the phone? It will only take a minute to call my husband," I said.

She paused for a minute, then she said, "Hold on."

When she went to get the phone, Sable and I entered. We could see the men with the guns standing over Trevor. They had their eyes on us and not on Trevor. They had their hands behind their backs, but their dirty minds were on me and Sable.

When the young lady came back with the phone, she reached out to give it to me. Before she had a chance to put it in my hand, Sable had her gun to the girl's temple.

"Don't fucking move," Sable said.

Before she could turn to look at Sable, my gun was pointed at her chest. The guys pulled their guns out and pointed them at us.

"If you don't drop your guns, this bitch is dead," I said.

Sable cocked her gun, then pulled her other gun and pointed it toward the men. "You better tell them to drop their guns, or I'll pull this trigger right now," Sable said as she hit the girl in the mouth with the other gun, still keeping her gun at her temple.

The girl yelled in pain and said, "Drop your guns, fools."

The two men laid their guns down.

"What's this about?" the girl managed to say through the blood-stained teeth in her mouth. "Who sent you here? I don't have any product here."

I didn't say a word. I walked over to where Trevor was sitting with his hands tied up. "You all right, boss?" I said.

The room was quiet. Sable pushed the young lady in the room with the other guys.

"They work for you?" the girl said.

Trevor tried to smile through bloody teeth and didn't say a word. I untied him, and he picked up the guns that the two men had.

"You want me to kill her, boss?" Sable asked.

The girl started pleading for her life. "Please, Trevor, I'm sorry. Don't do this, Trevor. Think of your son."

"Sherra, did you think of your baby daddy when you set me up?" Trevor said. "That is the only reason you are still breathing. I don't want my son to be motherless. But next time I catch you in my business, I'll raise my son by myself."

Sable and I kept our guns on the two men, who looked confused.

"She didn't tell you guys she had a son by me?" Trevor asked.

"No, I didn't know, but it wouldn't matter to me. I'm in it for the money," one of the guys said, trying to be hard. There are always those who believe that women are soft.

I walked over to the man, who was at least six foot three, and I stood there in all my five feet five inches. I looked up in his eyes, then shot him in his kneecap.

"You'll be walking with a limp for the rest of your life. Now, if you want me to solve that problem, say something else."

The man shivered in pain. The other man looked horrified.

"These bitches are your backup? Which one you fucking?" the woman screamed.

"That ain't any of your business. You need to worry about getting out of here alive, not who getting fucked," I said.

Trevor looked at me for an answer. He walked up to me and asked, "What you wanna do?"

"If we kill one of them, we got to kill them all. I'll do whatever you want," I said.

"You handle it," he said.

I whispered to him, "Trevor, you have to get a reputation and respect to be in this game."

"Just handle it any way you want!" he shouted.

Everybody could hear our conversation. Now they were uncertain as to what might happen to them. I looked at Sable, and she must have read my mind. You see, Sable's mother was raped while her father was killed watching. I was violated by some disgruntled workers. I guess somehow, we wanted some sort of revenge to make us feel better.

She again hit the woman with the gun on top of her head. The woman yelled out in pain. "Take your clothes off," Sable said. "Everybody take your clothes off. All of them."

Before the woman could complain, Sable hit her again. Blood was running down her forehead as she quickly started taking off her clothes.

"I'll be in the car. Give me your keys," Trevor said.

I tossed my keys to Trevor, and he left the house. Fear began to set in for the three people in the room. Two were bleeding, and the other one was standing mute and naked. Damn, he had a large tool.

"Since you worried about who Trevor is fucking, I wanna know who you fucking. Are you fucking either one of these guys?" I asked.

The woman just shook her head.

"What you think, girl?" I asked Sable. "You think she fucking one of these guys?" "I would fuck the one with the big dick. That's the one."

We both turned to look at the guy. "You, I want you to fuck this bitch right here, right now." Sable pushed the girl on the floor.

She was screaming, "No, don't rape me!"

"Girl, he ain't raping you. He keeping you from dying."

The girl lay on the floor and opened her legs.

"Put your legs behind your head. Lift them up," Sable said.

I went over to the guy and pushed him toward the floor. The other guy was staring and holding his bloody leg.

"You don't move." I pointed to the wounded guy.

The other guy started to get an erection, looking at the fine piece of ass in front of him.

When he got on top of the girl, she started screaming. "That's too big! I can't take that!" Sable bent down and put the barrel of the gun in her mouth. "Suck on this and be quiet."

The guy's dick wouldn't go in. It was too big. I walked behind him and hit him with the butt of my gun. "Force it in," I told him.

He pushed as hard as he could, and the girl screamed in pain as her insides were ripped wide open. The gun barrel Sable had in her mouth made her gag. Tears formed in her eyes, and the cries turned to joy as the pain subsided. The guy was pumping harder and harder. She began enjoying the moment. She was meeting him stroke for stroke.

Sable still had the gun in the girl's mouth. She was licking it like a Popsicle. I think Sable was getting turned on herself. She was sweating, and her eyes were getting bigger the more she watched. This was supposed to be torture, but everybody seemed to be enjoying it except me.

"All right, that's enough." I walked up to the man and woman lying together. "If you guys ever see Trevor, you need to cross the street, 'cause if our paths cross again, it will be a different ending. Come on, girl." I grabbed Sable by the arm, and we backed out of the house.

When we got back to the car, Trevor was sitting on the hood, smoking a cigarette.

"What was that about?" I asked.

"That was my son's mother trying to set me up. This is the second time she has done that," he said.

"You let her get away with it?" I said. "Look, I'm not trying to tell you what to do, but if you going to make money in this business, you have to be ruthless. You have to have a reputation."

"That's why I need people I can trust. I told you that. With me being white selling drugs in a black neighborhood, it gets me tried a lot. Again, you saved my life, Key. You girls are down. I need you around me 24/7," he said.

We all got in the car and took Trevor back to the restaurant to pick up his car. On the ride to his car, Trevor said, "Ladies, I have a proposition for you, if you are interested."

"What kind of proposition? We don't do threesomes," Sable said.

"Naw, I want you ladies to go in business with me."

"I don't know if we want to sell drugs, Trevor," I said.

"Not selling. Distributing and collecting. You think about it, and we'll talk tomorrow." He threw us a pack of money wrapped in a rubber band as he got out of the car and got in his own. "Nine o'clock tomorrow in Compton," he said as he pulled off, not waiting for an answer.

Sable and I looked at each other. "Do you think this town is ready for us?" she asked.

"Sable, we have to remember what our mission is. And by the way, I seen your ass getting hot in the panties back at the house. But I couldn't figure out, was you hot for the guy with the big dick or the girl who was sucking you off?"

"Fuck you, Krystal. She was sucking the gun, not me."

"Shit, I couldn't tell."

We both laughed.

"It has been a while without sex for both of us," I said.

We made it home and counted the money. It was five thousand dollars. We took a thousand each and a put three thousand away for a rainy day. We talked and plotted until the morning hours. Our lives were beginning to change.

CHAPTER THIRTY-ONE

It was a week before we heard from Trevor. He called me at 11:00 a.m. on a Sunday and asked me if I could meet him.

"I won't be alone," I told him.

So, Sable and I packed our arsenal and went to meet up with Trevor. We met in a park.

"I'm going to pick up a shipment of product," he told us.

I got in Trevor's car, and we drove about a mile away. Sable was following at a distance in our car. "When we stop," I told him, "I'm gonna act like your lady."

Sable stayed a block away in the background in case we were being set up. After fifteen minutes, a car pulled up, and two Mexicans got out.

"What's up?" one of them said.

"Everything's cool," Trevor said while handing them some dap.

"Who's the pretty girl, and why you with her here?" the second Mexican asked while he put his hand on his gun in his waist.

I put my hand in my purse as Trevor said, "Hold up, my man. This my woman." He reached over and stuck his hot tongue in my mouth. I must admit, he caught me off guard, and it felt good. "This is Shante," he said. "Ain't she fine?"

The Mexican looked at my reaction, and then looked at him.

Trevor said, "Let's get down to business."

The Mexican told him, "Follow me." He led the way to the back room in a vacant warehouse, and his partner followed us. I tried to sneak a look back to see if I could spot Sable.

When we entered the room, two more guys were standing around, holding automatic weapons. Trevor threw his suitcase on the table and said, "Here's the money."

One of the Mexicans reached for the suitcase. My gun met his temple before his hand reached the handle.

"Hold on, partner. We need to see the merchandise first," I said. I could hear each weapon being cocked. The tension was building.

"Hold on," Trevor said.

"Your lady comes in here and disrespects us by pulling a gun on my man," the Mexican said.

"You not going to get the bread until we see you got our merchandise. That's only business," I said.

"You bitch!" one of the Mexicans said as they pointed their guns at me.

"I'm not going to be too many bitches," I said.

"Hold on, Sammie," Trevor managed to say.

"I ought to blow you and this bitch away," he said while looking straight at me.

My hand was steady, and my gun was ready. "I won't be going by myself. We all be leaving here together," I said.

Sammie motioned for one of his boys with the automatic, but he didn't move because he noticed the red laser light on his chest. Then Sammie looked down to see a red light on his chest too. Everybody looked around to find where the laser lights were coming from.

"Can we just complete our business so we all can go home to our families?" I yelled and put my weapon down to my side.

"Come on, Sammie. This is my protection. Let's do our business and go," Trevor said.

Sammie was mad, but he was no fool. He didn't know how many guns were outside. "Go get the package," he told his man.

The man returned with two suitcases full of drugs. It had to be fifty kilos of cocaine.

"Everybody relax," Trevor said. "Here's your money. Let me test the drugs, and then we're outta here."

All the Mexicans were looking at Sammie. I don't think they really had the heart to die if it came to that.

Sammie waved his hand, and Trevor tested the drugs. He looked at me and said, "Everything's cool."

I pushed the suitcase to the man I had held the gun on, keeping my eyes on his every move. Sammie's men still watched the laser jumping on their chests.

"No disrespect, gentlemen. I have to protect my man's interest. Can we leave now?" I said.

"Trevor, you know we won't be doing business again," Sammie said.

"You right, Sammie. Next time I'll deal with your boss, not you." Trevor turned around to leave, and I eyed the other man and backed out of the room, following him. The laser light was still on the men as I left the room.

As soon as the laser faded away, Sammie yelled at his men in Spanish to get his drugs back. We had just gotten inside our car when the gunshots started pouring out.

"Come on, Trevor. Pull off!"

Sammie's bullets shattered the back window as we were speeding off.

After a block, I said, "Turn around."

"What? Why?"

"We left Sable back there!" I yelled.

"I'm not turning around," he said.

I pulled my gun out and shot in his direction, grazing his ear. Blood started flowing from the small wound.

"You shot me, you black bitch!"

"You better turn this motherfucking car around now, or I'll be the last bitch you see."

Trevor hit the brakes and turned the car around to the surprise of the guys shooting at us. I began shooting out the window, and the men started to fall.

Sable was hiding in a corner until she saw us turn around. Now, she was blasting away. Before the car got back down the block, two of the men were dead. I took out Sammie and the last guy standing before the car came to a stop.

After a few minutes, Sable came running to the car.

"Get in!" I said.

"Look, Key, all four men are dead. I'm going to see if anyone else is inside. I don't want to be looking over my shoulders because we left someone alive." Sable didn't even wait for an answer. She just ran into the warehouse.

Trevor was shaking like a leaf. I jumped out and followed her with both of my guns drawn. The scared-ass Trevor burned rubber, getting off the block.

"I should've killed that asshole," I said.

"In due time, Krystal. In due time," Sable said with a devilish look on her face.

"What's going on, Sable? You know we got everybody," I said.

She went in the warehouse with me close on her heels, guns ace-deuce like we were the police. We crept in slowly, in case someone was hiding. I was on one side of the room, and Sable was on the other.

Sable took off running to the table, and then it hit me. They left the money. The smile on her face spoke for itself when I reached the table and saw all the money in the suitcase. The gangster in us took over again as we ran out of the warehouse with the suitcase and guns drawn, ready to kill.

I walked back to her car, looking over my shoulder. We jumped in and sped off. Our adrenaline was in high gear, like we were high or something.

My heart was beating so hard. I looked at Sable. "Girl, we getting too old for this shit."

"Not when the rewards are this good," she said, still holding the suitcase in her hand. "Krystal, I knew you would come back for me."

"I will always have your back."

CHAPTER THIRTY-TWO

We counted the money at the house, which took us over two hours. It was two hundred and fifty thousand dollars. Sable and I just sat there, lost in our individual thoughts.

"This is a lot of money," she said, looking at the large numbers of stacked bills on the table. "We have enough money to start over anywhere, Krystal."

"Yeah, I know. Is that what you want?" I asked.

"Is that what *you* want?"

We were both silent for a few minutes. We knew that whatever decision we made, we both would have to honor it.

"Well, we have always had money. We have had a million dollars before that we made. We are always going to be able to make money. But this money won't bring my parents back." Tears formed in Sable's eyes. "But I would be able to have a little closure knowing that the people that were responsible for their deaths can join them in death."

"I don't care about the money, Sable. I want the people that did that to our parents dead. The cold-blooded way they were killed torches me every night. I want their whole family to feel this pain. I want revenge."

I didn't realize I was crying until Sable came over and hugged me. Our wet tears collided as we hugged tighter. We both knew that our lives would never be the same.

We both knew that we would die trying to avenge our family before we continued to live with this guilt and pain.

With tears in my eyes and snot running down my nose, I said, "If something should happen to me, could you please promise me to take care of my daughter?"

"Krystal, nothing is going to happen to you or me."

"Please just tell me you would," I begged.

"Okay, I promise."

"I'm going to take a long shower, and when I get back, we'll get our plan and priorities straight."

She smiled and sat down and started to put the money up.

When I got out of the shower, my cell phone was blowing up. Trevor had the nerve to call me twenty-four times. I didn't answer. I was going to let him wait a while.

"The nerve of his punk ass calling me after he left us in the middle of his bullshit. I can't wait to settle up with him," I said.

"Come on, Krystal," Sable said. "We got to keep thinking. We have to stay one step ahead of them. We have found his weakness, and it's you. I can't tell you how to play this, but if you let him get next to you, we could get his whole family. I don't want just him, because as you can see, he is too scared to hurt anybody, so he could not have killed our parents. I don't even see why he's in the game. His people set him up to be something that he's not."

"I see where you coming from."

"He doesn't have the heart. That's why he needs us to survive. So don't let our pride keep us from reaching our goal," Sable said.

"You're right. I just want him to think for a minute. Let him hold on to that dope that he can't get off without us. He will call us with a sweeter deal. Do you think that he thinks we took the money?" I asked.

"He didn't think about it when his ass left us, but I bet the boss of them Mexicans will be looking at him, thinking he double-crossed them," Sable said.

"That's more of a reason to make him sweat, at least until tomorrow. I don't want him to think that we got the money and left town," I said.

"Krystal, whatever you decide to do, either way I will be down all the way, till death if it goes that way. I'm getting ready to shower and get some sleep. I'll talk to you in the morning." Sable headed up the stairs.

My thoughts continued to the past. I thought about Ms. Lady and how she was always by my side and always gave us the right advice. I thought about Leon, the only man I ever loved. Tears ran down my face as I thought about my daughter. She didn't have a father, and she didn't have her mother with her. I wanted to call off all this revenge stuff and go get my baby.

The thoughts of my uncle and aunt being brutally murdered and my mother with the bullet hole in her head brought me back to reality. Rage built up inside me, and before I knew it, I was dialing Trevor's number.

"Hey, Trevor, this is me," I said, forgetting my alias for a minute.

"Damn, Key, you could have called and let me know if you were all right."

"If you were so worried about how I was, you wouldn't have left us," I snapped.

"My thoughts were on all the product I had. I couldn't get caught up by the po-po. You feel me?"

"I just know you left Sable and me in the middle of your mess."

"I'm sorry, Key."

"I think they had a lookout. We thought we saw a shadow," I said.

"Oh, naw. That's not good. When could we meet? We have to talk," he said.

"Sable just went to bed, and I'm not doing no business without her."

"This is not business. I want to see you and talk to you. You almost blew my head off. At least you can see if I'm okay," he said, trying to make me feel guilty.

"You aren't really cut out for this line of work. You should understand loyalty is with your people. You should have been loyal to us. We the ones got your back."

"Okay, Key, I'm sorry, but what I feel for you is not only business. I want you to get to know me better, meet my family, and be the woman I know you are," he said.

The key word that had my mind running was *family*. For me to get closer to his family, I would do anything— and I do mean anything.

"Trevor, we said we would do business together. I didn't promise you anything," I said.

"I know what we talked about, but every time I see you and every time you prove how down you are for me, I only get more attached to you. I really care about you as a woman more than an associate," he said.

I remembered the kiss and how I felt. It almost took me off my square. This white boy had some game.

"Trevor, what do you want from me?"

"All I want is for you to have an open mind and give a brother a chance," he said. We both had to chuckle about the last part. "Please, Key, meet me for a little while. When you ready to come back, I will let you go. It's only eleven thirty. I know you don't go to bed this time."

I couldn't let him think he could control me with his game. "Trevor, I'm a little worn out from the day. You can call me in the morning, and we can spend time together tomorrow. I hope your ear is all right. Remember, if I wanted to hurt you, I wouldn't have grazed your ear." I hung up the phone, not waiting for an answer.

I could almost see Trevor looking at the phone, wondering what to take from what I said. I knew he would have a lot of questions when he saw me. I had questions for him also about his family. I would sleep that night knowing I was getting closer to my goal.

CHAPTER THIRTY-THREE

The phone rang at exactly eleven o'clock. Of course, I didn't answer the first call. When he called back, I picked up the phone.

"Hi, Key. We on for this morning?" he asked.

"Yes. Where do you want to meet me?"

"I'm in downtown Los Angeles. You can meet me on Beverly Boulevard across from the Sofitel Hotel. There's a nice little restaurant on the corner."

"Okay, I know where that is. I'll be there at one."

"That's cool. You'll know who I am. I'll be the one smiling so much with a patched-up ear," he said.

"That's funny. I'll see you later."

He hung up, and I started to get ready. I had a lot of clothes that I never wore in California because I never had anywhere to go. I got out a two-piece pants suit with a low back and showing just enough cleavage in the front. I let my hair drop across my left eye, which made me look like a model off the runway with my short haircut. I put on some two-inch pumps just in case I had to get away fast. I was ready at 12:45.

I talked to Sable and told her, "Call me in two hours. If I'm not ready to come home, I will let you know by asking, 'How's the dog?' That will let you know I'm all right."

"Take you .380 revolver with you," she said.

So, I put it in my Prada purse. I arrived at the restaurant at 1:15 just a little fashionably late. Trevor was sitting in the back booth. I must admit he looked good.

He had on a nice pair of expensive jeans with a dress shirt and a jacket. His cologne smell was inviting. I don't know if it was the lack of male attention or if I was really beginning to feel him, but I was surprised that I was happy to see him. Again, I had to remind myself of the mission at hand and that I didn't do white boys.

"Rose, you look great. These flowers are for you," he said.

"Thanks. Why do you call me Key sometimes, then other times you call me Rose?" I asked while smelling the flowers.

"Well, when I call you Key, we are usually working or doing work. When I call you Rose, that is a form of respect I have for you as a woman. I separate the two because I have the ultimate respect for you, and I want to get to know Rose as the woman."

I blushed. This guy was beginning to make me tingle inside.

I noticed the looks we were getting from other people in the restaurant. The black women were looking at me mean. The black men had smirks on their faces. The white women looked at Trevor with disgust. The white men looked at Trevor and smiled, wishing they could be in his shoes.

The waitress was very pleasant, as though she knew about the looks we were receiving. We ate our meal and left.

Trevor said, "I want to take you on Sunset Boulevard to see the Hollywood Walk of Fame."

We walked and talked. He grabbed my hand, and I started to melt. I was really feeling good.

We were sharing each other's company, getting to know each other. We walked up to La Brea Avenue, then back to Vine Street. I had never seen this side of the world. I enjoyed seeing the different nationalities and people.

We turned on Vine and walked down a block from the avenue where Trevor said he had parked his car. We were still holding hands, and he had me smiling from ear to ear. He really was a funny guy.

A horn blew and startled both of us. We looked to the street, where the sound came from. The next think I knew, someone hit Trevor in the head with a gun, pushing him forward. Trevor released my hand, and he was struck again. I felt a hand smash me in the face. I put my purse up, shielding my face from another hit. The Mexican caught the purse with his hand, and the force knocked me to the ground.

The other guy got out of the car, and both men approached Trevor. "Where is my money?" the Mexican said.

"Where is my dope?" Trevor answered.

"I'm not bullshitting with you, Trevor. I don't care who your family is. I want my money or my drugs."

The second guy put his gun to Trevor's head. I pulled my purse down and acted like I was crying while grabbing my .380 automatic. I unlocked the safety, but I keep my hand on the gun while it was in my purse. The guys were not paying any attention to me like I wasn't there.

"Rico," Trevor said. "I lost two hundred and fifty K the other night, and I still didn't get my stuff. Some brothers were waiting on us. I barely made it out alive. Look, they almost shot my ear off." Trevor took the bandage off his ear to show the men.

I kept my ground, waiting to see how this would play out. I knew I could get one guy, but both guys had their guns out.

"Somebody set us up. Did you talk to Sammie?" Trevor asked.

"Sammie is dead. All my guys are dead. You are the only one alive."

Trevor said, "That sounds like an inside job. Your boy Sammie was mad when I told him I was only going to deal with you. You can kill me now if you want to, but I already told my uncles that I was set up, so they put a contract on your organization. You and your people won't be able to make no money. I want my two hundred fifty K or my product."

"I ain't got your money," Rico said.

"Let me kill him, Rico," the other guy said.

While Rico thought about his consequences, the other Mexican cocked his gun and put it to Trevor's temple. I aimed and shot him once in the head. My bullet caught him behind his right ear, and he fell to the ground.

Rico turned around and attempted to shoot me. He didn't have time. He had dropped his gun to his side while he was thinking. He didn't react in time. Trevor pulled a small gun from under his jacket and shot two times. Rico fell to the ground and clutched his stomach.

Trevor kicked him and said, "You better get me my money."

I was looking at the action when my phone rang. My instincts took over. "Come on, Trevor. We have to get out of here," I said.

It was like Trevor was in a trance, but he finally looked at me and reacted. We walked slowly up the street as the crowd began to surround the Mexicans. By the time we got to Trevor's car, we heard the police sirens. Trevor started the car, and we drove off like we weren't in a hurry.

My cell phone rang again.

"Hi, Sable. Yes, I'm fine. How's the dog? I'll feed him when I get back home. I'll call you when I'm on my way." I hung up. My message in girl talk was: *I'm okay. I have something to tell you when I get home. Don't wait up for me.*

Trevor drove up on the hill, and we looked at the stars' homes. We saw Halle Berry's and Bruce Willis's home sitting off what looked like a cliff. It was so beautiful. We rode down to Wilshire Boulevard.

"Trevor, you know, I underestimated you. I didn't think you had the heart to be in this game," I said.

"Thanks, but I was trying to protect you, Rose. I don't want anything to happen to you."

My heart sank. I hadn't heard that since Leon told me that. I was silent.

Trevor asked, "What's wrong? Did I say something wrong?"

"No, I was just thinking about my past. My last man said he would protect me, then he left me."

"I'm sorry, Rose. I got something that's going to cheer you up."

I didn't tell him that my man had died trying to protect me from Trevor's uncle.

We pulled up on a side street and got out. We walked up Wilshire Boulevard, and the stores looked like a magazine picture. Although the streets were full of people, none were going in the stores.

I didn't want to feel stupid, but I had to ask. "I know the prices in these stores must be high. Why isn't anyone going in the stores?"

Trevor looked at me with a puzzled look. "They don't let you in the stores unless you have an appointment or unless you are Paris Hilton." He smiled.

I hadn't noticed how handsome he really was. His smile was perfect. He had a dimple on his left side. If you saw him on the street dressed up, you would think he was a model or entertainer.

"Come on," he said as he pulled me into a boutique.

When we got inside, the lady said, "Mr. Ridgeway, how are you? And how is the family?"

"Hi, Denise. Everybody is fine. This is my friend, Rose. She wants to try on some dresses."

"Hi, Rose. Follow me. Trevor, you can sit in the parlor, and I'll have her model them for you. There is some coffee and donuts in there. Help yourself," the saleslady said.

She pulled me in the back room and showed me countless dresses and gowns, none of them under a thousand dollars. I tried the first one on, and she pointed me to a section that had mirrors.

Trevor was sitting there, smiling. "You like that one?" he asked.

"I don't know. They are expensive."

"Rose, I didn't ask you the price. Do you like it?"

"Yes, it's okay, but let me try on the rest," I said.

"Okay, but you choose any of them you like."

"Trevor, I can't let you buy these for me."

"Just try the dresses on," he said. "Let me decide what I can do." Trevor had another side that I had never seen before that day. I liked it.

I tried on all the dresses and could not choose one out of the four I liked the most. The saleslady was very attentive. I wasn't used to that.

Trevor got up and said, "I'll be right back." He went over to the saleslady. I didn't see any money or credit cards exchanged, but he came back and said, "Let's go."

I knew I couldn't afford the dresses, but what woman doesn't like shopping? I told myself I would be coming back to buy the dresses before I left California.

Trevor held the door open for me as we were leaving the store. He watched my demeanor. I couldn't help but to look disappointed.

When I stepped out, he said, "Rose, you forgetting your dresses."

I turn around, and the saleslady was rushing to the door with four bags. A big smile covered my face.

"Thank you!" I told Trevor and reached out for his hand.

He grabbed my hand and put his arm around my shoulder. We walked back to the car like we were so in love.

I cannot forget the mission. I cannot lose focus, I told myself.

We drove back down Beverly Boulevard. The police were everywhere.

"Damn, Key, where you park?" Trevor asked.

"I parked in the mall parking lot across from the hotel. Turn in the next driveway."

This was different than back in Memphis. The police usually didn't show up for hours. These police were out here like it was a riot.

Trevor must have noticed my far-away thoughts. "This is a rich neighborhood. They try to keep the peace down here. Do you think anyone saw us leaving the scene?" he asked.

"Trevor, you should always look at your surroundings when you doing dirt. I didn't see anybody around when I fired my gun. The side street was deserted. We were walking away when people started to gather."

"Which way should I go?" he asked.

"My car is right there on the left."

Trevor pulled up next to my car and put his car in park.

"Look, Trevor, thank you for the dresses, but I don't think I'm ready for all this. I don't think I can separate the lady you want and the woman that works for you," I said.

"Rose, I'm really feeling you, and I need you around me. I want you as my business partner and my life partner. Shit, I can't decide either. I lay at night and think about you. Then I think about how down to earth you are. I never met anyone like you. It's like you put some sort of trance over me. I don't know what to do. But I'm willing to try anything to be in your presence."

"Trevor, I thought I would never even look at a man outside my race. When you kissed me in the warehouse, I lost my cool. I'm usually in control of my emotions, but around you, I melt. I don't think I can love another man, because I'm still in love with the man I lost. I just want to be up front with you."

He moved closer to me in the car and said, "Rose, I'm not rushing you. All I want you to do is have an open mind." He leaned over touched my face and gently kissed my lips. I think he was trying to see my reaction.

I opened my mouth and accepted his hot lips. I pushed my tongue to meet his as we exchange the hot saliva that made us one. My lust was spilling out of the pores of my body. His passion for me was evident from the hot moans coming from him as we kissed for twenty minutes.

His hand slid under my shirt and gripped my breast. The wetness in my pants was pouring out. I couldn't give myself to him on the first date.

He felt me tense up with my thoughts. He grabbed my hand and put it on his thigh. I slowly moved my hand up his thigh while his tongue infiltrated the inner parts of my mouth. His breath was like a fresh breeze that had me sucking on his tongue to get the taste.

My body was shaking, and when I felt that hard dick that felt so big, I had to open my eyes. When I pulled away, my cell phone rang. We both came out of our little intimate moment.

I looked at the phone. It was Sable with a 999 call. That meant an emergency. I answered, and before I could say hello, Sable was talking.

"Krystal, you all right? They had a news flash that some people got killed in downtown LA. I know you went downtown. I was worried."

"I'm all right, girl. I'll be home in an hour. Trevor and I are just chilling."

"That sounds good. Tell Trevor I said what up," Sable said.

"My girl said what's up, Trevor. I'll holler at you soon. Bye."

I hung up the phone and said, "Trevor, I got to go. I really enjoyed your company. About today, we got some things to talk about."

"Tomorrow, Rose. I want to remember this beautiful day we had together. I'll call Key tomorrow." He smiled and kissed me goodbye.

CHAPTER THIRTY-FOUR

When I arrived home, Sable had a lot of questions. She looked at me and said, "You are glowing. Did you give him some?"

"No, I didn't, but damn, Sable, he had me wetting my panties. He is so romantic. He treated me like a real queen."

"White boy got you sprung already, Krystal. Don't get caught up. We on a mission," she said.

"I know, sis. Trust me. No one will stop us from our mission, especially not a man." I thought about the bags I had left in the car. "I forgot something in the car. I'll be right back."

I went and retrieved the bags from the car and threw them on Sable's lap.

"What is this? Trevor bought these for you? This is almost ten thousand dollars' worth of dresses that still got the price tags on them," she said. "You must have gave him some pussy, some head, or something," Sable said while laughing and looking at the dresses. "Which one is mine?"

"You can have any two. I was thinking about you when I tried them on."

"For real?" She was so excited, she just started taking her clothes off to try on the dresses.

I sat down and enjoyed the way Sable looked so happy. I thought about a few months ago, when I had found her on the street. She had made so much progress. I smiled and again vowed to myself that nothing or nobody would stop us from getting revenge for our parents and the suffering of our lives that were affected.

"Sable, you look so beautiful in that dress. You going to hurt somebody."

We both laughed. After she finished trying on the dresses, we sat down and talked. I told her what happened, every detail of my day with Trevor. We also talked about our mission, and I assured her, "I will always stay focused."

It was about four o'clock in the morning before we finally went to bed. I think we both missed the long talks we used to have. The only missing ingredient was Ms. Lady. I feel asleep crying softly, thinking about my mother and being without my own child.

The next morning, Trevor called again at eleven o'clock on the dot. I think he had a thing for punctuality.

"Meet me at the house where we first met in Compton," he said.

"We'll be there by two o'clock," I told him.

Sable and I got dressed in blue jeans, gym shoes, and big shirts. I couldn't believe Sable had actually dressed down. I couldn't get her to do that years ago. I guess now every day was a mission.

We met Trevor at the house. When he opened the door, there were six guys in there, looking at us funny. I could tell that they were users by the look in their eyes.

"This is Key and Racquel. These are my partners. I do not mean workers. I said partners. So, if you fuck up our money, you will have to deal with them, and I promise you, you don't want that. This is Lester, Stan, Jay, Renard, JB, and Ton," Trevor said.

"Hi," I said.

"What's up?" Sable said.

"Okay, this is the deal. I will have three houses that will be run by you six guys. This house will be the money drop-off house only. There will never be any product here. I'll give each house a cell phone only to be used to call for a money drop, when you out of product, or if you have a problem. I don't foresee any problems.

"When you call for a drop-off, someone will meet you here. One person will come. The other stays at the house. We won't have more than one drop-off at a time. Remember, I pay some of the police, so don't get any ideas. Any questions?"

Lester said, "Where do we get the product from?"

"You will pick up your product and be responsible for getting it to your house. If you get jacked, you pay for it. I know everything about each one of you, your mamas, your daddies, and your brothers, sisters, and kids, so don't play with us.

"If you don't want to be a part of this, you can leave and never come back. If you down, come back here in two hours to get your first package."

Trevor finished talking to them and turned to me and Sable. "You ladies have any questions for these gentlemen or anything to say?"

Sable said, "No."

I said, "I do. Don't try to play us. We will not take any shorts, and don't try to skim off the top of the package. That's it."

"And please don't take us for granted," Sable chimed in.

"Here are your phones. If I don't call you before five o'clock, I'll meet you here. All right, you can leave now," Trevor said as he went to the door and opened it.

All the men left the house.

"We need to talk," Trevor said. "Damn, Rose, you look good even when you trying not to."

"Oh, I'm Rose now?" I said.

We both laughed. Sable didn't get it.

"You ladies know I got all this product that I'm not supposed to have. I told my connection I got jacked, and I told my family I got jacked. All eyes will be on me to see if I'm moving all this weight. That's where you ladies come in. I need you to be my partners. I know this is a lot for you, but the reward is all the profit. That could be a lot of money. If my connect gives me the product back or my money, then everything is profit. If not, as long as I get my two hundred fifty K back, the rest is still yours. That may seem like a lot, but this is California, and most of my clientele is millionaires. I think we should be finished with this package in sixty days. What you ladies think?"

"It looks like we are going to be taking all the risk," I said. "If you're not around, nobody going to trust us."

"I will always be around. I'll be in the background. I'll bring the product for you to distribute, and they will bring you the money, and I'll be there," he said.

"Suppose we have some conflict? And we will," Sable said.

"Then we will deal with it. I have some soldiers, but their loyalty is to the drugs. You need to find someone you can build some trust in, and we all can make lots of money," Trevor said.

"How much money will we make?" Sable asked.

"The package should bring in one point five million. If I somehow get my money back or they replace my package, that's a half million each. If not, you should get about three hundred seventy five K. How does that sound?" Trevor asked.

"Trevor, we are not staying in Cali for too long. This might be a one-time thing. Can you handle that?" I asked.

"I should hope to change your mind," he said, looking directly at me.

"You might change her mind, but not mine. I have to leave in a few months. My parents are sick," Sable said.

"I will not leave my sister again, Trevor. You must understand that. If not, we walk now." I said. We both got up to leave.

"Hold on, ladies. I will just have to deal with that. With that cash each of you, wherever you go, will be happy," he said. "Now, let's get this product separated and to these houses. We will drop each off at the houses, so you will know where they are. This will be the only time you should have to handle any product. You are to make sure the money is right and make sure we don't have any problems."

After getting all the houses started, Trevor wanted to go out, but Sable and I declined.

Trevor pulled me to the side and asked, "Can we hang out?"

"Not tonight. We have to get our mind set for the next day," I said.

Things took off. The next few weeks went by fast. Sable and I could not believe that this many drugs were sold in this rich California area.

We hadn't forgotten about our mission. We decided that we could make the money and get deeper in the organization.

Our job was to get the money from the house after the drop-off and keep it until we saw Trevor. I hired Claython, the first guy I met in Cali. I had used him to get me hooked up with Trevor. I kept him at the drop spot only on the days of drop-off. I paid him well, and he stayed high, which made him loyal to me. I also got him a little apartment and an old, raggedy car. I also had him put my car in his name and told him when we left, he could have it.

Everything went smooth for the first thirty days or so.

One particular day, I woke up with a knot in my stomach. Sable and I showered and dressed, then headed for the drop spot. Both of us had our usual arsenal of weapons. Sable had her two Glocks, and I had my two chrome-handle nine millimeters. This day, I grabbed my .380 and stuck it in the small of my back.

Our usual procedure was to go to the house, call the person who wanted to drop their money off, then wait for the drop-off. The workers would come in the house, and Claython would search them, then bring them in the dining room so Sable could count the money in front of them, while I stayed on guard.

We called Lester to meet us at the house. As soon as we got inside the house, the doorbell rang.

Claython answered the door and said it was Lester.

When Lester entered, Jay came in with him.

"Hold on. What you doing here?" I asked.

Jay said, "We waiting for product. I called Trevor. He said make my drop."

"Sable, get both the drops, and I'll call Trevor," I said.

I called Trevor and got his voicemail.

Claython had a shotgun on his lap, pointed in the direction of Lester, who stood next to him. When Jay came over to put his drop on the table, I turned to call Trevor again. In an instant, Jay drew a gun and put it to Sable's chest. When Claython raised his shotgun, Lester pulled a gun and shot Claython in his shoulder.

"Okay, Miss Key," Jay said, "put your guns on the table. One at a time. I know you carry two. If not, I'll blow this bitch's head off."

Claython was hollering in pain. Sable's eyes were on me like she was ready to go for her gun and die, waiting on me to give her the go-ahead.

"All right, relax. Claython, you okay?" I asked while pulling my guns from my purse.

"I'm okay, Key. Just losing a lot of blood," he said.

"You lucky I didn't dead your punk ass," Lester said.

"We just want the money." Jay put the gun to Sable's head and told her, "Put your gun on the table."

Sable always kept a gun taped under the table just in case. She took the gun out of her purse and put in on the table.

He swatted Sable with his other hand, causing her to fall to the floor. "Where is your other gun?" he asked.

"I don't have but one. You wanna search me?" She unbuttoned her blouse, revealing her firm 34D titties. She never wore bras.

"I might want to do that," he said with lust in his eyes as Sable got off the floor.

"Get the money, Jay. That's what we came here for," his partner said.

My instinct told me that they were going to kill us. They had the money when they came in. They could have easily just not showed up. They were going to kill us and take the money and go back to work to make it look like an inside job.

"Where is the other gun, hot mess?" Jay's mind was on his other head. "Turn around. Let me search you," Jay said.

"Grab the money and let's go," Lester said, moving closer to Jay.

"She got another gun. I want to search her, man," Jay said. He hit Sable again and turned her around, facing the table. He started to feel on her chest as though he was searching. He patted her down on her sides and back.

Sable had on a skirt, so he reached under her skirt. Sable never wore any underwear, and his hand hit a wet pussy. I could tell he didn't want to bring his hand up. His finger found the spot.

Lester was looking at him, smiling, and they didn't notice Sable reach under the table and pull out the gun. With one motion, she slapped his hand from under her skirt, then spun around and shot him in the head with the gun in her other hand. The second Lester saw the gun blast, he couldn't react fast enough before I pulled my .380 automatic from my back and shot twice, hitting him in the chest and forehead. His body hit the floor with a thump.

Claython was in shock. We needed to get him to a hospital or kill him and leave him there.

"They were going to kill us, Krystal—I mean Key," Sable said, forgetting my alias for a minute.

"Let's think for a minute. Claython knows better than to let more than one person in at a time," I said.

"You're right. He let both of them in. You think he is part of it?" Sable asked while walking over to Claython.

Claython was fading in and out. I went and got some towels and put pressure on his wound. "Claython, you can live or die right now. I could take you to the hospital, or I can leave you here to die. Now, tell me. Are you part of this?" I asked.

Claython started coughing as Sable put her gun to his head. "Naw, Key, I wouldn't hurt you."

"So why you let Lester and Jay in, and you didn't search them, and you know we only allow one person in at a time? Why?" I asked.

"Okay, sis, you can go ahead and do him." Sable cocked her gun, ready to pull the trigger.

"Wait, Key. Trevor came by before you got here and told me to let both of them drop. He said they were cool."

"What? Let's kill him. He going to tell Trevor he told us," Sable said.

"Key, no! I'm your boy. I was set up too. They was going to kill me too. I know they wouldn't have let me walk."

"If we take you to the hospital, you tell Trevor that you didn't tell us nothing, okay?" I asked.

Sable removed the towel from his wound and put her gun where the bullet was. She pressed it real hard. "Do you understand us? We helped you so much."

"I'm so hurt. I should kill you," I said.

"Key, I swear to God. I'll tell him what you want. I owe you. Please take me to the hospital," Claython asked.

"Go get in your car. I'll drive you, and sis will follow us," I said.

Claython left and went to start his car.

"Should we call Trevor?" Sable asked.

"Naw, let's wait for him to call. Let's see how this plays out. Get the money," I said.

I drove Claython to the hospital, parked his car, and gave him the keys. "Claython, I don't want to come looking for you," I said.

"Key I'll be back to work as soon as you need me. I'm in your corner. Please believe me. I'll prove it to you. Thanks."

Claython walked to the emergency entrance, and Sable and I pulled off. We decided to go get something to eat. Since we were in Compton, we stopped at a restaurant on the way back home. We must have really been turning into hard-nose killers. How we could kill someone then go eat is beyond me.

We needed something to stop our adrenaline. Sable wanted some coffee, and I needed some tea. We didn't eat. We had to think.

"If Trevor is in the middle of this, he might know who we are. Then we will be set up eventually," I said, talking to Sable but really thinking out loud.

"Maybe he was at the drop, waiting on you and got a call and had to leave. Then he told Claython everything is cool, not knowing about the stickup," Sable answered.

"If he didn't know, then why didn't he answer his phone?"

"He could have been getting busy. You won't give him none," Sable said, trying to lighten our tension.

"Seriously, we almost got blown away, and we haven't reached our goal. Sable, we here back in the game, and we are no closer to finding the killers of our parents. We need to change our tactics. Let's get out of here. We need to go home and put a plan together," I said. "I need to get this money together for your boy anyway."

We had so much money that we were beginning to get careless. We should have taken that drop money home first.

After we left the restaurant, we turned the corner, walking toward the car. I saw a man leaning on the car, smoking on the passenger side.

Sable said, "We getting jacked. They trying to steal our car."

"Hey, that's my car," I said.

The lookout man stood straight up and told his accomplice to hurry up. As we ran to the car, Sable had her gun out. The guy under the wheel jumped up and took off running. The lookout guy tried to be hard and looked at me and laughed while he backed away. Sable let off a couple of rounds in his direction, and he ran away, ducking and hollering like a little bitch.

Our steering column was broken, but we could still use the key.

"The money. Where is it?" Sable asked.

I dug under the passenger seat and found the bag. Sable and I looked at each other and started laughing at the thought of the thieves working so hard to steal the car and not noticing that over forty thousand dollars was under the seat.

We rode in silence, both deep in thought, until my cell phone rang. It was Trevor.

"Hey, Key. You count up yet? What's my take?" he asked.

I just looked at the phone, trying to find an answer. "We had an issue at the house. You need to go clean it up. Call me later." Then I hung up. I didn't let him ask any questions.

He called back over and over again for the next ten minutes. Then, I guess, he arrived at the house and found his answer.

CHAPTER THIRTY-FIVE

Sable and I went into the living room, where she had all these papers with numbers. She had the money stacked up in three piles.

"Okay, Krystal," she said. "We have a hundred twenty-five thousand dollars each, and Trevor has the same. We already had two hundred fifty thousand in a safe deposit vault. We made a million dollars in forty days."

"None of that money will do us any good if we dead. I have a plan. You down with it?" I asked.

"Hey, I told you we're a team. Whatever you do, I got your back."

"Trevor has been blowing my phone up," I told her. "I'm gonna make him wait until we get our plan together. We're not gonna get caught up like that again."

I picked up my phone and dialed a number.

"What's up, cuz?" I said when the person answered.

"Who this?"

"This is your cousin, Krystal."

Sable looked at me strangely. She knew I didn't have any other relatives but her sister. She kept her ears open, listening to my every word.

I moved into another room so I could talk in private. "Tyrell, you told me I could call you when I needed you," I said.

"What's wrong? Somebody hurt you?" Tyrell asked.

"I'm in California with my cousin. I can't talk on the phone. Can you come spend some time with us until we get control of this situation?" I asked.

"Should I drive up?" he asked.

"I need you to fly and bring at least two of your loyal friends that don't mind putting in work. They might have to stay couple months. I'll take care of all expenses, and you'll make a hundred thousand if things go right."

"Give me time to set up, and I'll be there in three days. Is that cool?"

"Fine," I said. "Call me when you ready, and I'll pick you up at the airport. See you soon."

"I told you I would always be there for you. I'll call you. Bye."

I hung up and returned to the living room. Sable was standing there with her hands on her hips.

"Were you talking to my sister?" she asked.

"Naw, I was talking to Tyrell. You remember him. Leon's cousin."

"Yes, I remember him."

"I called to get us some backup. I have a plan, and we should be out of this town one way or the other in three months," I said.

"What's the plan?" Sable asked.

I broke it down to her. She agreed with some parts and disagreed with others, but we both agreed on the mission. After hours of talking, we both fell asleep on the sofas. It had been a long day.

My phone woke me up around three o'clock in the morning. It was Trevor. I wanted to make him wait, but I had to get a feel for if he had set us up before Tyrell got there.

"What's up?"

"Damn, girl, why you didn't answer my calls? I didn't know if you were hurt or if someone kidnapped you. You had me worried," he said.

"Well, I didn't know if you set us up or not, and I still don't know!" I yelled at him.

"What? Why would you think that?"

"Because Claython said you okayed them guys to come together."

"No! Jay called me and said he had too much money over at the house," he explained. "I told him to drop it off. I was there, but I had to leave." He sounded aggravated. "Look, I can't talk over the phone. Can you meet me for lunch later?"

"I don't know. Call me later. Did you clean up the house?" I asked.

"Yes, but we got to move. I'll call you later. Hope you're all right."

He hung up, and I went back to sleep.

Later, I woke to the smell of breakfast being cooked by Sable. I went and showered and brushed my teeth, put on a robe, and went down to eat breakfast with Sable.

"What's the agenda for today?" she asked.

"We having lunch with Trevor. I want you to see if you can read him. Get a feel to see if he was involved."

"That's cool. Dress up or down?"

"Sexy," I said. "We going to change our tactics. Be ready about one."

At 12:30, Sable was downstairs, looking like she had stepped out of a fashion magazine. She had gained her weight back, and her hair was flawless. Her makeup was perfect, and she was dressed to kill.

"Damn, Sable, who are you going to meet looking that good?"

We both laughed.

Trevor made his usual eleven o'clock call, and I told him we would meet him downtown at one o'clock. He picked a quiet restaurant that was almost empty, so we could talk.

When we walked into the restaurant, all heads turned. I must admit, we were looking good. I decided to wear one of the dresses Trevor had bought for me. It fit me good and showed all the curves my body could afford to show. We were getting looks from the two couples on each side of the restaurant and all the staff, women and men.

Trevor saw us and signaled for us to join him. "You ladies look beautiful. I am honored to grace the same room as you, let alone have the pleasure of dining with you."

"Thanks, Trevor. I needed that," Sable said.

"You look handsome yourself," I said.

"I cleaned the house. So, what happened the other day?" he asked.

"We will never be caught with our panties down again. We don't know if we were set up or that your crew is not loyal to you and tried to set you up," I said.

"Here is your take for the last forty days. A hundred and twenty-five. We both got the same," Sable said, pushing a small leather bag to Trevor.

"My sister and I are thinking about moving on. Even though the money is good, the risk to our lives mean more to us," I told him.

"Wait. Hold on a minute. I don't know what or how that went down, but it will never happen again," Trevor said.

"We don't know if you were a part of it or not, but I don't like to be slapped around," I said.

Sable's mindset was different. She pulled her gun from her purse, cocked it, and put it under the table. She said, "Keep your hands on the table where I can see them. I really believe you had something to do with this, but unless you can convince me otherwise, my sister and I will be the only ones walking out of here today."

"What the fuck is this, Key? I'm trying to trust you guys, but you got to trust me too. I just want to find out who is behind this shit." Trevor sounded nervous. "Look, I came to also tell you ladies that I got the product replaced, and as we agreed, that makes your profit more."

"It ain't about no money, Trevor. What the fuck we need money for if we can't spend it?" I asked.

"Whatever you want to do, I'm down with it. We are in this together. I need both of you, but you got to trust me." Trevor was beginning to almost beg.

The look in Sable's eyes was death. She wanted to kill him while she had a chance.

"Sis," I said, putting my hand on her arm, "let's think about this for a minute. You know whatever you do, I got your back. We haven't reached our goal yet. We need that money for your sick parents. Come on, girl. Put the gun down. We'll handle things our own way now. Is that cool with you, Trevor?"

Trevor had to agree reluctantly Sable put the gun back in her purse without taking her eyes off Trevor.

"Everybody is a little tense. We need to relax a little," I said. "Let's order some food."

Everybody ate in silence. After lunch, Trevor said, "I got the perfect idea. They have a red carpet gathering at the Kodak Theatre a few miles away. You ladies want to go?"

I just stared at him.

"I don't hold any grudges," he continued. "I'm trying to build the trust between us. We can hang out with the stars, and you ladies look like you belong with them. Would you like that?"

Sable looked at me. Her eyes said, *Hell yes!*

"Yes, we can do that," I said.

"Rose, Racquel, no more business until tomorrow. And I apologize for what happened. I promise I will find out who set us up. Now, let me take you ladies out on the town. Enjoy the day. Relax a little."

For the next few hours, we went shopping and went to a special screening of a movie. I was around all these celebrities. Sable and I felt good. This did a lot to boost our confidence.

In the evening, we walked the red carpet at the Kodak, and people thought we were celebrities. They kept taking pictures, asking us who were our agents. It was a fantastic night. Trevor was a great host. He knew everybody.

After everybody was leaving, Trevor asked, "You mind if I stop by my house before I drop you at your car?"

We agreed, since knowing where he lived would help us reach our ultimate goal someday. We drove for a while and talked about the celebrities we had seen. I noticed a sign that read: HUNTINGTON PARK.

We pulled up in a beautiful neighborhood. I didn't see any cars. Everybody owned large garages, and no one parked on the street. This told me it was an influential place.

Trevor pushed his garage opener, and we pulled into an eight-car garage with all different kinds of luxury cars in it—a Porsche, a Bentley, Benz, BMW, and a few more I couldn't name.

When we got out, Trevor noticed the shocked looks on our faces. "These are my dad's and my uncle's cars. My dad used to stay here, but I took over because he's down for a while," he said.

We took an elevator up to the third floor. The house was beautiful. We could see the two floors below as we walked around the catwalk. The family room where he took us was decorated in a modern design. Expensive art hung on the walls, along with the biggest television I had ever seen. When he hit a button on the remote, soft music came from every angle of the room.

We sat on the couch and fell deep into the soft cushions. The fireplace was as big as the television, and it, too, turned on with a remote. We looked around, enjoying the scenery.

"You want a drink?" Trevor asked.

"Sure." We had already had a couple, and I was feeling pretty good. I knew Sable had her buzz on.

He pushed another button on his remote, the wall came down, and the glass bar pushed out with everything you could want to drink. He mixed us martinis, and we had a toast to our future.

"We must have each other's backs and trust each other," Trevor said.

We touched glasses and drank to our new alliance. I was all smiles because I was feeling we were getting closer to the family.

I wasn't sure, but I suspected that Trevor's father was Mark Ridgeway, the person charged with killing our parents. Sable must have sensed something too. She was giggling and dancing to the music all sexy. She kept looking at me and then at Trevor, as though she wanted my approval. I nodded at her. As I said, we were getting so close that I would do anything to complete our mission.

After a couple more drinks, Trevor and Sable were buzzed and started dancing together.

Trevor said, "Come on, Rose. Join us."

I got up and started feeling the music also. Sable started to undo her clothes. By the next song, both of us were in our panties and bras.

"Trevor, come on and join us?" I asked.

Trevor took off his shirt and pants, revealing his erection. Sable and I stood there, amazed by how large he was. Sable danced over to him and turned her butt around. I went to his back and started kissing on his neck. I put my arms around his waist and grinded to the beat of the music from behind him. I could see how turned on his was. He was moving with his eyes closed like he was in a dream and didn't want to wake up.

My body was sweating, and my insides were wet. My panties were wet also. I took them off. I grabbed Trevor's hand and put it on my wet pussy. His finger felt the inside walls of my vagina. I was feeling his nipples with my other hand. I looked down to see Sable pulling his boxers down and inserting his huge dick in her mouth.

Trevor's eyes were getting bigger, and he was losing control. He lay down on the plush carpet while he pulled me close to him and instructed me to sit on his face. I felt his warm lips on my inner thigh. I jerked slightly as his hot tongue went deep inside my pussy. I moaned to each lick of his tongue, until I climaxed on his face.

Sable took off her panties while still holding and rubbing his big, white dick. It looked like an ice cream stick, and Sable must have thought so too, because she was sucking, gagging, and licking for a while.

After making me climax, he pushed me off of him and looked into my eyes. "Rose, I want you. Let's go to the bedroom. I got some rubbers up there."

That was the magic word. I liked him, but I wasn't doing nothing if he didn't have any protection. I don't want no baby by a Ridgeway that I knew was going to die.

We went down the hall to the bedroom. We were high and feeling good.

Sable fixed herself another drink and joined us. Trevor laid me down on the bed. After he put the rubber on, he tried to put that big dick inside me.

"It hurts, Trevor. Take it slow," I said. I had only had a couple of men in my life, but none were that damn big. It was really hurting.

Sable stood next to me, seeing the pain I was in. After a few minutes of seeing me being tortured with that big dick, Sable lay on the bed next to me and pulled Trevor toward her.

"Let me have some, big daddy," she said.

Trevor took out what little he had in me and inserted his manhood into Sable. She moved a little, and then she put her legs up higher and grabbed Trevor and pulled him closer to her. Trevor pushed his thick dick inside her, and she took every inch of it. She looked into his eyes while moving her body.

Trevor couldn't take it. He was about to cum. All that, and he couldn't last more than three minutes. He started to shake, and spit came out of his mouth and dropped down on Sable's chest as he came all inside his rubber.

"Damn," she cursed. Sable was frustrated, and Trevor could sense it. He came too fast, and she didn't get hers.

Trevor got up and laid Sable on the bed and started eating her wet pussy. For twenty minutes, Sable moaned and finally begin to shake. She squeezed his head between her legs and yelled out in ecstasy.

Trevor rolled over and fell straight to sleep. Sable and I looked at each other, not believing we had just done this to the son of the man that killed our parents.

I motioned for her to follow me to the bathroom. When we got in there, I asked, "Are you she all right?"

She nodded.

"I'm gonna look around. Keep an eye on Trevor to make sure he doesn't wake up," I said.

I went down the hall and looked in the other bedrooms. They were clean, with no pictures on the walls or clothes in the closets. I went downstairs and looked in the other bedrooms. I didn't see anything.

I went down on the first floor and into the spacious living room. There were pictures on the wall. I began to tremble when I saw John and Desmond Ridgeway in a picture with three other young men. They all looked like brothers. I saw more pictures of their mother and father with Trevor and Mark Ridgeway, the man who could be his father. I saw pictures of little kids with each family. Then I saw a picture of Trevor with a little kid and the girl who had set him up.

I had seen enough. I went back upstairs without touching anything. When I reached the room, Trevor was sitting up in the bed.

"Rose, you didn't bring my clothes," Sable said.

Trevor looked at my empty hands.

"I was trying to find some water or juice. My sugar is kicking up," I said.

"I'll get you something," Trevor said.

I turned around and went to get the clothes. Trevor went to the bathroom, then to the kitchen. He returned with a pitcher of juice and a couple of glasses.

"Where can I shower?" I asked after I drank some juice.

He showed me the bathroom and where to get towels. I showered, and Sable showered in another bedroom. Trevor went downstairs, and I guess he showered down there, because when he came back, he was fully dressed.

"I know you guys are ready for me to take you back. We got to get busy tomorrow, and I have to get some product ready," he said.

We rode back, listening to the music and talking about the beautiful day we'd had.

When we reached our car, Trevor said, "Rose, let me holler at you for a minute."

Sable got out, and I gave her the keys to start the car.

"What's up, Trevor?"

"Rose, I really dig you, and I am sorry for what happened tonight. I was caught up in the moment. I never had two women before. I just want to let you know that you are the one I want. I'm really feeling you," he said.

"Don't sweat it. Me and my sister is cool. We're down with each other. I do like you, Trevor. Everything is cool," I said as I opened the car door. "But you're going to have to take it slow with me with that tool you carrying down there."

He smiled and said, "I will, baby."

CHAPTER THIRTY-SIX

Sable was silent on the ride home. When we arrived, she went upstairs and took another shower. She was in there for over an hour. I pulled my thoughts together and went to bed.

The next morning, I woke up at eight. Sable was already up, drinking coffee in the kitchen.

"You want to roll with me to take care of our own business?" I asked.

"Cool," she said. "I have to put some money in the safe deposit vault, and I want you to sign in case something happens to me."

We went to the bank. Then we went to pay for an apartment I had rented in a house two doors from ours, and also to pick up the keys. Then we went to buy a car. Sable picked out a triple black BMW with tinted windows. She pulled the salesman outside and told him she would pay cash and give him an extra three thousand if he could get my plates and put the car in a dummy corporation. We got the car, and Sable drove it home and put it in the garage.

I called Tyrell to see what his status was.

"I'll be in tomorrow night. LAX at nine thirty," he told me.

When I hung up, Trevor called and said he had a new home. Sable and I met him at the new drop house, which was in a good neighborhood. It looked too good to be used only for dropping off money.

Trevor met us there, driving the Bentley that we had seen in his garage. He had on a suit and tie, looking like a cool Robin Thicke.

"You wanna hang with me?" he asked.

"Nah, me and my sister have plans," I told him.

He looked so disappointed. I kissed him on the cheek and told him, "I'll call you later."

Sable and I got in my car and left. We went and bought three beds and a living room and dining room set. I paid the company extra to have it delivered the next day.

Trevor called and said, "I have a couple of money drops."

I asked him, "Can you handle it? We're kinda busy. We will be available day after tomorrow."

He was mad. "Shit, what am I supposed to do?" he asked.

"You have your loyal crew," I said. "See how loyal they are. We'll be back," I said.

"You're not leaving me, are you? What about our plans? I told my grandparents about you," he said. "They want to meet you."

"Trevor, sweetheart, I'll be back. You can take me where you want and do what you want to me. Of course, after we handle our business, we still partners."

"All right, I guess I can hold it down without you, but it's gonna be hard. See you soon." He hung up.

Sable and I wanted to clean the apartment and get some essentials for the boys. The next day, the furniture arrived, and Sable and I put our women's touch on the apartment. It was ready for the guys to crash for a couple of months.

Sable and I stayed there overnight, and we both slept like babies. The next morning, we went home, showered, and changed clothes. Sable wanted to go the grocery store, but I asked her to sit down so we could talk before the guys came.

"Sable, we must not forget what we are here for," I said.

"You don't have to remind me. You don't have to ever worry about anybody coming between us again," she said.

"I love you, and we should be out of this town in a couple of months. Trevor wants to introduce me to his grandparents, so we're getting closer to the family, and our plan will come together when the guys get here."

"Good," she said.

"The only thing I didn't tell you about is what I said to Tyrell. I told him I'll give him a hundred K out my money when the job is complete," I said.

"That's cool. If we get out alive, I'll give a hundred K too. The other guys can split it up."

"You sure?" I asked.

"Krystal, it's not about the money. I just want closure. Please understand that whatever we have to do, I'm down with it. I love you too, Krystal. You are the sister that I always wanted to be close to," she said.

CHAPTER THIRTY-SEVEN

We were at the airport at nine o'clock, a half hour before their flight was supposed to arrive. We were excited about seeing people we knew and, of course, someone down with us to give us more strength and have our backs.

The plane arrived, and Tyrell was the first one off. He must have been in first class. He saw me and smiled. He looked good, dressed in a business suit. Behind him was a big white guy and then two brothers followed in business suits. So many people got off the plane with suits on I thought it was a convention.

Tyrell walked over to me and hugged me right off the floor.

"Tyrell, the last time I saw you I was being carried in your arms. Put me down."

"I'm sorry," he said. "I'm just happy to see you alive. I heard you got killed in a fire."

"I never did thank you. Thanks," I said.

He looked over at Sable.

"I'm sorry. You remember my cousin Sable?"

"Sure I do. I must say, you look more beautiful today than the last time I saw you." He took her hand and spun her around. "Damn, I always thought you were attractive, but you have taken it to another level."

"Flattery will get you everywhere. You better be aware," Sable said.

"Give me a hug." He pulled her close to him.

We were so into each other we forgot about the other guys standing around.

"Oh, I'm sorry. Where are my manners? This is my man Sandy Boy, Quan, and this is Lorenzo. These are my enforcers, and Lorenzo is also my attorney," Tyrell said. "He can get me into places I couldn't get into. He also knows how to invest our money. Just in case you are wondering, he has a black daddy, so don't his looks fool you. He is as deadly as all of us."

We all laughed. Everybody spoke to each other, then I said, "Let's get out of here."

As we walked out of the airport to the car, I pulled Tyrell back to talk to him privately.

"I need to tell you what's going on, and I don't want to talk in front of your crew," I said.

"It's cool. These guys ain't my crew," he said.

"You said they were your enforcers."

"They are my enforcers because that's their role. They are my partners, Krystal. They share equal in all the profits, and everybody puts up their share to buy. Each of us has a role, and we all make money, which bonds us together. It's a win-win situation. They are completely down with me as was I to Leon."

The mention of Leon's name brought tears to my eyes. Tyrell noticed and put his arm around my shoulder as we walked.

"So, I can talk freely in front of them?" I asked.

"Anything you got to say to me, you can say it in front of them. We've been a team for five years, ever since you put me down with the game. And oh yeah, I never told you thanks. So, thanks," he said.

That made me smile. I had forgotten how funny he was.

Back at our building, I showed the guys where we lived and told them they were always welcome. We arrived at their apartment, and we could smell the food before we opened the door. Sable was a very good cook.

The guys couldn't believe how the apartment was laid out.

"I'm sorry, Tyrell. I only got three bedrooms because I thought you were only bringing two guys," I said.

"Don't sweat it," Lorenzo said. "One of us will always be on the couch for lookout. We been doing it that way for years"

After twenty minutes, Sable said the food was ready. She made fried chicken, macaroni and cheese, yams, corn bread, and peach cobbler. We all ate until we were full, drank wine, and talked. The guys were talking about each other the way only true friends can.

I left and went home to my place for a minute. I wanted to put on some comfortable clothes. When I returned, everybody was laughing and having a good time. Sable and Tyrell seemed to be bonding.

"I hate to interrupt your party, but we got business to handle. Everybody come in the dining room."

They all sat down around the dining room table.

"First of all, I have to tell you guys that whatever we tell you has to stay between us. Tyrell says you guys are cool, so I have to learn to trust you, because I trust him with my life."

They nodded in agreement.

"We have a situation that we didn't ask for out here. I'm going to try to explain why we have to do what we're doing. This is our problem. If you feel you can't put in the work, you can leave tomorrow."

"We all with you, Krystal," Quan said.

"Cuz, let me explain," Sable said. I gave her the okay, and she turned to the guys and started telling them what was up.

"You guys know me and my cousin Krystal ran the Bottom Barrel and part of the Midwest?"

"Yeah," one of the guys said.

"Well, I gave up on the life and moved to California with my mother and father. Then Krystal gave up on the game and moved out here to raise her daughter by Leon."

"Hold up. You got a daughter, Krystal? I have a cousin?" Tyrell asked. He was surprised.

"Let me finish, please," Sable said. "Tyrell, you remember the Ridgeway brothers, don't you?"

"Yeah, I remember who they were."

"Well, their family came and killed my mother and father. They also killed Krystal's mother and almost killed her daughter, Leethia." Sable started to shed tears but continued talking.

"They raped my mother and tied my father up, duct-taped his eyes open, and made him watch as they violated her and killed her." Sable started crying uncontrollable. "They killed our family! They killed our family."

Tears began to form in my eyes. I went over to hug Sable. Tyrell came over and hugged me.

After a couple minutes of letting it out, I pulled myself together. Wiping my face, I said, "This is the deal. We got back in the game through our research and creativity. Our partner is Trevor Ridgeway, the nephew of the man accused of killing our parents. We have made over three hundred seventy-five K in three months. All the rich people out here use cocaine. But our mission is to avenge our parents. The money is icing on the cake."

No one spoke. The guys were mesmerized by the story.

"We won't leave until it's done. We want their whole family. We have been waiting patiently, and we are getting so close. Trevor calls his self liking me because he thinks I saved his life. So, he trusts us. We need backup because we were set up and almost got killed. We don't know who to trust."

"Krystal, whatever you need, I'll help you. Even if it means my life for yours, I'm down," Tyrell said.

"I'm in all the way," Quan said.

Sandy Boy said, "I'm in."

Lorenzo said, "I'm down all the way. I have to protect my investment."

Everybody laughed. This guy was cool. The fact that he was white and let people call him Lorenzo meant a lot.

I pulled out four envelopes. "This is part of the money you make. There's twenty-five thousand for the guys and fifty thousand for Tyrell. You will get the same when we leave. Our goal is sixty days. If we reach our goal before then, we can leave."

I put the money down and slapped my hands on the table. "We are about to turn this town upside down. The police here respond very fast, so whatever you do, remember that."

I said thanks to everybody. "We're going home. We got plans for tomorrow, so be ready about ten o'clock."

Sable got up and hugged everybody and said good night.

We were walking out the door. Tyrell and Sandy Boy were right behind us.

"We'll be all right," I said.

"You will never be by yourself in these streets again while we're here," Sandy Boy said. They walked us to the door while watching their surroundings.

I was feeling secure. I leaned over and kissed Tyrell on the cheek. "Thanks. Good night."

CHAPTER THIRTY-EIGHT

The next morning, the guys were at the front door at ten o'clock. Sable and I were waiting downstairs, ready to go.

Sable called all the guys in the bedroom and showed them our arsenal.

"Damn, ladies, are we going to war," Quan said, smiling. He ran to get something he liked before someone else got it. "This is me," he said, holding a .45. "This just came out."

Everybody found something they liked.

"You need to pick two. Sable and I always double up," I said.

Everybody picked another gun, and each person grabbed a bulletproof vest.

"Follow me to the garage," I said.

Once inside, I gave Tyrell the keys to the BMW and broke it all down to them. "This is yours. I got a special job for you and Lorenzo. This Cutlass is for doing work. No one has seen these cars. They are not in my name, so if you have to leave them to save your ass, it's okay. The first thing we gonna do is get closer to the family. This week, we're going to post up just in case we are set up again.

"Sandy Boy and Quan, you guys will go with us to the drop house. Tyrell, you and Lorenzo will be close by. We need you watching our backs just in case someone has the nerve to stick us up.

"You guys get our cell numbers. One more thing—we use aliases so no one knows our real names and puts two and two together. I am Key, and Sable's name is Racquel. So, don't say our names."

They stood there and stared at me. It was a lot of information I had just given them.

"I hope you don't think I'm trying to control you guys," I said. "I just know the plan. I'm sure you will do your own thing once you feel where things are going. I ain't trying to hurt your manly egos by telling you what to do."

"Krystal, it's not like that. We all understand," Sandy Boy said.

We made it to the drop house, and I called Trevor again. I had talked to him that morning.

"Where are you?" I asked. "It's the first of the month and all the celebrities get paid, so I know you got mad drops coming in today."

"Yeah, I got three, but I purposely didn't pick up the drops so I could see how loyal my other crew is. But if you want, I'll come by," he said.

I didn't want him there, so I said, "Nah, it's cool. I got some backup."

I was relived when he didn't ask any more questions. "Okay. Call me later," he said and hung up.

Quan stood at the front door. Sandy Boy and I stayed in the dining room with our guns out. Within ten minutes, there was a knock on the door.

Sable went to the door. She recognized Renard. "He's cool," she told Quan.

Sandy Boy walked to the door as Renard was coming in. He grabbed Renard and threw him against the wall.

Sable and I had our guns out, not knowing what was going on. Quan's gun was at Renard's head, while Sandy Boy searched him hard.

"He's clean," he said.

Quan put his gun down and said, "Go in the dining room."

Sandy Boy followed Renard closely, seeing that he was nervous. "Where is your drop?" Sandy Boy asked.

Renard took the paper bag out of his pocket and threw it on the table. He was shaking when he pulled out a cigarette to relax himself.

"No fucking smoking in here," Sandy Boy said.

Sable counted the money and asked, "How many drops are you supposed to have?"

"I'm supposed to have two. I gave one to Trevor."

Sandy Boy swatted Renard on the back of his head with the gun. "Your drops supposed to come here. Nowhere else. We understand each other?"

Renard, rubbing the knot on his head, said, "Yeah, man."

"I'm calling Trevor," I said, going with the flow. "If you lying, you got a problem. If he doesn't answer his phone, you got a problem."

I dialed Trevor's number. It was tense in the house. Everyone was on alert. The phone kept ringing. I let it ring a few more times, looking straight at Renard.

I hung up the phone. Sandy Boy and Quan cocked their guns and moved toward Renard.

"Wait a minute. I ain't lying!" he yelled.

My phone rang, and everybody froze. It was Trevor.

"Hello, Trevor. Renard is here saying you picked up a drop from him. You told me to pick up all drops," I said.

"No, I got the drop. He had too much money for me to let him hold it," Trevor said.

"Look, Trevor, if I'm getting the drops, then let me deal with that," I said, annoyed. "I'm not going to be going back and forth. We pick up all drops from this point on, all right?"

"Okay, Key," he said.

Then I hung up the phone. I had to let everybody know we were still in control.

"He's cool. Let him get out of here," I told the guys.

After two more drops, we all left. Tyrell and Lorenzo were still posted up outside until we left. I contemplated counting the money in front of the guys, but I had to see if they were going to be part of this team. I hoped that we would not have any problems between us.

We went back to the house and ate, drank wine, and talked. It was really good having some friendly faces around again.

Trevor kept trying to get with me, and I kept putting him off. I only saw him when we met to give him the money. I told him I had my cousin there helping me out, but I never let him see none of the guys.

The next couple of weeks went smooth. I called Tyrell one evening and told him to come over because I needed to talk to him.

When he came over, I told him I had a special project. He looked nervous.

"What's up? You look worried," I said.

He looked down and said, "I'm cool."

"We family, Tyrell. I trust you with my life. There is nothing you can tell me that we can't work out. What's up?" I asked.

"Krystal, I'm sorry," he said.

I reached for my purse with my gun in it, thinking I was getting ready to be robbed.

He saw my reaction and said, "Hold on! It ain't like that."

My hand was on my gun. I uncocked it inside my purse. With a hardness in my voice, ready to go out blazing if he made the wrong move, I asked, "So, what you sorry for?"

"I'm really feeling Sable. I know we family and we're on a mission, but I really like her."

I jumped up with my gun out.

"What the fuck?" Tyrell backed away, trying to reach for his gun in his back.

"Why you—I'm, I'm really happy for you."

He looked at me to see if I was serious.

I smiled and put my gun down. "I was just fucking with you. I know Sable been sneaking somewhere in the middle of the night. I thought Lorenzo was hitting it."

He came over and lifted me off the ground and gave me a big hug. "I love you like my big sister, Krystal. Nothing will come between our family."

"I love you too, Tyrell. Where is that hot-ass Sable?" I asked.

Sable came running down the stairs and hugged Tyrell, then hugged me.

"What you think, Sable, I was going to shoot you?" I asked.

They both said, "Yeah."

We all started laughing. We stayed up playing cards and talking about the old neighborhood. I finally went to bed and left the lovers hugging on the couch. I was truly happy for Sable.

CHAPTER THIRTY-NINE

The next day, we had to pick up drops again. We all went to the house and posted up as usual. After a few minutes, the doorbell rang. Ton came in and was searched. The word had gotten out that the people running the drops were killers, so we hadn't had an incident since the guys arrived. Ton dropped his money, and it was obvious he couldn't wait to get out of there.

My phone rang, and it was Tyrell. "Two guys coming your way. Salt and pepper," he said then hung up.

"Quan, you and Sandy Boy come in here quickly," I yelled out.

The guys came in the dining room with their guns out. "What's up?" they asked.

I pushed Sable in the kitchen and waved for the guys to hurry up. Before we got the door closed, shooting began. I had to stop the guys from running out there.

"Hold on. Not yet." Everybody looked at me and knew I had a plan.

"Tyrell is outside," Sable said.

"He's all right. Wait until the shooting stops. Then we go out," I explained.

The shooting stopped, and everybody ran outside with guns out, only to see Trevor hiding in the bushes. There was a body at the front door.

I looked around and didn't see Tyrell or Lorenzo, so I knew everything went right.

"Trevor, you okay?" I asked.

"Somebody tried to kill me. I bet it was them damn Mexicans!" he yelled.

"Get that guy in the house," I told the guys, pointing to the body.

"That's JB," Trevor said. "He was with me. He was bringing his drop."

JB had been shot in the head and the chest. He was dead.

I introduced Sandy Boy and Quan to Trevor and told him they were my cousins. Trevor was shaking and repeatedly saying that someone was trying to kill him.

This was all part of my plan. I had thought that he would call his family and they would come to get him. Then Tyrell and Lorenzo could follow them and find out where they lived. Or else he would beg Sable and me to ride him to his house or to his family's home. Either way was okay with us. That meant we were getting closer to his family.

Trevor went in the kitchen to make a phone call.

Across town, two men walked up to a house with a circular driveway. There was a hard knock on the door.

When the young lady peered through her open blinds, she asked, "Who is it?"

The burly white man said, "Police, miss. We need to ask you a couple of questions. There was a shooting a couple doors down, and we're talking to all the neighbors."

"Hold on a minute." Sherra rushed into her bedroom to hide the cocaine she had been sniffing. She peeped in to see her son playing video games and went to answer the door.

She cracked the door to see to two large men dressed in business suits, one white and one black, with badges chained around their necks.

"I'm sorry to bother you. We just need five minutes. May we come in?" the white man asked politely.

She thought it was safe to let them in. "Sure, but I have to take my son to the doctor in a few minutes, so please hurry."

The two men entered the house and she led them to the dining room.

"What's this about?" the lady asked.

Both guys pulled out their guns. Before she could scream, a large hand was around her mouth, and the cold steel gun was against her temple. "Do not scream or I'll kill you, then your son. You understand?"

She shook her head in agreement.

"Call your son."

Tears formed in her eyes as she did what she was told. "DJ, get down here right now!" she yelled in panic.

The man moved behind her and let her feel the gun at her neck. The kid came running to the sound of his mother's panicked voice. Before he could reach her, the other man put a cloth around his mouth and held her son until he fell limp into his arms, knocked out.

"No, not my son! What the fuck you want? You aren't police." She looked at the fake toy badges through tears running down her face.

"Shut up."

She watched the other man tie her son up and lay him on the couch. He then put his gun to the kid's head and looked at Tyrell for instructions.

"I know you are Trevor's baby momma. Where is his stash?" he asked rather calmly.

"I don't know," was all she said before she felt the back side of the gun clash with her head. She put her hand up, feeling a big knot swelling there.

Lorenzo took the safety off his gun and cocked it. He put it on the boy's forehead as he lay there unconscious.

"No!" the mother screamed. "Okay, it's in the safe. Please don't hurt my baby."

Tyrell yanked her up and pushed her. She led him in the back bedroom and opened the closet full of men's clothes, where she didn't hesitate to open the safe. She didn't tell them about the drugs in the other bedroom, hoping that she could keep that for herself when they left.

In the safe was a large bag full of money and some stocks and bonds. Lorenzo gathered up everything and stuffed it in the bag.

"That's it. That's all he left. He just left here a couple of hours ago, and he took everything else with him. Please don't hurt us," she said.

Tyrell pushed her back in the dining room. Lorenzo went and stood over the kid and put his gun to his chest.

Tyrell made the young lady sit down. "Now, I can kill you or your son. I'll let you decide."

"No, wait! The drugs are in the closet in the other bedroom. Please don't hurt me," she said, tears running down her face.

Tyrell shot her once in the head, then he waved off Lorenzo. He was mad that she was more concerned about herself than her child.

Lorenzo went in the bedroom and found the drugs. Tyrell untied the kid hands and feet. He left the knots loose enough so he could get free when he woke up. They took the drugs and money and left the house nice and neat, except for the dead body.

CHAPTER FORTY

Back at the drop house, Trevor called for his cleanup crew to take care of JB's body. He also called his uncle to let him know what was going on. His uncle said he was on his way. Trevor returned to the dining room and informed us.

While I was trying to think of a plan to get going, Sable's cell phone rang. She had a surprised look on her face, and she looked at me. I read her eyes as she continued her conversation in private.

She came back. "Key, that was the nurse. I have to leave," she said.

"Is everything all right?" I asked.

"Dad is getting worse. Are you coming with me?" she asked.

"Trevor, we got to roll. You going to take care of everything here?" I said.

Before he could answer, his phone went off. His eyes got bigger as he listened to the person on the other end. Tears formed in his eyes as he whispered, "Sherra is dead? Is my son all right?" He looked like he stopped breathing while he waited for the answer.

"Wow, where is he?" he asked. "I'll be right there." Trevor hung up the phone.

"That was my uncle. Someone killed my baby momma and tied up my son. I have to go to my uncle's house. He's waiting there for me. I want someone to follow me to watch my back."

I told him, "We only have one car, and Racquel needs to go see about her dad."

"You ride with me. It will only take an extra fifteen minutes out your way. Please, Rose. I need you. I need to think, not drive," he pleaded.

"Okay." I said. "Sandy Boy, you ride with me, and Quan, you ride with Racquel. You guys can follow me. After I drop off Trevor, we'll take the money and put it at the drop. Then we can go see your dad," I said.

We closed the house down. In the driveway, I told Sable, "Call me and keep me posted if anything changes. Keep me close."

Sable called Tyrell to let him know what was going on. I knew that was who Sable had been talking to when she said her dad was sick. He told Sable what happened on his end.

Trevor showed me the directions to his uncle's house. Sable and Quan were following us in their car, and Tyrell and Lorenzo were following them a block behind.

As we pulled up to the gated house, there were two cars facing the exit. I had a nervous feeling inside. We pulled to the entrance, and two guys armed with AK assault rifles met us. They saw Trevor and waved us through. When Sable pulled up behind us, the other car moved backward and blocked us in. The guys with the assault rifles stuck their guns in the car and had Quan and Sable on lock. If they moved, they would be killed. The next thing I knew, two more guys drew guns on me and Sandy Boy. I could see Sandy Boy getting ready to make a move for his gun. I reached to my purse and had my hand on my 9 millimeter.

"Hold the fuck up. What are you doing? This is my crew. They're protecting me!" Trevor yelled.

Nobody moved. They weren't listening to Trevor. I could see in my rearview mirror that Tyrell and Lorenzo were outside the gate. They got out of the car and had their guns on the two guys with the assault rifles who had their backs to them.

I probably can take this guy by surprise, I thought, *but I think Sandy Boy is going to get hit.* One guy had a gun to Sandy Boy's head. Everything was moving slow.

"Terry, what the fuck you doing? They with me," Trevor said directly to the guy standing by my window.

The guy didn't answer. He just picked up his phone and dialed a number. Everyone was at a standstill.

"We got a situation," he said into the phone. Then he hung up.

A short, bald-headed man came down the driveway. He looked at us, then at Trevor.

"Uncle James, what is this? They're with me."

"Boy, you were almost assassinated. How do I know they didn't set you up?" Trevor's uncle said.

"This lady took a bullet for me a couple of months ago. She saved my life. You know I must trust her to bring her here. This is the young lady I told you about. This is my partner," Trevor pleaded.

Uncle James looked at us. He looked at me a little longer than the others. He looked inside the car and noticed my hand in my purse and Sandy Boy's hand under the seat with his gun out.

"If they had wanted me dead, Uncle, I would have been dead already. How is my son?" Trevor asked.

Uncle James waved his men off, and before he turned around, Tyrell and Lorenzo were gone.

I got out of the car. "Nice to meet you, sir. Trevor, please call me later. Hope your son is okay," I said before I walked over to the car Sable was driving.

"Let's get the fuck out of here before he remembers me," I said when I got in her car.

We backed out of the driveway as soon as his goons moved the car that had us blocked in. I could see one of them write down my license plate number. We drove off, burning rubber.

After a mile, I looked back and saw Tyrell was following us. The long ride home was silent. Facing death like that makes you think. I believe everybody was thinking that sooner or later death was going to catch up with us.

When we arrived at the house, I told the guys we were going to shower, and we would be over to their house to talk in about an hour. I went to my room to shower, and Sable did the same. We both were back downstairs in about forty minutes.

We were chilling on the couch when the doorbell rang. Sable ran to the door and opened it. Tyrell and Lorenzo walked in, smiling.

Lorenzo had two bottles of champagne, and he was carrying a big duffle bag.

"What's going on? I thought we was coming over to your house," I said.

Tyrell didn't answer. He just pulled Sable and me into the dining room.

Lorenzo opened the bag and poured the contents onto the table. My eyes got as big as melons. Sable was holding her hand over her mouth. It was a lot of money and at least fifty kilos of drugs and some stocks and bonds.

"Homeboy was living with his baby momma, and he used it as his stash house," Tyrell said.

"Damn," was all I could say.

"I didn't tell the other guys. I figure we could work something out between the four of us," Tyrell said.

"My thoughts are, you girls can have most of the money, and we will take the drugs," Lorenzo said.

"First, let's count the money," I said.

We spent the next few hours counting money and drinking champagne. We talked about what Trevor would do when he found out the money and drugs were gone.

Lorenzo said, "He'll think the police got it, since they were the first to arrive on the scene."

I was beginning to feel Lorenzo. He was so down to earth. It might have been the champagne working on me, but I was looking at him differently.

When we finished counting the money, it totaled one point three million. That was a lot of money to have lying around.

"What do you ladies think?"

Sable said, "The money is cool, but we are here for a purpose. The drugs won't do us any good, because our plans are not to get back in the game. I got money. I just want revenge and closure." Tears began to build in her eyes as she thought about her parents.

"Look, guys. We have to close this up in this town. I want to go see my child and start building my life back up," I said. "You guys can take the three hundred thousand and split it up between all of you, and you guys can also keep the drugs."

"Anything you want, Krystal," Lorenzo said.

Tyrell said, "Lorenzo and I agreed that the stocks and bonds go to our great cousin Leethia. Is that all right with you?" he asked.

"Yeah, that's cool, but the one thing Sable and I want is for this to end in two weeks. Whatever way this is going to play out, we want to be out of California in two weeks," I said.

"Can we do this, Tyrell? You got a couple of leads? Can we make it happen so Sable and I can go back to living normal again?"

"Yes, we can make it happen. A lot of bodies going to fall. I don't want you or Sable in the middle," Tyrell said.

"We already in the middle," Sable said. "I want to pull the trigger."

"All right, we need to relax. Here, Krystal, have some more champagne," Lorenzo said. He poured me a glass as he continued to look into my eyes. I didn't know if he was reading my mind, or I was reading his. It seemed like we were both on the same page.

We all drank and talked until early in the morning. Sable pulled Tyrell by the hand and disappeared up the stairs. I heard the door close, and then I heard the sexy sounds.

Lorenzo came and sat next to me on the couch and asked, "What do you want out of life?"

I was shocked. Since I had never been asked that question, I didn't know how to answer it. I thought for a minute.

"I just want to be happy. I want to raise my daughter in an upper-class community, away from all the violence I've been through in my life. I want to settle down and spend my life with one person."

"You taking applications?" he said.

We both laughed. That was the ice breaker. I laid my head on his chest, and he put his arms around me. He told me about his life, about his family, and about what he wanted in life. We talked and listened to music until I fell asleep in his arms. I must admit that was the most peaceful sleep I'd had in a long time.

CHAPTER FORTY-ONE

The smell of breakfast woke me up. I looked around and saw Sable in the kitchen.

"Hey, where is everybody?" I asked.

"Tyrell and Lorenzo got up this morning and left. They took the drugs and said they had some business to take care of."

Since it was Sunday, I decided that I would stay at home and watch TV. My phone rang. It was Trevor.

"Somebody ripped me off!" Trevor yelled. "They took all my money and my entire product. I need to talk to you in person."

"Hold on, Trevor. I've had a hard week, and I'm trying to rest."

"I need to talk to you. Please meet me," he begged.

I finally gave in. "I just got up. I'll call you back in an hour," I said and hung up.

I sat there looking at the phone for a minute, trying to gather my thoughts. Something didn't feel right. I told Sable, and she suggested I call the guys and they could follow me. I called Tyrell.

"I went on a mission with Lorenzo," he said he. "I should be back by tomorrow."

I knew they had to get that product working before it went bad.

I called Quan and Sandy Boy, and they said they would be ready in an hour, so I went upstairs to take a shower.

When I heard Sable yelling my name, I came running down the stairs, naked, with my gun in my hand. "What's wrong?" I asked.

"The news. Somebody killed Claython," she said.

"Claython? I thought he got straight and went back to his family."

"He did, and his family got killed. Two little girls and a woman were killed," Sable said while holding her mouth in disbelief.

The newscaster said they were shot execution style, and it looked like Claython was tortured. This wasn't good for us. Did he talk? Did he tell them my real name? Did he tell them how we met?

I called Tyrell back and told him what had happened.

"Just chill until I get back in the morning," he said.

"But if I don't meet Trevor, he'll think something is up."

"Okay, but don't go nowhere alone," he said before he hung up.

Trevor called me back, and we set up a meeting in a public place. We took Sable's car, and I had Quan follow us in the black car. Sandy Boy stayed at the house so he could keep an eye on the money. We left my car for Sandy Boy because he said he wanted to make a quick run to the store to get some cigarettes.

Sable and I met with Trevor. I think he wanted me to come by myself, but Ms. Lady didn't raise no dummy. Sable had her guns inside her jacket pocket, and I had one in my purse and the other in my back under my blouse. We approached Trevor with caution and our eyes open, ready for battle if necessary.

Trevor was sitting on a park bench with a lot of kids playing around. Sable sat on one side of him, and I sat on the other. Trevor didn't look good. He looked like he hadn't been sleeping or he was getting high. He looked worried.

"What's wrong, Trevor? You look terrible," I said.

"I hired you girls to protect me, and now that you haven't been around so much, somebody is trying to kill me."

"Trevor, you don't know what you want. You want us to be your partners, or you want us to watch your back? We can't do both," Sable said.

"I know, but so much is going on," he said.

"So, what do you want from us?" Sable asked.

"My uncle thinks that you set me up to get robbed," Trevor said.

"How can I set you up, stupid? I was with you. I was collecting your money," I said.

"I know. That's what I told my uncle. I just wanted to let you know to watch your back. My family is ruthless, and sometimes I don't agree with their tactics." He looked at me. "I still want you ladies to watch my back with no strings attached. We'll split all the profits. But you have to roll where I roll. Is that cool?"

"I don't know. I can't trust you. You been lying to us. You lied to me when you said you didn't care about your baby's mother. Plus, we're only going to be here a month or so. Sable's dad is getting worse, and when we leave, we're not coming back. We have to watch her mother," I said.

"Okay, but when they robbed me, they took all my product and money. I will have to get twenty kilos from my uncle. I just want to flip that. Please, can we do that?" he asked.

"Trevor, this shit is getting too confusing. You say your uncle thinks we set you up. Then you say you want us to go with you to get twenty K from your uncle. You think we stupid." Sable pulled her gun out of her jacket and stuck it in Trevor's back.

"I'm tired of being caught in the middle," she said to me. "Sis, why don't we just do him here and leave?"

Trevor got nervous as I pondered the answer. He jumped up and turned toward Sable "I'm getting tired of you pulling guns on me. You think I'm some punk," he said.

A man appeared from behind the bench with his gun out, pointing it at Sable's head. "You all right, Trevorinique?" he asked.

Before I could draw my gun and Trevor could answer, the man was struck in the head with the butt of a gun. The kids on the playground started yelling and screaming. The parents were running, scooping up their kids. Quan had his gun in the man's face.

"Hold on. Wait. We are all family up here. I'm sorry, Sable," Trevor yelled.

"Relax, Quan. Everything is cool," I said.

Quan put his gun down to his side and helped the man up. He just looked at him and didn't say a word. The man looked at Quan with revenge in his eyes.

Sable put her gun up and just looked at me. She really wanted to blow Trevor away.

"We got to get out of here. The police will be here in a minute," I said. Everybody started walking away.

Trevor stopped me and said, "Meet me at the house tomorrow at one o'clock." He kissed me on the cheek and asked, "Are we cool, Rose?"

"I'm sorry for not being sensitive to what you're going through. I guess I like you more than I thought. I'll see you tomorrow," I walked said.

Sable, Quan, and I walked around the park first to make sure no one was following us. Sable and I got in her car, and Quan followed in the Cutlass.

"Sable, don't worry. The right time will come. I know you wanted to dead Trevor. But see, we didn't even know he had backup, and you would have got hurt before we could respond," I said.

"I know, but I'm getting frustrated. I want to finish this so I can live my own life. Try to be happy," she said.

"We have to concentrate on the big picture. We want all their family. Just be patient, girl."

"I'm trying."

On the ride back, we talked about happiness. We talked about what we wanted to be doing in the next five years. We talked about Leethia and how old she would be soon, and about Sable's sister, Judge Thomas. I knew Sable really missed her sister.

We turned the music up and sang with Melanie Fiona. "If you can't give it to me right, don't give it to me at all." Our mood had change, and we were laughing and joking by the time we got to the house.

CHAPTER FORTY-TWO

Quan parked the Cutlass in my garage.

He asked Sable, "You feel like fixing something to eat?"

Sable said, "Okay. Come back in an hour." She looked in his eyes. "And thanks, Quan, for having my back."

"We all fam here. I will always have your back," he said as he walked toward his apartment.

Neither Sable nor I had our keys out, so we both looked at each other and laughed. I reached in my purse.

"The fuck?" is all we heard coming from two doors down. It was Quan's voice. "Hell naw!" he yelled.

Both Sable and I ran over to the guys' apartment two doors down with our guns out.

"They killed Sandy Boy. They killed my boy!" he yelled.

When we entered the apartment, we saw Sandy Boy's body close to the back door. We carefully went inside, holding our guns up like veteran police officers. The house was torn up. Everything was broken.

We searched the house in every corner before we returned to where Sandy Boy's body was. Quan was still holding him like he was expecting him to wake up.

We tried to talk to Quan for a minute. He was ranting about going to find the motherfuckers who did this and kill them. He had a theory about who it was.

I pulled out my phone and called Tyrell. "Tyrell, Sandy Boy's dead."

"What? How?"

"Somebody killed him at the apartment while we were meeting Trevor. I don't know what happened. We left him at my house, so I don't know why he was back here. They tore up the house and furniture looking for something. I hope you didn't have anything there," I said.

"I left the money you gave me. That's it. Fifty thousand. Are you and Sable all right? How's Quan?"

"Tyrell, he messed up, man. He wants to go kill everybody at that house we were at. He said he just feels they got something to do with it. He saw the guy write down my license number."

"Krystal, keep him at your house. I think these guys are smarter than we think. We got to move. But nobody leaves the house until we get there. Let me talk to Quan."

I gave Quan the phone and heard him say "okay," over and over. Then he said, "I'm cool."

He gave me the phone back.

"I'll bring some recruits. Don't let anybody leave the house. Gather up all the essentials, and tonight will be your last night there," Tyrell said to me.

"Okay," I answered.

He asked to talk to Sable, so I handed her the phone. Sable took the phone as we walked back to our house.

Quan picked up Sandy Boy's guns, took Sandy Boy's wallet, and wiped down the apartment before he came down to our house.

Sable went upstairs and took a shower. I stayed downstairs and talked to Quan. He was withdrawn. I asked him again who he thought did it and why.

"I think it was Trevor's uncle, trying to see if we set him up. I found some cigarettes in Sandy Boy's pocket, so he must have went to the store to buy them, because he didn't have any before. They must have noticed your car and followed him from the store."

"Damn," I said. "That makes sense."

"Tell me about Claython and what happened to him," he asked.

Sable came back down and joined us.

"Don't forget you put that car in Claython's name," she reminded me. "That might be how they tracked us so fast."

She fixed a couple of sandwiches, and we ate and drank wine. We told Quan everything. We told him about why we were in California and how we got to California. Sable told him about the deaths of her parents, every detail. We told him about my mother being killed protecting my daughter. Quan told us about his past with Tyrell. He and Sandy Boy were basically the enforcers for the last few years.

We talked until early in the morning, when Quan said, "I'm all right. Y'all should go to bed."

We gave him some covers, and he asked me for some duct tape.

When I got it for him, I asked, "What you need it for?"

"I will protect you. If you hear shots, come down shooting." He showed us how he wrapped the tape around his hand with the gun. He taped his trigger finger so that the gun wouldn't fall out of his hand if he fell asleep.

I liked that. "Show me how to do that," I asked, holding out my hand. He wrapped mine, and I went to bed with my gun. It was uncomfortable at first, but soon I was asleep. I never had to sleep with a gun before, but I wanted to make sure that I could if I had to.

It was 9:30 before we were awakened by a heavy knock on the door. Quan jumped up, gun pointing at the door. I guess this was the only downfall with having your gun taped to your hand. You could wake up and start shooting before you realize it.

Tyrell and Lorenzo came into the house, followed by six other gentlemen. I heard them talking. Tyrell said,

"We cleaned everything out of the apartment and wiped everything down with bleach. Packed all the clothes up and put them in the van."

They made plans on the next move. Their plans were well thought out and put us out of California in two weeks.

I cleaned up and came downstairs just as Sable was walking out of her room.

"Good morning. You all right?" I asked. She looked a little pale.

"I'm fine. Didn't sleep too well. Need to get me something to eat," she said as she headed straight for the kitchen, not noticing the guys in the dining room.

Tyrell followed her in the kitchen, and he came out smiling. I didn't pay too much attention to what was going on with them because Lorenzo was introducing me to the other guys. Two of them I knew from back in the day. They were Leon and Tyrell's cousins. I knew by the looks on their faces that somebody was going to pay for Sandy Boy's death.

I looked at Sable, and she had a look of contentment, something I hadn't seen on her face in years. We all sat down and listened to Tyrell explain his plan. He assumed his old role of the top enforcer.

He told all the eight guys that were present, "Sable and Krystal are our main concern. We must protect the ladies at all costs, by any means necessary."

Sable and I got dressed, and we all left. Quan rode with Sable and me. Tyrell and Lorenzo rode in their BMW. The six guys followed us, keeping a block distance in the van.

I had an appointment with Trevor at the house. We rode to the drop house cautiously. Quan, Sable, and I got out to enter the house. Quan pushed us back and made us wait until he saw that no one was inside. We went in to set up.

My cell phone that was on vibrate rang twice. I knew Trevor was on his way in. The two rings meant he had two guys with him.

When they arrived, Quan stopped them at the door.

"Who the fuck you think you are going to search?" Trevor asked.

Sable and I had our guns drawn. "Trevor, everybody coming in this door here is getting searched. They killed one of my cousins, and my family is very upset," I said.

"I run this shit, Key, not you. You can't search my people," he said.

Quan and Sable had his two men against the wall. Quan turned around and hit Trevor with his fist. Blood splattered from his nose.

When one of the guys reached for his gun, Sable shot him point blank. The bullet went through his neck as he fell to the ground. The other guy put his hands up in the air.

Quan put his gun to Trevor's temple.

"You want to talk," I said. "Let's talk."

"What's going down, Key? You trying to take over my business?" he asked.

"I don't want your business. If I had wanted it, I would have *been* took it from you. You brought two of your goons in here to talk to me. What you wanna talk about, Trevor? You want to talk about why you killed my cousin? If I had been driving my car, you would have killed me too," I yelled.

"Key, it's not like that. I didn't know they were going to kill your cousin. They were just making sure you didn't set me up and take my money."

"So, you had something to do with that?" I asked.

"No, that was my uncle. You know I wouldn't hurt you," he said.

"But you would kill my cousin. Trevor, you have a problem."

The man on the floor took his last breath. The second man pushed Sable hard, and she fell to the floor. Quan and I turned around just in time to see the man bolt out the front door.

We heard gunshots, and then the door opened. The man entered, holding his leg. Two men, dressed in all black with scarfs over their faces, came in behind him. They held AK assault rifles against his back.

"Don't nobody move. Everybody drop their guns," one of the masked men said.

Quan went for his gun, and the assault rifle let off between four and ten shots. Everybody ducked for cover as Quan fell to the floor and didn't move.

"What's going on, Key? Racquel?" Trevor asked. He was scared. The words were stuttering out. "I'll give you money. Anything you want," Trevor told the masked men.

"I know you will give us what we want, but for now, you call your uncle and your mother and tell them you have been kidnapped," the strong voice said.

Our guns were no match for the assault rifles, so Sable and I pulled our guns out and threw them on the table. One of the masked men went to the back door and let in two more men. They were also dressed in black with scarves and bulletproof vests.

"Tie them up," he said, pointing to Sable and me.

The men tied us up and went over to Trevor.

"It's time for you to make that call." The man pulled his cell phone from his case on his side and gave it to Trevor.

Trevor dialed a number and spoke into the phone. "I have been kidnapped, and I don't know what they want. Yes, I'm at my drop house."

The man took the phone from Trevor. "We will be in contact and tell you what we want. Yes, I know who the fuck I'm talking to. James Ridgeway. Now, you wait for my call. We won't be here when you get here." The man hung up.

He told his men, "Take him out the back door and wait." Then he looked at us. "We will leave them here for the Ridgeway family to find."

"No!" I yelled at them. "They are going to kill us."

Sable yelled, "Untie us so we can leave."

The man just looked at us and then left. One of Trevor's men was dead, and the other one was lying in a pool of blood. Sable was tied up, and I was tied up. Quan was lying on the floor.

He started to move. He began to cough, and he sat up, pulled his shirt off, and looked at his bulletproof vest that had saved his life. He untied Sable and me. He searched the other man again to make sure he wasn't armed. Then he went outside to his car.

He returned with a gallon of gasoline. Quan pulled the dead man to the middle of the living room, and he went over to the other man and helped him in the living room. Sable poured the gasoline on the dead man as the other man begin to plead.

"Please, don't. What you want?" he asked.

"We only got a few minutes before your boss get here. Now, I'm only going to ask one time. How long have you been working for the Ridgeways?"

The man said, "Ten years."

I told him, "I want the addresses of all the Ridgeway family members, including parents. If you give it to us, we'll leave now. You have one minute."

Quan took the gas can from Sable and started pouring gasoline on the man's wound. He started yelling and screaming from the burning on his leg.

He gave in, stating addresses and streets, hoping the pain would stop. He even told us who lived at each address. Sable wrote everything down.

Twenty minutes had passed, and we had to leave before reinforcements came.

Quan took his gun out and shot the man in the head twice, saying, "This is for Sandy Boy."

Sable and I ran outside to the car and noticed Tyrell and Lorenzo standing guard. Quan threw his cigarette at the man and watched as the flames started. He slammed the door and jumped in the car. We drove off, and Tyrell and Lorenzo followed in their car.

CHAPTER FORTY-THREE

On the other side of town, the guys in the van pulled up to a warehouse. They pushed a button on the remote, and the large door opened. Trevor could hear the sound of the door chains cranking up. He feared for his life.

The van stopped, and Trevor heard footsteps as the door opened. The guys pulled him out of the van and put him in a chair that already had handcuffs on it. It was cuffed to an iron pipe coming out of the wall.

"Sit there and don't make a sound," they told Trevor. They put a blindfold over Trevor's eyes as he started screaming. One blow to Trevor's head silenced him as he fell unconscious.

A cell phone rang, and one of the guys answered. Three of the guys jumped in the truck, opened the door, and left. The guy who stayed behind closed the door and told Trevor to be quiet.

Just as Felix and Smitty, James Ridgeway's hired killers with a badge, reached the drop house, they saw fire trucks and a lot of police vehicles. They took their badges out and approached the house.

A couple of the police officers spoke, and another one asked "Felix, what you doing here? I thought you were on a case."

"Me and Smitty was going to a see an informant when we heard the call. Just want to see what happened, then we're out of here," Felix said.

"All right. Let them in."

The house fire was in one room. In that room, two charcoaled bodies lay in the middle of the floor.

"You guys ID them yet?" Smitty asked.

"Not yet. We can't tell if they are white or black," one of the policemen said.

Smitty and Felix left and went to call James Ridgeway. They didn't know if one of the dead bodies was Trevor, their boss's nephew.

The phone kept ringing and ringing. Back at James Ridgeway's house, two men entered with their badges around their neck. They were let in by the bodyguard. Then they were taken to the den to see James.

James was at his desk, and he had his back to the two men. "I'm not paying another one of you guys. I got four badge-toting killers, and my nephew still gets kidnapped."

"We have a little news about your nephew," Lorenzo said.

James turned around in his chair. Just when he looked up, Tyrell put two bullets in his bodyguard, one in his chest, and one in his forehead. The guns had silencers on them, so the only sound heard was a thump.

Lorenzo pulled his gun as James Ridgeway watched his bodyguard fall to the floor. He got focused when Lorenzo swatted him in the face with his gun. Blood came out of his nose, and he tried to go into his desk to get a hanky.

His hand touched his gun. He pulled it out of the desk drawer, but he felt a hot sting in his shoulder, which caused him to drop the gun to the floor.

Tyrell said, "Next one is for keeps. Who else is in the house?"

James started to say no one, but Lorenzo's gun caught him again across the top of his head. James screamed in pain.

"Who else is in the house?" Tyrell asked.

With blood streaming from his head and his face, James said, "My wife and daughter are upstairs. Please don't hurt them. What is this about?"

Lorenzo went upstairs and got the woman and the girl, who was about eighteen years old. They came down screaming.

Lorenzo hit the lady. "Shut the fuck up," he said.

James was begging. "What is this about? I got money. You want money?"

"I'm not going to tell you again. Everybody shut up," Tyrell said.

"Please just tell me what this is about?" James said in a mild voice.

Lorenzo walked up to James like they had rehearsed this. "About a year ago, three people were killed at a beach house in Fresno. They had large sums of money and drugs in the house. Somebody took my five million dollars. Your brother Mark got knocked for the job, so I figure you must have my money."

James took the bait like a baby taking his bottle. He thought that he could save his family by telling the truth. "There was no money in that house," he said before he realized that he was snitching.

Tyrell and Lorenzo looked at each other as Lorenzo kept probing. "We had ten kilos in there and five million. You are trying to tell me that nothing was there, even though I dropped the money off myself that morning at nine o'clock?"

Lorenzo turned around and shot the woman in the chest. James tried to get up, but Tyrell hit him with the butt of the gun. "Where is the money?" he asked.

James screamed in terror, watching his wife's eyes fade off to the other side of life. "There was no money. We went in the house looking for the girl that killed my brothers. They wouldn't talk, so we killed the rest of the family."

Tyrell shot James in his other shoulder.

Lorenzo walked over to the front door and peeked out the window. He waved to Quan, who was standing on the porch with his gun to his side, signaling him to come in.

The door opened, and Sable and I came in with Quan. The look on James's face told the story. He knew who I was. His daughter, kneeling over her mother's lifeless body, looked up and saw the look on her father's face. Fear began to take its toll, and she cried loudly.

James looked into my eyes as I looked in his. I pulled my gun and walked over to the daughter.

"Get up," I said. I pushed her to where James was sitting. I grabbed her hair and banged her head on the desk. Then I put my gun to the back of her head. I cocked the gun to put a bullet in the chamber. "I want to know exactly what happened on my family's last day. Don't leave anything out, because if you do, I'll kill your daughter right here," I said.

James Ridgeway started ratting like he had some cheese waiting on him. He told us every little detail.

I didn't even notice Sable walk over to my side. She held my hand and cried. When I turned toward her to give her a hug, she pulled the gun out with her other hand and shot the girl four times. Blood splattered all over me and her. She looked like she was in a trance.

Tyrell cocked his gun and asked James, "Who else was with you?"

"It was the two policemen, Felix and Smitty," James said.

"Why did your brother Mark get locked up on that case?" I asked.

"He is only going to do three years. Somebody had to take the fall," James admitted.

"Who killed my cousin yesterday?" Tyrell asked.

"The same two guys." James started crying and screaming, looking at the dead girl in front of him. "I told my brother I'd watch out for his daughter, and you killed her."

That brought some sort of closure to Sable. She wiped away the tears and pulled the trigger again. The bullet hit James in the head. It caught all of us by surprise. I turned and emptied my gun in James's body.

Quan was at the front door. He opened it and went outside to see if everything was cool.

We all walked out and got in our cars. As we drove down the big driveway, I saw the van on the outside of the gate with four heavily armed guys in it.

I thought to myself, *It is good to have family that has your back.*

CHAPTER FORTY-FOUR

Felix and Smitty made their way back to James Ridgeway's house. They had called James numerous times and also called the bodyguard watching him. They didn't get an answer from either. Their suspicious were getting to them. As police officers, they had a gut feeling something was wrong.

They pulled up the driveway, and everything was quiet. They drew their guns and approached the house. They tried to open the door, but it was locked. They decided to call for backup and kicked the door in.

The sight of the three bodies lying there brought a tear to Felix's eyes. He had grown up with the Ridgeways and also promised Mark that he would look after his daughter. To see her lying there in a pool of blood with bullet holes in her head caught him off guard.

Police were everywhere in three minutes. A sergeant came in and asked Felix and Smitty if they knew who was responsible for these gruesome murders.

Smitty said, "I don't know."

"Why are you two here?" he sergeant asked, since these two weren't assigned to this precinct.

"The victim's nephew had been kidnapped. We came by to talk to James about that," Smitty answered.

Felix and Smitty were most upset when they thought about not being able to get the twenty-five thousand a month that they had been receiving from the Ridgeway family for protection. Ahead of them were a lot of sleepless nights following this case.

CHAPTER FORTY-FIVE

At the vacant warehouse, Trevor asked the man watching him for a cigarette. The man gave him a lighted cigarette. Trevor tried to make small talk.

"You ever had a million dollars?" he asked the man.

"No."

"I could get you a million in thirty minutes. You could be in the Bahamas by nightfall," Trevor said.

The man listened. He had thought about getting out of the game. To have a million to his self would mean no more taking orders.

"We could be back at my house in a few minutes. I got two million there. You can take one," Trevor suggested. "I'll take the other, and we will never see each other again."

"You want me to cross my family?" the man asked.

"Has your family ever given you that much money? What's your name?"

The man was silent for a minute before he said his name was Craig.

"So, you want me to let you go? My family will kill me," Craig said.

"No," Trevor said. "We leave together. My family is the connection on the West Coast. We will protect you and get you out the country."

"I can't spend any money if I'm dead," Craig said.

Trevor's mind was spinning. He knew he might die. He was trying to bargain a way to stay alive.

"Are you with the Mexicans?" Trevor asked.

Craig didn't answer.

"I tell you what, Craig, or whatever your name is. I'm going to trust you and tell you where the money is. Shit, I can't spend it if I'm dead, like you said. You feel me?" Trevor asked.

Craig shook his head, letting him know he was listening.

"I'm going to have to trust in you. Trust that if you have an opportunity after you get the money, you will let me go. Is that fair?"

Craig just looked at Trevor strangely.

Trevor kept talking. Craig asked a few questions to get the information he needed without letting Trevor know he was really interested. Trevor gave the man so much information about his family, where everybody lived, and where the millions were stashed. All the while, Craig had his phone recording everything.

Craig still didn't let on that he was really listening that closely. He looked Trevor in his eyes. "I will think about it."

"That's all I can ask. When you get the money, you will see I'm serious," Trevor said.

The door to the warehouse opened, and three guys came in, still in all black, with scarves on their faces, the same as Craig.

"The boss giving you a break. We are going to watch him for a while," one guy left, and Craig followed him, then the door closed behind them.

Outside the warehouse, Tyrell, Lorenzo, Quan, Sable, and I were waiting. Craig gave us his phone and told us how to listen to all the information he got from Trevor.

CHAPTER FORTY-SIX

After we listened to the information on the phone a few times, Sable asked, "Where we going next?" We now had four addresses for Ridgeway family members.

I took a moment to think. We had to work this plan perfect. If we didn't hit each house at the right time, the others would be notified. Then the element of surprise would no longer be in our favor.

We decided to hit Tommy Ridgeway's house. He was the last brother out of the five. He would be the easiest one, because he was a lawyer and not directly in the game. He handled all the legal matters for the family. He lived in the suburbs.

It took us about an hour before we started seeing all the beautiful homes and mansions. Lorenzo had a GPS, and we followed the black BMW that he was driving. Tyrell rode with him. I was with Sable and Quan in Sable's car. The black van with the heavily armed men was trailing us by a block.

We came up on the block, looking for the address. Tyrell called my cell phone.

"It is not the right time," he said.

"What you mean? What's wrong?" I asked.

"Look around. It must be a hundred cars on this block and the last one. People are over here paying their respects," he said.

"Oh, yeah. They did lose a few relatives in the last couple of days."

"We have to be patient. Our time will come," he said.

"What you want to do?" I asked.

"Lorenzo had an idea. We going to stop and get something to eat before we get back to LA," he said.

"Let me talk to Lorenzo?" I asked.

Lorenzo got on the phone. "You all right?" he asked me. Then he said, "I can still smell your scent on my body."

We both laughed.

He then told me, "Don't worry. We're still gonna get Tommy Ridgeway. I went to school at UCLA. I can get a lead on where Tommy Ridgeway's office is. I just need a day or so."

"Cool," I said.

"Anything for you," he said. "Krystal, I just want to hold you and talk like we did the other night. I really enjoyed your company."

"I'd like that. We will follow you back," I said then hung up the phone.

The car was silent, but I could feel Sable looking at me, wanting to ask me something, or else tease me, but Quan was in the car, so I escaped that one.

We drove for about twenty minutes. Then we pulled up to a nice restaurant off the highway. Tyrell and Lorenzo got out of their car and approached ours. They told us to come on in we could sit down and talk.

Quan said, "I'm going with the guys in the van." They went to the Mc Donald's next to the restaurant.

We went in and were seated in the back. The place was an Italian restaurant and reminded me of one of those restaurants in the movies about Al Capone. It was a nice family restaurant. We sat in a booth. Tyrell sat next to Sable, and Lorenzo sat next to me, smiling.

"What you smiling for?" I asked.

"I have been waiting on this moment for a while," he said. "You deserve to be dining in nice restaurants like this, not always caught up in so much drama."

Sable and Tyrell just laughed. I looked deep in Lorenzo's eyes. I could see softness and gentleness, like I was looking at the inside of his heart. But I knew on the outside, he was a natural born killer. My mind was deep in thought, looking in his eyes, as he was still looking in mine.

The waitress came over and asked if we would like something to drink. To my surprise, everybody ordered water. We all thought alike. We knew we had to keep our minds focused.

When the waitress came back, we ordered food. We sat and talked and just enjoyed our lunch. We didn't talk any business.

Lorenzo got up to call some guys he went to school with to see if he could get a lead on Tommy Ridgeway.

My cell phone startled me, since I didn't think it would ring when I was with everybody close to me. I looked at the caller ID. It was Quan.

"Krystal, four guys pulled up in a Hummer. One of them looked just like Trevor. Before I did something, one of the guys in the van called the garage. Trevor is still tied up. What you want me to do?" he asked.

"Stay on point," I said and hung up.

I told Sable and Tyrell what he'd said just as the men entered the restaurant. Two of them went and sat at the bar, and two others sat by the door. The young guy did look like Trevor, but he was flashier. He looked like a drug dealer with lots of jewelry, new clothes and gym shoes. He acted like he was in control.

Sable looked at me. "Who is that? You think they came here for us?" she asked.

"Sable, how they know where or who we are? He probably doesn't know anything about us."

We could see them from where we were seated, but they couldn't see us. I could tell this wasn't Trevor. This guy was loud and mouthy.

Tyrell took out his cell phone and called Lorenzo, who was still in the restroom on the phone. We were through eating and as we got ready to leave, everybody had their hands on their guns. I put one in my chamber after unlocking it. We got up, ready to face our destiny.

"Wait a minute," Tyrell said. "You ladies wait here until after we leave. Quan and the guys in the van will make sure you make it back to LA. We'll meet up at the warehouse again." He didn't wait for an answer.

He got up to head toward the restroom. Lorenzo was already out and walking toward the men. I pulled my gun out and put it under the table. Sable did the same.

Before he could reach the guy that looked like Trevor, the two guys at the door were up in front of him.

"Trevor," Lorenzo said. "Trevor, you not going to holla at your boy?"

The guy turned around as the two guys stopped Lorenzo from reaching the young man.

"Oh, it's like this, Trevor?" Lorenzo said.

"Look, my man, I'm not Trevor."

"Oh, now you don't know me after I hooked you up with them fine sisters in LA?" Lorenzo said, sounding so convincing.

"Let him go," the young man said to his bodyguards.

Lorenzo sat down on the seat next to him.

"Look, dude, let me buy you a drink. I'm not Trevor. I'm his cousin JJ. John, Junior," he said.

"For real, man? You two look like twins," Lorenzo said.

"Our fathers were twins."

"Man, that's deep," Lorenzo said as he watched Tyrell pass him and go outside. That was his cue to leave. "Hey, I'll take a rain check on that drink. Tell Trevor that Tyrone said get at me," Lorenzo said as he got up and extended his hand to the young man. They gave each other the brothers handshake. It looked funny for two white-looking guys to be giving each other dap.

"Be cool," the young man said as Lorenzo walked out the door.

After ten minutes, the young man and his crew got up and left. Sable and I put our guns back in our purses and left a few minutes later. Lorenzo and Tyrell were gone, following the Hummer. Quan was posted outside the door of the restaurant, waiting on us. We got in Sable's car and drove back to LA with the van following a block behind.

CHAPTER FORTY-SEVEN

When we all met up at the warehouse again, I looked at Lorenzo and saw he was now in a "don't fuck with me" mood. Maybe he was mad because our nice time at the restaurant had been cut short by some more Ridgeways. He wanted it to end, and so did I.

He walked into the warehouse with a purpose. I followed behind him, while Sable and Quan stayed outside talking. Trevor looked up and saw Lorenzo and probably thought he was being rescued. Those thoughts soon faded when Lorenzo spoke to the guys who were guarding Trevor.

"Take them damn scarves off," he said to the guards.

Tyrell walked to the back of the warehouse and joined the others. I knew right away that Trevor was going to die in this warehouse. He would never be able to leave since he had seen everybody's faces.

The guards were off to the side, talking to Tyrell and Lorenzo. Sable and Quan came in and closed the gate.

Lorenzo told the guys loudly, "Come on. We're going to get that money, since this punk ass told Craig where everything was."

Trevor yelled, "That's my money!"

The guys ignored him as they left. Quan went outside to guard the door, leaving me and Sable alone with Trevor.

Sable walked over to him. "Don't worry about the money. You're not gonna need it."

Trevor was puzzled. I guess he still thought we were on his team. When he saw me walk up with my gun out, he just shook his head.

"Rose, what's this about? You know I'm falling in love with you. I would never do anything to hurt you," Trevor said. "I didn't set you up. I was always real with you. I really do care about you girls."

I laughed. "Do you think I could really fall in love with you?"

I looked at Sable, and she was looking so serious.

"Do you know who I am, Trevor?" I asked.

"What's this about?"

"I am the woman that killed your Uncle," I told him.

"What? My Uncle?"

"I killed your Uncle John, and I made Desmond jump out a window before I killed him."

"So what does that got to do with me?" he asked.

"You was born in the wrong family. You see, your daddy and your uncle James and those policemen your family pays killed my mother and Sable's mother and father."

Trevor looked confused as I finally revealed her true name. Then she spoke, and he suddenly knew I was not really Key.

Sable eyes got watery, and the tears started flowing. "Fuck this, Krystal," she said. "I let this motherfucker have sex with me knowing his family killed my parents. Now I want it back."

"You want what back?" Trevor asked.

Sable shot Trevor in his leg. "Stand up, motherfucker!" she yelled.

I put my gun to Trevor's head as he tried to stand up. His hands were tied in front of him. I looked at Sable. I didn't know what she was about to do.

"Pull your pants and underwear down," she said.

Trevor yelled, "No! I'm sorry about your parents, but I didn't do it. Please, don't do this to me."

"You did it to me, didn't you?" Sable shot Trevor in his foot.

Trevor screamed in agony. I hit him with my gun butt. "Pull your pants off before I drop you right here." I said.

Trevor pulled his pants down, and Sable pulled a bag out of her purse. She had a big meat cleaver in the bag and a pair of gloves. She slowly put the gloves on and said, "Your daddy raped my mother and made my father watch. Then he killed both of them. He them killed my aunt, Krystal's mother, and tried to kill her child. After all that, I laid down and fucked you. I want it back."

"What back?" Trevor said.

With one swipe, she cut off his dick and his nuts. Part of his leg was open. Her cut was so swift and fast that the blood didn't come out right away.

Sable held his bloodied dick in her hand. She pulled out a pickle jar from her purse, threw his genitals in the jar, and screwed the top on. "I'm going to send this to your daddy to see if he likes pickles."

Trevor fell to the floor, screaming in pain. Blood started gushing out of his body like water. He screamed and moaned until he took his last breath.

Sable stood over him and shot him once in the head, and I shot him two more times. We hugged each other and cried for a few minutes. I spit on his dead body, and Sable did also. We walked to the gate, holding each other tight, tears pouring out.

We had never had the time to mourn the death of our family. To us, this was our way.

CHAPTER FORTY-EIGHT

We went outside and Quan put us in one of the cars. He told us the guys had gone to one of the addresses that Trevor had given to Craig, where there was supposed to be a lot of money. None of us felt safe going back to our house, so we decided to go stay in a hotel in Santa Monica until it was the right time to go get the rest of the Ridgeways and be done with this. Quan called the guys to tell them where we were going.

Everyone met up at the hotel later, and we found out that Trevor had been telling the truth about the money. The guys found two million dollars and about a hundred thousand in jewelry. Everybody's mood was upbeat, even with all the drama going on.

Tyrell and Sable got a suite, and I had a connecting suite. I knew in my heart that Lorenzo would end up in my room, but I let him wait a minute. Only a minute, though. He really excited me.

All the guys went shopping and to the titty bar. Lorenzo and I were in Tyrell and Sable's room, just chilling and talking.

Lorenzo said, "I got something to tell you guys. My friend called and told me where Tommy Ridgeway's office is. The guy that looked like Trevor was John Jr. He's John Ridgeway's son. He runs a drug ring in Inglewood."

"So when we going to get him?" I asked.

"That's all the business we talking tonight," he answered. "We can plan tomorrow. Is that cool with you guys? I just want to relax and watch some TV."

"Let's go get some movies," Sable said.

We left to get some food and some movies.

I asked Lorenzo, "Are you going to watch them with me?"

He looked at me like I was crazy. "I can't do that. I might fall asleep," he said.

"So, what's wrong with that?" I asked.

He just smiled. He grabbed my hand as we walked through Wal-Mart, looking for movies. His touch made me feel so alive. I was blushing all over as he kept making me laugh. He was really a silly man.

Sable saw that I was actually letting myself have fun. She looked at me and gave her approval as only close friends can.

We went to a restaurant, but we got carryout. Sable and Tyrell were kissing and hugging like they hadn't seen each other in months. I couldn't really blame them. We all hadn't slept much in a couple of days.

"Damn, Sable, get a room," I said, giving her a jealous look. She just looked at me a laughed.

We got our food and drove back to the hotel. Sable and Tyrell disappeared in their room, leaving Lorenzo and me standing in the hallway.

"Well, are you going to watch a movie with me?" I asked Lorenzo."

"Yes, I want to, but I need to take a shower first," he said.

"You can take a shower in my room," I said, not knowing where that came from.

He just smiled and said he had to go get something from his room. Ten minutes later, Lorenzo knocked on the door. When he came in, he had on some shorts and a wife beater. I had never really looked at his body because he always had on big clothes or a jacket to hide his gun. This man was looking good.

I stood there looking at his features, and I could notice the black blood in his face. He had a thin nose and straight hair, but his lips were fuller than a white man, and the dimple made me blush.

"Are you going to let me in, or are you going to just stare at me?" he asked.

"I'm sorry," I said as I let him in, checking out his butt that was also made like a black man.

"I'm going to take a shower. I'll be out in a minute," he said as he disappeared in the bathroom and closed the door.

I just stood there letting my thoughts consume me. The lust in my body was pouring out. The pent-up sexual desire was about to burst out of me. I almost came just thinking about his body and anticipating him making love to me.

As my body burned with passion, I walked to the bathroom, hoping he hadn't locked the door. I turned the knob slowly. I didn't want to make any noise in case he wanted his privacy. I pushed the door slowly open and saw the shadow of Lorenzo through the steamy shower doors.

I stood there taking my clothes off piece by piece, building up excitement, watching this man rub his body down with soap. When I pulled my panties down, they were sticking to my leg.

I opened the shower door. Lorenzo looked at me with his sexiest smile. "I been waiting on you," he said. He helped me in the shower and pulled me under the water.

He kissed my lips for the first time, and my body and my heart immediately became his. I don't know if this was love at first kiss, lust, or destiny, but at that moment, I knew I would be all his.

We didn't watch movies that night. When we finally got out of the shower after he gave me at least ten orgasms, we just got in the bed and fell asleep in each other's arms.

I woke up just as daylight was creeping in. I looked at Lorenzo, laying on his stomach, sleeping hard. I looked at all the scratches on his back and felt a little guilty—but only a little, because I enjoyed every minute that we shared in that shower. I pulled the sheet back and exposed his entire body. I was about to start kissing all over his body to wake him up for another round when I heard a knock on the adjoining suite door.

I got up and put on a robe to let Sable in.

"Tyrell wants a meeting with us in the parking lot around four o'clock," she said.

"What time is it?" I asked.

"It's after two. I see a glow in your eyes," she said. "Lorenzo must have hit that spot."

I smiled and held my head down.

Sable just laughed and said, "Meet us downstairs at four. Make sure you bring Lorenzo." She closed the door, laughing.

CHAPTER FORTY-NINE

Everybody was in the parking lot when Lorenzo and I arrived. It was the four guys from the van, Quan, Tyrell, and Sable. Tyrell got us together and started his speech.

"While we took a day to relax, these guys have been working. I had them keep an eye on John Jr. They have been staked out, watching his operation in Inglewood. Quan reported that he usually watches his money. He is usually at the spot most of the day with two or three guys. He sends one out to lunch around three o'clock every day. Drug traffic is usually heavy, so our window of opportunity is slim. We have to get in and get out quick.

"I suggest, if it's all right with you ladies, that we hit two places at one time. That way, they won't have time to communicate with other family members. We should hit John Jr. and Tommy Ridgeway at the same time. Then we go to the parents, and then get out of this city, one way or the other. What you ladies think?" Tyrell finished.

"I think that's a good idea. Krystal, what you want to do?" Sable asked.

"I wanna go to John Jr.," I said.

Sable said, "I'm going wherever you're going."

Quan opened the van door, and there was an arsenal of weapons. There were guns of different sizes mounted on the walls of the truck. There were automatic weapons and ammunition on the back walls. On the open doors were bulletproof vest and silencers.

Quan told Sable and I to put on vests. All the other guys already had their vests on. Tyrell told everybody to put silencers on their weapons. That would buy us time, because no one would hear the shootings.

When Tyrell finished telling us his plan, we went and cleaned the hotel rooms down. We wiped down all flat surfaces, taking the sheets with us and emptying the waste baskets. We didn't leave any evidence or DNA that could be traced back to us.

Tyrell and Lorenzo went to take care of Tommy Ridgeway as we made our way to Inglewood, California.

While we were making our way to Inglewood, Felix and Smitty, the two policemen who worked with the Ridgeways, were going to Tommy Ridgeway's office to talk about the recent murders.

Tyrell and Lorenzo made it to the tenth floor of the office building. They checked the exits and remembered where they were. They reached the law offices of Tommy Ridgeway and partners. The receptionist was very polite.

"Yes, Mr. Ridgeway is in. Can I tell him your name, please?" she asked.

Lorenzo said, "We are friends of the family."

The receptionist turned around to go get Mr. Ridgeway, and Lorenzo was right on her heels. When she reached the door, Lorenzo pushed her in. Tyrell came in behind him.

"What's the meaning of—" was all Tommy could get out before Tyrell shot him in the forehead.

As the woman attempted to scream, Lorenzo shot her in the back of her head. She fell to the nice plush white carpet, blood quickly flowing on the carpet and turning it red. She just happened to be in the wrong place at the wrong time. They couldn't afford to leave any witnesses to identify them.

Both guys had on gloves, so they picked up the shell casings and walked out of his office.

Felix and Smitty had just stepped off the elevator on the tenth floor.

"I got to take a leak," Felix said, heading in the opposite direction of Tommy Ridgeway's office.

"I'll meet you in his office. I want to flirt with his fine secretary," Smitty said as he walked toward the office. He saw the two well-dressed men come out of Tommy Ridgeway's office. He didn't pay much attention to them, until he looked down and noticed they had on gloves.

Smitty reached for his service revolver just as Lorenzo turned and fired a shot that caught him on his arm. Smitty fell down to grab his extra gun on his ankle. Tyrell let off three shots, killing him instantly.

Lorenzo walked over and snatched his badge from around his neck. Both Tyrell and Lorenzo took off for the exit. They had to run down ten flights of stairs before the place would be swarming with cops.

Felix came around the corner and saw Smitty lying there in a pool of blood. He drew his gun. Felix called 911 and yelled "Policeman down!" and blurted out the address.

He walked in the office with his gun ready to fire, and he saw Tommy Ridgeway and his secretary lying in a pool of blood. He ran out and looked at the elevator. Then he ran to the exits. He cautiously moved through the staircase, looking for the shooter.

Tyrell and Lorenzo had made it to the first floor. They wiped the sweat off their foreheads and fixed their ties. They walked through the lobby nonchalantly, talking about the Los Angeles Lakers. When they got to the door, four policemen almost knocked them down. They pushed right past them, running up the stairs.

Within two minutes, the office building would be on lockdown. Tyrell and Lorenzo walked casually back to their car, which was parked two blocks away. They headed toward Inglewood.

CHAPTER FIFTY

Quan, Sable, and I parked a half block away from the drug house of John Ridgeway Jr. We watched to see if we could find a way in other than just blasting our way in. That way, we might have some casualties. We watched as dope fiend after dope fiend went in and out of the house.

Suddenly, I had an idea. I got out of the car, pulled my pants down past my belt buckle. I told Sable to get out, and she pulled her blouse out and messed up her hair. I messed up mine and picked up some dirt off the ground and put it on my face. Sable looked at me and did the same. We looked like two drug addicts looking to cop some dope.

We walked up the block with Quan trailing us half a block away. The van was watching all of our moves, ready for any hint of trouble.

I spotted a dope fiend leaving the house. He had to pass Sable and me on his route.

"Hey, bro, can you cop for us? We'll make it worth your while," I said, rubbing my hand and scratching my nose.

"They don't sell no dope in there. Just crack," he said.

"We know, man. We just had too much H, and we want to get some good stuff."

Sable said, "Here. I'll give you fifty dollars."

He took the money and tried to walk away.

"Wait. We're going with you. We spending two hundred. You can get high with us, but we got to go with you," Sable said.

"Yeah, last time we did this, we got ripped off," I said.

The dope fiend looked at the money in his hand. He could get high with us, then buy a rock to take home. This was a win-win for him. "Okay, girls, let's go. These guys don't like new people, but you lucky I grew up with the family," he said.

"What family?" I asked.

"The Ridgeway family. They run all the drugs in Cali. I went to school with JJ and Trevor," he bragged.

Sable looked at me, and I just kept scratching my nose.

We got to the door. He knocked, and the door was opened. We walked in, and the guy at the door had a shotgun. The other guy was by a kitchen door, and I guessed that JJ was in the kitchen.

"Give me the money," the dope fiend said. I reached in my pocket and gave him two hundred-dollar bills. The guy at the door was looking at my roll of hundred-dollar bills.

"What you girls do, rob a trick?" he said, laughing.

"I'll stay here, girl. You go with him to make sure he don't rip us off. Is that okay, cutey?" I asked the man at the door.

"That's cool. You can keep me company."

I watched as Sable disappeared in the kitchen with the dope fiend. The guys looked down on us like we were just a couple of dope fiend hoes. It was another case where males underestimate females, but it would not turn out well for them.

There was a knock at the door. At the same time, Sable stumbled out of the kitchen. The guy at the kitchen entrance was watching the door. When he saw Sable fall to the ground, he tried to pick her up, but he was met with a bullet in his stomach.

I pulled my gun out and put it to the back of the other guy's head.

"Open the door," I said.

He opened the door, and Quan burst in with his gun out. The guy figured out what was going on and turned like he wanted to run or warn John Jr. He took two more steps before Quan's bullet caught him in the back on his right side. The bullet went straight through. I could hear it hit the wall. He dropped dead on the spot.

I ran over to Sable while Quan watched the door. "Where is John Jr.?" I asked.

I walked past Sable to the kitchen. John Jr. was at the table, slumped over with two bullets in both his eyes. The poor dope fiend was sitting there with a crack pipe in his hand, but he never got to use it. He had one bullet in his head. Now, I was really beginning to worry about Sable. It just seemed she snapped in and out when she was near any Ridgeway family member. She would need some psychiatric help when we got back to Memphis.

"All right, let's clean up and get out of here," Quan said. He picked up all the shell casings and left.

Outside, the guys in the van were redirecting traffic. The crackheads turned the corner when they saw the van and the guys. They looked like police officers, still wearing their gear and scarves.

We got in the car and pulled off. The van followed us.

I called Tyrell to see if everything went smoothly for them. He said he would meet us in East Los Angeles.

CHAPTER FIFTY-ONE

We drove to East Los Angeles and got a hotel on the outskirts of the city. Sable communicated with Tyrell, and he met us in the parking lot. When he and Lorenzo got out of the BMW with suits on, I almost melted. Lorenzo looked so good. I just ran up to him and hugged him.

"You all right, baby?" I said.

He hugged me so tight, like he thought he wasn't going to see me again. Tyrell and Sable were hugged up too.

"Look, can we take care of this business so you guys can get a room?" Quan said, laughing.

Tyrell broke free from Sable. He walked over to the van and opened the door. "Everybody put all the guns that have been used in this bag. Wipe them off first," he said. He took out a bag from the van and loaded his weapon in it. Lorenzo, Quan, and I put our weapons in there.

"All California is swarming with cops. We need to lay low for at least a day," Lorenzo said.

"I don't want anybody to go further than walking distance. Quan, you and Marv go bury these guns," Tyrell said. "One more thing. This is our final stand. If anybody wants to pull out, I won't be mad at you. You have earned your hundred twenty-five thousand dollars. This last fight is for the ladies. You can leave now, and I'll meet you in Memphis."

"I'm staying with you," Lorenzo said.

Quan said, "I'm staying."

All the guys said they were in it until the end. It felt good inside to know that someone would go all the way for us. I looked at Sable with tears in my eyes. Sable understood and came over hugged me.

We left the guys standing there and walked to the hotel up to my room. Sable and I hadn't really talked in about a week. So much had happened.

When we got to the room, I asked Sable, "Do you think you have closure?"

She looked at me with tears in her eyes. "My daddy would be proud of us, knowing we didn't let this rest until the people responsible for their deaths paid for it." She cried on my shoulders as she said, "After tomorrow, their spirits can rest in peace."

I hadn't thought about it like that, but she was right. Sable and I let all our tears out that night. The mourning for our parents was over. We talked like we used to for hours. This time, we were talking about the future. I was getting excited knowing I was going to see my daughter. Sable wanted to mend things with her sister.

We counted up the money we had in a safe deposit box that Sable kept track of in her notebook. We had a cool five point three million dollars. She had it written down to the dollar.

We both laughed. I hadn't seen Sable look so happy in a long time. She told me that she hadn't seen me this happy in a long time either. She also told me that she was pregnant with Tyrell's child.

"That's why you're glowing so much," I said.

We talked until four in the morning, when Lorenzo and Tyrell came to the room. I think all the guys had been drinking at the bar together, planning their next move.

I looked at Lorenzo from the couch and smiled. *I think I got a new man,* I thought. Sable and Tyrell was hugging and kissing on the couch, so I pulled Lorenzo in the bedroom.

I looked into his eyes and said, "I want to thank you for having my back. I want to be with you forever."

He held me and kissed me on my forehead and said, "I will always have your back."

Tears began to fill my eyes, and my heart opened up. I let Leon out, closed that chapter, and let Lorenzo into my heart forever. I cried as he held me.

"Are you all right?" he asked me.

"I am now."

We laid on the bed. He put in a movie, and I just snuggled up next to him.

He whispered in my ear, "I'm falling in love with you, Krystal Love Davenport."

I just held him tight as I drifted off to sleep.

I woke up the next morning and took a long, hot shower. I had some nervous tension in my stomach. Usually that meant something bad was going to happen. I woke Lorenzo up with kisses all over his body, and he made sweet love to me until I forgot all about that nervous feeling.

My phone rang about an hour later. It was Sable. She said that we were supposed to meet the guys in the parking lot at one o'clock. We got up, took a shower together, and got dressed.

When we got downstairs, everybody was waiting on us. They all laughed and clapped. Lorenzo and I just smiled.

Tyrell gave us instructions, and we all put on our game faces. We loaded up our arsenal and headed to an exclusive neighborhood of Los Angeles.

CHAPTER FIFTY-TWO

Felix was camped out by the Ridgeways' parents' home. He had been there for a couple of days, ever since he found his partner dead at Tommy's office. He figured that whoever was killing all these Ridgeways would come after the parents eventually, and he wanted to be there when they did.

He was beginning to think that he was on the wrong trail. He started his car and went to get some coffee and donuts. "This will be my last day," he told himself. When he got up the block, he noticed a black BMW pass him. He looked at it and kept going.

He turned at the next corner, not noticing the black van go right past him. Felix pulled up to the donut shop as Tyrell and Lorenzo were pulling up to the large house. The neighborhood was filled mostly with older people out cutting their grass of working in their gardens.

Lorenzo walked to the door as Tyrell and Quan went around the back. Lorenzo rang the doorbell. A large man answered. He looked like he used to be one of the goodfellas back in the day.

Lorenzo showed him his badge. The guy looked at it, making sure it was authentic, then let him in.

"Can I speak to Mr. and Mrs. Ridgeway?" he asked.

"What precinct you from?" the man asked.

"I'm with homicide downtown," Lorenzo answered.

"I used to work in Compton," the man said. He was trying to intimidate Lorenzo.

"Is Mr. and Mrs. Ridgeway here? I really need to talk to them," Lorenzo said, watching every move the man made.

Finally, he said, "They are upstairs. You wait here."

"You got a restroom?" Lorenzo asked. "It's been a long drive, and I have to piss."

The man looked at Lorenzo, then said, "It's in the back by the kitchen." He didn't want Lorenzo to use the main bathroom up the hall.

The man headed upstairs to get the Ridgeways, and Lorenzo went through the kitchen. He looked for and found the back door. He let Quan and Tyrell in and went back in the front foyer to wait for the Ridgeways to come down.

By the time the large man and Mr. and Mrs. Ridgeway came down the stairs, Lorenzo had on his face mask. The bodyguard reached for his gun just as Quan and Tyrell became visible.

"I wouldn't do that," Quan yelled.

The bodyguard still tried to pull out his gun. The first bullet from Tyrell caught him in the chest. Lorenzo's bullet hit him in his arm where he was reaching for his gun. Quan's deadly bullet hit him on the left side of his temple and went right though his brain. Blood and brain splattered on the wall. He fell down the rest of the stairs, dead before he hit the bottom stair.

Mrs. Ridgeway started yelling and holding her chest. Mr. Ridgeway held his wife as the blood rushed to her brain. Her heart stopped beating, and her eyes rolled to the back of her head.

"Help my wife!" he said.

She fell down the rest of the stairs, almost landing on top of the bodyguard.

Quan walked to the door and let Sable and me in. We walked over to the foyer and looked at the old man.

He was crying, "Please help my wife." Tears were flowing down his face as he tried to give his wife mouth to mouth resuscitation. "Please help me," he said between tears.

Sable and I looked at each other with tears in our eyes. I felt that this was enough. We had gotten our revenge.

Sable must have had the same thoughts. She had her gun in her hand, but she put it down to her side.

"Please, please," the man begged. He looked at his wife, dead in his arms, blue in the face and cold. He kissed her on the lips. "I love you, Lucinda," he said as he cried.

He looked up at Tyrell and Lorenzo. "Please kill me. I don't want to live anymore. She was my everything. I can't go on without her. Please kill me," he begged.

Sable looked at me, tears rolling down her face. "I'm done, sister. This is enough for me. I want to start the healing process," she said.

Everybody looked at me for the final answer. Lorenzo and Tyrell had their guns ready to end this man's life. I looked at Sable, and her eyes told me it was over. I just shook my head at Tyrell and Lorenzo. As I turned around to leave, we heard sirens in the distance.

Quan said, "We need to go."

Tyrell and Lorenzo ran to the door and looked out. "We got to roll out of here," he said.

Sable was standing off to the side, wiping her face with tissue.

The old man reached for the bodyguard's gun and pointed it at my back.

Bang, bang!

The noise caused us all to turn around as Sable was unloading her automatic weapon in the man's body. She didn't stop firing until I came and got the gun out of her hand. She still was pulling the trigger even though there were no bullets in the gun.

"Thank you, Sable," I said after I took the gun out of her hand.

"Let's go," Quan said as he opened the door.

Two gunshots went off, and Quan fell back in the house. We then heard a lot of shots being fired. We knew it was the guys in the van.

Tyrell grabbed Sable and said, "Come on!"

Lorenzo snatched my arm and headed for the kitchen. He said, "Wait a minute." He went back to the foyer and dropped the police badge he had after he wiped it off.

Quan followed us out. He was bleeding.

We walked through three or four back yards and walked out front just as more police were arriving. Quan got in our car, and Tyrell and Lorenzo got in theirs. He always said they would stop two men before two women. We pulled off and we could see the guys in the van in our rearview mirror. They had the entrance blocked with the van, and they were on each side, firing at the police. It looked like something out of a movie.

Tyrell's car was noticed by a police cruiser coming in that direction. They turned around and gave pursuit. Sable drove down the next block. She was driving fast.

"Slow down, girl," I said.

Just as I said it, Felix was coming from the coffee shop. He looked at me and Sable as he passed us. Then he noticed Quan slumped in the back seat. His police scanner was dispatching SWAT teams. His police instincts kicked in. He spun around and put the siren on.

"Shit!" Sable said as she put her foot on the gas. "Put your seatbelt on!" she yelled.

I put my belt on and turned around to see Quan lying in the back seat. I think he was dead after losing so much blood.

Sable turned corner after corner doing ninety miles an hour. The police were a block behind. Sable acted like she knew the area because she was losing them. After a couple of miles, I could hear more sirens.

I thought to myself, *If I gotta go out, this is the way I want it.* I pulled my guns out and made sure I had bullets in both of them. I had two clips in my vest and one inside each gun.

Somebody is leaving here with me, I thought to myself.

While looking at my guns, I didn't notice where Sable was going. I looked up to see that she had stopped after pulling into some garage. I could hear the police sirens speeding past us.

"Look, Krystal, both of us don't have to die. You have your daughter to live for," she said.

"No, you have your new baby and Tyrell to live for. I'm not going to leave you," I said.

"Krystal, I love you and want to give my life for yours."

"Sable, I've been so proud of you and how you fought back for your life. I want you to enjoy the rest of your life," I said. "I'm not leaving you."

"We've avenged our parents' lives, and now they can rest in peace. I want to join them," she said.

"If you go, I'm going too."

We sat there, holding each other, saying our last good-byes. The police sirens were coming back our way.

She looked at me and said, "I love you."

She pulled off, and I cocked my gun, ready to go out in a blaze of bullets. She suddenly stopped. The police sirens were getting closer, maybe a block away.

"What's wrong?" I asked.

"I need some more ammunition," she said. "My gun clips are in the car trunk. Grab them right quick."

I sprang the door open and headed for the trunk that Sable had popped open. I was looking in the trunk for the clips when Sable burned rubber and sped off.

"Sable, no!" I cried. I stood there with my gun in my hand, yelling. "Sable, please don't leave me!"

I ran to the entrance and watched Sable flying up the block with six police cars following her. Their sirens were blaring. I could hear the tires of the cars burning the streets while turning the corners.

As the sirens were fading, I heard gunshots and then a large crash. I dropped to the sidewalk and cried.

After a few minutes, I called Tyrell to see if they made it. The phone just rang and rang. I cried for Lorenzo, sad I didn't get the opportunity to really love him. I dialed the phone again and again.

The End